TURBULENT WATERS

ALSO BY MELODY ANNE

The Billionaire Aviators series

Turbulent Intentions

Turbulent Desires

TURBULENT WATERS

A Billionaire Aviator Novel

MELODY ANNE

Montlake
Romance

Published by Montlake Romance, Seattle

www.apub.com

Amazon, the Amazon logo, and Montlake Romance are trademarks of Amazon.com, Inc., or its affiliates.

ISBN-13: 9781503943285
ISBN-10: 1503943283

Cover design by Jason Blackburn

Cover photography by Regina Wamba of MaeIDesign.com

Printed in the United States of America

This book is dedicated to another pilot, Adam Ragle.
This series wouldn't have happened without you.
Here's to a long friendship with many, many more
years to come.

PROLOGUE

Somewhere in the recesses of Captain Nick Armstrong's brain he knew he was in a very bad situation. Pain radiated from every square inch of his body, and even with his adrenaline on overload, he was aware that there was a good chance he was about to die.

The turbulent waters of the ocean were thrashing him, trying desperately to take him below the surface. Each wave slammed into him with a harsh slap that radiated through his entire body. He went under, taking in huge mouthfuls of the Pacific Ocean before surfacing, gasping for air.

Pulling out a flare from his jacket, he set it off, the crimson light nearly blinding as he looked around for other survivors from the Coast Guard helicopter crash. He couldn't find another soul. His crew. Where was his crew? Shouting for minutes, he felt defeat try to overtake him when there was no answer.

Nick wanted to let the sea take him, as he knew it had taken the other members of his crew, people who were more family to him than friends. It had all gone so wrong—and it was his fault.

Another wave surged over him, and for the briefest of moments Nick considered not fighting the strong pull. But a flash of his mother and brothers ran through his mind, and he knew he couldn't give up.

The Guard would know exactly where he was. They'd already have dispatched a rescue. They didn't leave their own behind. But at this particular moment, Nick was all alone in the vast sea. They might not make it in time.

The protective suit Nick wore kept him afloat, but the injuries he'd sustained in the crash were taking him in and out of consciousness. When a hundred feet away from him there was a popping noise, he pulled himself together and almost felt like weeping. That sound meant a boat had been dropped.

Pulling himself across the pummeling waves, he managed to arrive at the inflatable boat one of his fellow Coast Guardsmen had dropped from a jet high in the sky. Luck was on his side that a carrier jet had been in the vicinity. It hadn't taken long. They knew where he was. They were giving him hope. Now he knew what the people he'd saved had felt in those moments when they were ready to give up.

Grabbing the side of the rocking boat, he pulled himself up and over, his leg scraping against the rubber. Nick's vision blackened as his shattered knee made contact with the edge of the boat, his body barely making it inside before he collapsed.

When he came to again, Nick was in the small vessel still being tossed about, but he was alive. He didn't know if the sea was pushing him farther out or closer to land. It didn't matter. His beacon would allow the Guard to follow him when the seawater pulled the small vessel in new directions. With the force of the waves and the strong winds, it might be a while before they could get there. He almost didn't want them to attempt the rescue. He didn't want any more deaths on his bloody hands.

Trying to stay conscious, he searched the black water until he couldn't sit up any longer. If any of his other crew had survived the crash, the waves had taken them far away from him. Maybe they were floating on their own rafts miles away. That was the hope he clung to.

Closing his eyes, Nick thought of his family, his career, and his life. At thirty-two years old, he was the second oldest brother out of four.

His relationship with Cooper and Maverick was perfect. All three of them missed their youngest brother, Ace, who had been gone for years.

Nick couldn't give in to the sea, couldn't let her take him yet, not until he could mend the fences that had been put up between Ace and the rest of the family.

Being a Coast Guard pilot was hazardous. Nick was well aware of that. He loved the danger and adventure of it all, loved knowing he was heading out into the fray when the rest of the world was boarding up their windows. He loved being a hero.

He also knew the Coast Guard motto, *Semper Paratus* (Always Ready), was that they *had* to go out; yet, they didn't have to come back home. But knowing you can die, and the reality of losing your life, were two entirely different feelings.

He wasn't ready to let go—not yet. He refused to continue to allow himself to think negatively. If he gave up, then he would be lost. Nick closed his eyes as the sea whipped him around. He lost track of time as shades of black formed into circles before his eyes. He didn't know when they were open or when they were closed.

As an hour passed and then two, he felt like the waves were calming, like the wind was settling. But he didn't have the energy to pull himself up and check. His leg was broken. He was sure of it, along with other injuries throughout his body. He'd most likely lost a lot of blood, and with the intake of the salty water, he was dehydrated and he was fading.

Nick tried to focus on his family. That would give him the will to go on. His mother would be traumatized to lose him. She might not be able to bear it. His brother Cooper would be frantic by now, most likely down at the station demanding they let him come on the rescue mission.

Cooper owned an airline and loved to fly. But flying jets and choppers were two different things. If anyone could figure out a chopper's controls on the spur of the moment, it would be Cooper, though, Nick thought with almost the hint of a smile.

Maverick would be at his base. Even being retired wouldn't stop him from getting into the cockpit of his favorite F-18 to search for his brother. He'd grab one and dump it in the ocean just to get to Nick. Hell, his brother would probably reason that he could afford to replace the ridiculously expensive piece of military equipment anyway. That did bring a small grin to Nick's cracked lips.

And then there was Ace. Being so helpless made Nick even more determined than ever to find his brother, to mend those fences. He swore to himself he would get home and he would find Ace.

Hell, with the names their parents had given them, it was no wonder they'd all ended up pilots, Nick thought. Their father had enjoyed flying, but the favorite of their relatives, Uncle Sherman, had really loved it. He'd been the one to give the boys the bug to be above the land and sea.

Their mother worried about their chosen professions, but she was loving and supportive. She still would be when Nick got home safe, healed, and went right back to work. She would never guilt him into quitting the job that had ultimately saved his life.

It was almost ironic that joining the Coast Guard had saved him from wandering down a dark path but also might be what took his life. But safe wasn't in his vocabulary. Life was too short to simply exist—it was worth living for.

The brothers had all vowed to each other that no matter how dangerous a situation they were ever in, they wouldn't give up. It was that promise that kept Nick holding on to his fading life.

He wouldn't give up. The pain in his body was simply a reminder that he was still alive. It was a good reminder. Was he awake? Nick didn't know anymore. But when he heard a faint noise in the distance, a familiar noise, his brain was shutting down and he couldn't focus on it. He needed to rest. A small nap wouldn't hurt . . .

His head spinning, Nick tried to move and found himself unable to do so. Confusion swirled as he tried desperately to remember why he was hurting and where he was.

Nothing was coming to him. Nick didn't appreciate the unfamiliar panic beginning to creep up into his throat. He couldn't even remember what day of the week it was, or for that matter, what month.

"I'm Captain Nick Armstrong, US Coast Guard helicopter pilot," he said out loud, but his voice was weak and scratchy, and he wasn't even sure if the words were audible to anyone who might be nearby.

He opened his mouth to speak again, but ended up in a coughing fit that sent spasms of pain splintering through him. Shutting his eyes, he tried to concentrate, tried to get his befuddled mind to begin making sense.

"You're going to be okay. Hold on for just a while longer. You'll be fine."

Nick clung to the voice, which seemed to be coming to him through a long tunnel, the words echoing as the blinding sun burned through his closed eyelids. But just as he was turning his head, a shadow passed over his face, instantly shading him from the fiery sensation.

He cracked his lids, and gasped.

"I'm dead," he croaked, again not sure if his words had even come out.

A light chuckle sounded like music to his ears. The angel hovering above him had an ethereal glow about her, her features blurred. Her concerned eyes were the only feature he could see clearly. He tried to lift his hand to her, telling her it was okay to take him home. Even that effort was too much for him.

With a shaking smile on his lips, he closed his eyes—and the pain faded away.

CHAPTER ONE

The wind blew briskly as Nick sat on the back deck of his house, his throbbing knee making him take a needed break. Frustration was brewing inside him as strongly as the waves crashing against the shore and the ominous clouds billowing above. The promise of a brilliant storm in the air seemed to be mirroring his life.

Though Nick was content to be out in the open, he would be much happier if he could walk through the rain and lightning, through a freaking hurricane if need be. If he could just get off of the damn deck for more than a few minutes at a time.

Nick was itching to go back to work, but his shattered knee, broken arm, three cracked ribs, and concussion had left him with limited mobility. There was something seriously wrong with the entire situation.

Nick tossed rocks off his deck, aiming for the turbulent waters off the coast of his place on San Juan Island not far from Seattle, Washington. He sighed in frustration at how far away the ocean seemed. With a shake of his head, he closed his eyes and growled. Unable to help it, he found himself thinking back six weeks earlier. It was almost as if he were back there in the hospital.

Confusion had swirled around him as he had tried to get his bearings. The bright lights had made it nearly impossible for him to open his eyes. They'd crack the slightest bit, and shooting pain would scorch from his head to his toes, so he'd shut them again.

But Nick was a Coast Guard pilot. He wasn't afraid of pain, and he certainly didn't fear death. He knew that every mission could be his last. He didn't care. He'd known what he was signing up for from the moment he'd stepped into that recruiter's office.

Blurred visions of the crew who had rescued him flittered through his muddled brain, but no matter how much he tried to focus, the images wouldn't become clearer. By the time the medical staff had steadied him, the world had gone out of focus.

He'd lain in that hospital bed for two weeks. They'd called him a miracle. He'd been the only survivor. In his book, that wasn't a miracle at all. And now Nick was bored and angry. That wasn't a good combination for him. In the past, those emotions had led him down roads best never traveled again. It had gotten him into trouble. But maybe that was exactly what he was looking for now.

At least he was beginning to see improvements. His ribs didn't hurt nearly as badly. The cast was off his arm, and though it was still slightly tender, he refused to give his body mercy. He was lifting weights mostly from a sitting position, had the pool in his house installed with special equipment, and he was pushing the upper half of his body relentlessly. His lower half wasn't responding as well as he'd like. He'd gone through three physical therapists, all of whom had practically run from his place screaming. But Nick always searched for that sweet spot of pain while working out that reminded him he was very much alive.

He didn't need to prolong his forced leave any longer than necessary.

Along with a weaker body, though, he was having trouble sleeping. Nightmares of his lost crew flooded him whenever he shut his eyes. So he pushed himself harder. Maybe he just needed something else to occupy his mind. His brothers sure as hell thought so. They'd told him repeatedly that even if his knee was broken, that didn't mean all of him was.

They wanted him to let go of the anger and start living his life again. Nick wasn't sure exactly how to do that without his job. The Coast Guard was a calling, not an employer. His brothers had told him repeatedly that he needed to enjoy the forced vacation—that he needed a woman. Nick scoffed at them. But their point was abundantly clear.

He needed sex—and lots of it. Sex was therapy, but it wasn't necessarily the answer to everything. That thought made him laugh out loud. Maybe that had been too hasty a thought. Sex sure seemed to cure a hell of a lot, actually.

It was early morning, and the storm was growing in force. The torrential rains hadn't started up yet, but it wouldn't be long now. He hoped the lightning would be right on top of him, the clap of thunder shaking the windows of his place. There was nothing quite like a good coastal storm. Of course, that meant he should be performing rescues for those foolish enough to get caught out in the unforgiving sea.

Soon, he promised himself. Very soon. Taking a deep breath, he inhaled the sweet scent of the storm and then turned away from the progressively aggressive sea. It was only depressing him that he wasn't flying over her deep waves in search of lost vessels.

"Are you done feeling sorry for yourself out here?" The sweet voice of his brother's wife, Stormy, actually made his frown disappear.

"Don't you think I deserve to have a bit of self-pity?" he countered as he turned to give Stormy his most charming smile.

Nick couldn't help but notice his brother's wife was just as beautiful as ever, with a glow in her cheeks and her lips twisted up into a warm smile. If Nick weren't so determined to sow as many oats as possible, he'd hope to find a woman just like her. But since she was taken, he'd have to be a lone wolf.

"I think pity time is over. You're a pain in the ass, Nick, but you're also a great man. Your brothers want to talk to you, so get your butt inside," she told him as she held open the back door.

He put on his most pathetic expression. "Can't you give a guy a hand?" he asked her with a waggle of his brows.

"You are utterly hopeless," she said with a laugh. But she did step out and lean down to help him up. Of course, he could almost get around faster in the wheelchair since he'd been using it for a few weeks. That wasn't the point, though. Nick had lost a lot in the past six weeks. He didn't want any more backsliding.

Once Stormy got her arms around him, he grabbed the crutch that was resting beside his chair and leaned on her with his other arm until they got inside. His knee was killing him. She led him to the wheelchair.

"Sit," she commanded. He wanted to refuse, but he'd pushed himself too hard the day before and he knew she was right.

With a glare sent her way, he plopped into the chair. But just to prove his manliness, he reached out to her with his good arm and tugged, making her fall into him, landing on his lap. His knee was well protected in the brace, plus the impact hit his thighs. There was a slight stirring of pain, but he ignored it as he kissed her forehead.

"Thanks, beautiful," he said with a chuckle as she huffed at him before quickly jumping back to her feet.

"Nick Armstrong, you are going to hurt yourself," she scolded him as she straightened out her clothes. He laughed and shrugged.

"Sorry. I couldn't resist," he said with a wink.

"If you would settle down and find a good woman to keep you in line, you wouldn't be such a pain in the butt," she said with a smile.

"I would gladly settle down if you would wise up and leave my brother," he told her with a wiggle of his brows.

"Tempting," she said with a laugh.

"You've got my number, darling," he told her.

"Trying to steal my wife yet again, Nick?" Cooper asked with a growl as he stepped into the living room to join them before moving toward the kitchen. Nick wheeled his chair forward and followed them. Stormy was chuckling.

"Always," Nick told his older brother.

"I think I'm going to have to whip your ass again in the ring to show you how effective that might be," Cooper warned.

"As soon as I'm on my feet again," Nick said with a glint in his eyes. He would love to get back in the ring. "On second thought, I'm sure I could kick your ass even *while* sitting down."

"I'm going to leave you boys to battle it out. A woman does love to be fought over," Stormy said before softly kissing Cooper, then patting Nick on the arm. It felt as if the light dimmed a bit when she walked away.

"You truly are a lucky man, Coop," Nick told his brother as Stormy's scent lingered in the room.

"That I know, little bro," Cooper said with a smile as he opened the fridge and looked inside at the contents, acting a bit lost.

"Get out of the way, Coop. Even injured, I cook better than you," Nick said with a laugh as he moved to the fridge, pushing Cooper aside. He scanned the shelves before pulling a few items out. Cooper took a seat.

"I see you're starting without me again," Maverick said as he stepped into the kitchen and lit the stove, pulling out a pan as he eyed the food Nick had pulled out.

"Forgot you were even here," Nick told Mav.

"I am anything but forgettable," Mav said with a wink. "Just ask my *very* satisfied wife."

"Spare us," Coop said with a chuckle.

"Yeah, this morning after I got done—"

"Stop!" both Nick and Coop yelled at the same time. Maverick busted up laughing as he added oil to a pan and let it warm.

"Fine. I won't embarrass you by showing you your own inadequacies," Mav said.

"Miracles really do happen," Nick told him with a roll of his eyes.

Mav's expression became serious all of a sudden. "Yes, they do. You're proof of that."

The brothers might joke a hell of a lot, and they might get into some pretty damn big brawls, but when it came down to it, they were family, not just because they'd been born into it, but because they were also friends who would die for each other. Nick felt his throat tighten and he cleared it to cover up the emotion.

"Don't be getting all mushy on me. I'm not married like you two idiots, so I haven't tapped into my feminine side," Nick said with a laugh to cover up the awkward moment.

"Wouldn't even think about such an emotion," Mav said with a smile.

"You really are looking better, though," Coop said.

Mav pushed Nick's wheelchair aside as he threw steaks into the pan and began cutting up vegetables. Nick decided to back off. It was hard to do anything while sitting.

"I'm getting stronger every day. My arm and ribs are as good as new, and I'm lasting longer and longer on the crutches. I'll be back to work soon," Nick boasted.

"Want me to test the arm for you?" Coop pointedly asked.

Nick sent him a glare. The words didn't warrant a reply.

"Fine, I might not want to take a hit in the arm or ribs right now, but that damn well doesn't mean I can't fly," he said.

"You know you do a lot more than fly," Coop asserted.

"I try to," Nick admitted.

"Well, your commander knows you well enough to realize that light duty isn't something that appeals to you. Sherman is bringing in a new therapist. If you behave this time, you can get your strength back in your knee, then maybe, just maybe, you can get out there on a few dates before you're back to saving those lost at sea," Mav said.

Nick glared at both his brothers. "I really don't need therapy or dating advice," he warned.

But the reality was, he needed help—maybe in both areas. There was something missing in his life. He was sure it was just because he hadn't been able to work, hadn't truly been able to say good-bye to his crew.

His copilot, Gail, had a six-year-old daughter who was now being raised without a mother. When her husband had come to see him in the hospital, Nick had been mortified when he'd felt a tear wet his cheek. Gail's strong husband had placed his hand on Nick's shoulder and told him Gail would want him to survive. He'd known Nick hadn't been able to continue speaking, and he'd left, leaving Nick lying there trying not to fall apart.

His young paramedic, John Francis, had only been with them six months. He'd been so happy to be a part of the Coast Guard, and he'd been far too young to die. His parents' lives had been forever altered by his loss. Secretly, Nick had paid for his funeral and left a fund for the parents, whose son had been taking care of them. They were lost without him.

Then there was his rescue swimmer, Pat, who had been so damn brave. He'd jumped into the water no matter the risk to himself. He'd always cracked jokes and had come up with the most insane songs to torment them with through their headsets.

And they were all gone while Nick lived. *It wasn't right.*

Nick realized that as he'd been reflecting on his crew, his brothers had stopped speaking and were staring at him.

"What?" he grumpily asked.

"We're not trying to be a-holes, we're just trying to help you out," Coop said as he gave a far-too-understanding look to Nick. Nick shook his head and sent each brother a stare that was sure to make them stop meddling.

"Since you and Mav married, you've been pestering the hell out of me to do the same. I'm perfectly content to be single," Nick warned.

Cooper looked as if he was going to keep pestering him, but then he sighed and sat back. Mav continued cooking. But Nick didn't miss the glance that passed between the two brothers. Something else was going on that they didn't want to share with him. He was immediately on alert.

Mav turned off the stove and put their lunch on plates, then they all moved to the dining table. Nick waited to see if they would say something. They didn't and he lost patience.

"What's going on, guys? I know it's not my lack of a dating life," Nick said when the room remained too silent. Mav and Coop looked at each other and Nick grew frustrated. "I was injured, I'm not dead, and I don't need to be safeguarded. Don't leave me out of whatever is happening."

"It's about Ace," Cooper said with a sigh.

Nick sat at attention. Their brother had walked out years ago at the reading of their father's will. He'd been angry, and time had only made it worse. They had all tried reaching out to Ace, but he had only made a couple of appearances, and they hadn't been happy reunions.

"What's the news?" Nick asked.

"He's back in the States," Coop said.

Nick was silent for several moments. He took a few bites of food, not tasting it, eating on autopilot as his head spun.

"What does that mean?" Nick finally asked.

"He's been back for six weeks, living in Montana. I'm trying to get more information, but I don't understand why he's not trying to get ahold of us. He's not even pursuing the stipulations of the will anymore."

That was another contention among the brothers. Their father had left them all ultimatums upon his death. The four brothers had told their mother they wouldn't comply, but then life had happened, and whether they'd wanted to or not, they were doing exactly what their father had requested with his final words—leading more respectable lives, settling down—maturing. Coop and Mav had gotten married like their father had wanted. Nick and Ace were the only holdouts there, but it wasn't because of the will that Nick didn't marry. It was because the thought of settling down with only one woman made a cold sweat break out on his brow. His brothers made the actual act of matrimony seem appealing . . . but he kept going back to the only *one* woman for the rest of his life part. Damn! That seemed like shackling himself for sure.

"Should we go to him?" Nick asked, deciding he didn't want to focus on wedded bliss any more than he absolutely had to.

It was Cooper's time to be quiet. He pushed the rest of his food away, not able to even pretend he had the stomach to continue eating. He was the eldest of the brothers, and therefore always felt like he had to take on the brunt of the responsibility.

"I think we need to do that, but let's get some more information first. I think he might be mixed up in some shady dealings," Coop said with a sad sigh.

"Why does it have to be shady dealings?" Nick asked.

"Because he's been avoiding us. And now we find out he's back in the States and won't have anything to do with us? We don't ever see him anymore. To me that looks like shame," Coop said.

"We don't have enough information to determine that," Nick insisted. Why was he the only one defending Ace?

"I've used every connection I have, and I still can't get anywhere," Mav pointed out. "It's not that I want to think the worst. He's just not leaving us much of a choice anymore."

Nick shook his head. "No way. I don't care what he's done over the past few years. He's still Ace, and there's no way he would ever do anything illegal."

Nick and Ace had always been close. He had to have faith in his brother even if the rest of their family had lost theirs. Maybe he would go in secret and find out what was happening—that was, when he could walk again.

"There's not an official investigation," Cooper said. "It's just from some of the things I've been hearing from investigators. He can't even be pulled up in the system."

"That doesn't even make sense," Mav said. "Everyone leaves a paper trail whether they want to or not."

"I'm just telling you what I found," Coop said, holding up his hands.

"What does Uncle Sherman have to say about it?" Nick asked.

"He says to have faith in our brother," Mav said.

"Then maybe that's exactly what we should do," Nick said, his voice gruff. "I'm just saying there has to be more behind this. He's our brother, and I'm choosing to believe that he's still him—even if he got lost a bit along the way. We've all been lost and we're okay now. Let's have the same faith in him."

"I want to, I really do. But so much time has passed. I just don't know what to think now," Cooper said.

"We stick together no matter what," Nick said. It was pretty cut and dry in his book.

Coop shook his head. "We can't support something illegal."

"I'm not suggesting that," Nick snapped. "I'm just saying there has to be a reason behind what's been happening. I'm going to do my own research."

"Let's talk to Sherman, and we'll go from there," Coop said.

Nick was irritated at how logical Cooper was being. When it came to family, it wasn't always black and white. Maybe it was time for Ace to quit hiding and ask for help with whatever was going on. Had he lost his faith in his family? If so, they'd have to figure out a way to restore it.

"I'm sorry we upset you," Coop said.

"Yeah, we know how delicate you are," Mav added.

Nick glared at them both. He was injured, not incompetent.

"Quit treating me differently. It's pissing me off. Of course I'm upset. Ace is our brother," Nick spat out.

"None of us are giving up," Coop reassured Nick.

Nick knew that. His shoulders dropped as the anger drained from him. He smiled at his brothers. Cooper and Mav both nodded. Nick pushed away from the table and went over to his large windows. He could see the waters churning and the sky flashing, but his earlier excitement over the storm had evaporated.

It had already been a long day, and it wasn't even yet noon. It would be a long while before the hits stopped coming at him from every direction. For now, he needed to simply learn how to roll with the punches.

CHAPTER TWO

Chloe Reynolds stepped up to the monstrous-size house on San Juan Island. She wasn't happy about being pushed into taking the job for the wealthy, arrogant helicopter pilot for the US Coast Guard, but at the same time, she hadn't had a lot of choice.

It wasn't just about taking the job. Chloe knew a lot more about Nick Armstrong than she would ever want to know. He was a monster— as was his entire family. But she smiled as she took calming breaths outside his front door. She could put on a happy face, do her job, and be instrumental in making him pay for his crimes.

Having experience as an RN and being a board-certified orthopedic physical therapist had gained her access to his home. Because she was a professional, she would do her job and do it well, but that wouldn't stop her from completing her other mission.

Nick Armstrong was going down. That thought brought a smile to her full pink lips as she brushed back her blonde strands and took a step forward. The door opened before she even lifted her hand to knock, and then she was gazing at Nick Armstrong, the man she'd been sent to investigate—unofficially. Her stomach tightened and her muscles shook. So much emotion raged through her, she wasn't sure she actually would be able to do her job of helping him heal—not when she knew what he'd done. But she couldn't turn back now.

"Can I help you?" The deep timbre of his voice made her stomach clench. This wasn't starting off well at all: first the self-doubt, and now facing him, she felt something she most certainly didn't want to feel.

"I'm . . ." Her sentence fell away as she took a step forward, her foot sliding on a slick leaf. She tried to regain her balance, but she was suddenly tumbling. Nick held out his arms, either to help her or push her away. She wasn't exactly sure which.

With a rush of breath, Chloe landed in Nick's lap. With her face far too close to his for comfort, she saw momentary agony in his eyes. She was locked in place by his powerful arms as she watched a mixture of emotions cross his face.

Chloe knew she should jump up, demand he release her, apologize profusely, and run like hell in the other direction—she knew she should do anything other than lie there limply in the arms of the enemy. His arms tightened around her, and Chloe felt a stirring in her stomach that startled her. This was much different than the turmoil she'd felt just a few breaths before as they'd gazed at one another.

Besides the fact that this man was her enemy, had been her enemy before she'd ever even met him, she wasn't normally a foolish woman who fell into the arms of random men. So to have this reaction to *him* of all people was throwing her completely off balance.

His eyes were burning as he looked her over. Chloe shifted, wondering what in the world she was going to say after her noteworthy entrance. He smiled and she found herself having a difficult time breathing. Did her heart just skip a beat?

Nonsense!

Nick Armstrong was far too good-looking for the natural well-being of all women within a hundred yards of him. He had dark hair, smoldering green eyes, and a cocky tilt to his lips that made her want to lean forward and kiss him. Of course, she already knew all this, since she'd been studying the Armstrong family for quite some time.

As his arms tightened around her, Chloe's stomach continued to stir, coiling as unexpected sensations rushed to the rest of her body. She inhaled a breath of air, and Nick's scent permeated her system. She found her fingers tightening on his shirt as she pressed a little closer to him.

The shock of what she was doing stunned her into immobility, and she stiffened. She could have prevented the fall if she'd been more careful, but it had happened. However, her subsequent reaction to this man, who she was supposed to hate with every fiber of her being, was inexcusable.

Foolish, foolish, foolish.

She would be kicking her own butt for a while for her mistake. She most certainly wasn't going to be able to continue her self-loathing until she extricated herself from his arms. What was she doing? If this was playing with fire, she'd leapt in with both feet and was now scorched.

She raised an eyebrow at the man as Nick's head began leaning toward hers. For one moment she wanted the kiss he seemed about to give her. And then, thankfully, her brain cells began firing again. The shock of the moment had her heart thundering and her stomach doing a little dance.

"Let me go," she demanded, her voice coming out too squeaky for it to have any real impact.

He stopped, but he didn't look irritated, merely surprised. Maybe he hadn't thought his own actions through and had been going on impulse. His eyes twinkled as he gazed at her. No words beyond their quick greeting and her plea for release had been spoken. She moved while she tried to pull from him. That's when she felt a bulge pressing into the toned flesh of her thigh.

Her body tightened even more, and she knew she had to get away. Pushing against his chest, he finally loosened his grip and she scrambled to her feet.

Chloe raised a hand, wiping moisture off her face, realizing that the rain had started up again while she'd been in this surreal encounter. Why in the world were they simply staring at each other while the storm intensified? A crack of lightning flashed across the sky, and a boom of thunder quickly followed, making her jump.

She took a step back, not sure of what she was doing. Escape was on her mind, but she was stopped by the grip of his fingers on her arm. The touch sent more heat spiraling through her.

This so wasn't good.

"I'm assuming you came here for a reason," he said, tugging her back toward him. His eyes were raised as he waited for her to introduce herself.

As much as Chloe suddenly wanted to run, she knew her nerves were just a reaction to the unique situation. She was there for a job and she wasn't going anywhere. Putting her professional mask in place, she tugged against his hold to no avail as she looked down at him. Her aloof attitude had made many men walk away with their tails between their legs. She could handle Nick Armstrong—no problem. She'd been pushing men away since she'd developed early at the age of thirteen. Men with looks like Nick wanted one thing, and it wasn't something she was willing to offer.

"Yes, sorry. The fall startled me, that's all," she began, putting on her most professional smile—the do-not-touch-me smile that had always worked so well for her. "I'm Chloe Reynolds, your physical therapist," she said. She tugged on her arm again.

He didn't let her go, but he also didn't scowl at her like she'd been hoping. If he was irritated, he'd lose interest. Instead, her reaction seemed to amuse him. A brilliant smile lit up his lips as raindrops slid down the side of her face, making her think of entwined, sweating, naked bodies.

She was shocked by where her mind had wandered. She *never* thought this way. She was busy with her career and her family, two things she wanted this man to have nothing to do with. She didn't have time for men, and she *really* didn't have time for sex. So why would she be thinking of it with this particular man?

"You're a whole lot better looking than the last couple of therapists sent my way," he told her. Unexpectedly, the compliment made her glow just a little.

"I don't appreciate that. I'm here because of my qualifications," she said to him.

He smiled even more. "Uncle Sherman sent you, right?" he said, his eyes not straying from hers.

"Yes, Sherman Armstrong hired me for six weeks of intensive home care. He said you're impatient to get back to work, that you're a pain-in-the-ass patient—his words, not mine—and that if I can stick it out, I'll get paid triple."

She might as well let him know right up front this was about work. It was more than obvious the man was attracted to her, which should have made her angry instead of light-headed. It was better if she let him know nothing unprofessional was going to happen. At least, not the sexy kind of unprofessional . . . She wasn't here for that.

"Hmm, sounds about right," he told her. "Of course, you're not off to a very good start. I'm injured and you just crashed down on my lap." The smile in his voice took away any sympathy she might have felt for him.

"I apologize for that. Let me check to make sure you're okay. Maybe we can go inside," she pointed out. The rain was blowing right under the porch roof. He didn't seem to even notice.

"Yes, of course. Please come in."

He expertly backed his wheelchair up and spread a welcoming arm before him in a sweeping gesture. With reluctance she followed him inside his monstrous house. No one needed so much space, she thought as she looked around at the wide hallways and modern furniture. It appeared as if some of it had been rearranged—most likely to help him get around the place more efficiently.

Even though the rooms were open and large, Chloe felt as if the walls were closing in on her. Nick in a wheelchair was a force to be reckoned with. She couldn't imagine what he'd be like in full health. It was a good thing he would be locked away in jail by the time that point came.

"I get you all to myself for a full six weeks," Nick said, and Chloe whipped around to see he was far too close to her. She needed to nip this flirting in the bud right away.

She gave him a derisive look. "I'm not interested," she told him in her sternest voice.

His smile grew as he stared at her, not at all intimidated by her remark. Chloe found that she again wanted to retreat. Dammit. This was going all wrong.

"You know what, Chloe Reynolds, I think I like you," he said, his grin in place, his eyes darkening and his chest pushing out the slightest bit. Though he was affecting her in a way she didn't want to be affected, she'd rather be flung into the ocean than admit to it.

"You don't know me," she pointed out.

"Maybe I'd like to rectify that," he said with a wink.

A shudder passed through her, and she sent him her harshest glare. He didn't wither as intended. In fact, he didn't seem to be turned off even a little bit. Even though she was being her snarkiest, he didn't seem to mind. It appeared there was one part of his body that hadn't been injured in the crash.

"Have I given you even the slightest indication that I want that to happen?" she said, putting her most librarian tone into her voice.

He didn't even blink.

"Maybe," he said.

"Back off," she told him. "I'm a professional and I'm here to do a job—without the flirting."

"Maybe you need to loosen up a bit and enjoy life," he said.

Her back stiffened as she tried to pull herself under control. The last half hour or so had been more draining than she ever could have imagined. It was time for that retreat.

"Can you just tell me where my room is, please?" She decided the best option was to ignore the flirting, try to get him to open up to her about the crash, and tend to his wounds. But not until she had a few minutes to herself.

"I'll do better than that, I'll personally show you," he told her. She caught the twinkle in his eyes. She didn't want the man anywhere near where she'd be sleeping. She'd fought like hell not to have to stay at his house, but Sherman had insisted the therapy would be an all-day thing. He'd also insisted on having someone there in case Nick had problems at night.

Chloe had pointed out that she wasn't a nurse. Of course, he'd called her on that. She'd been a nurse before she'd decided to go into physical therapy. That's when he'd offered to triple the pay for a job well done. And Chloe had a lot of school debt the job would help pay off.

"Let me go and get my bag first," she said, then spun around and dashed back out the front door. She was soaked when she came back to a scowling Nick. She had no idea what she'd done now.

"What?" she finally asked.

"I'm just sick of being this incapable," Nick said as he slammed his hand down against the arm of the chair.

"What do you mean?" Immediate concern filled her. After all, she was a therapist first.

"Never have I allowed a woman to carry her own bags before," he grumbled.

His angry words made her smile, which shocked Chloe. She didn't want to find an appealing trait about the man, but she couldn't help it.

"I'm perfectly capable of carrying my own bags," she informed him.

He reached over and took the handle from her, pulling the large suitcase to the side of his chair.

"I've got it from here," he said. "Though I should have had it from the car."

"Don't be ridiculous, Nick." She tried getting the bag back. He wasn't budging. They had a stare down until she was the one to break and look away.

His arm muscle bulging, he pushed the wheel of his chair, using his good leg to keep it straight while holding the handle of her bag with the other arm and tugging it beside him. She slowly trailed after him.

"Thank you." It was sincere. Silence surrounded them then as she tried to force herself to move away from him. This was going to be a trying job. That was for sure. But the sooner she found what she needed, the faster she would get away from him.

Nick was almost at a loss as he led Chloe through his large home. The woman had shown up on his porch like a present from the gods. He wasn't about to complain. Even with her uppity attitude, he was having more fun than he'd had in a while.

All it had taken was one look into Ms. Chloe Reynolds's eyes, and he'd felt warmth invade him as his heartbeat elevated its pulse. He'd been turned on by women before—many, *many* times—but he'd never had that knee-weakening feeling that had been coursing through him from the second he'd opened his front door to find her standing there.

The spark between them was undeniable. She might be trying to act like it wasn't there, but that only made Nick want to try that much harder to make her yield. She was guarded and stubborn all in one. She was a challenge.

Nick was a confident man—injured or healthy—and he certainly knew when a woman found him attractive. Chloe obviously did, whether she was willing to admit to that or not. It just made the game of cat and mouse that much more appealing.

Without the injury, he never would have met the physical therapist, which would have been a shame. He found her intriguing. It had been a while since someone had piqued his interest so quickly.

Chloe scowled at him as he led her down the hallway. Was she really this standoffish or was it him? He couldn't imagine it being *him*—he was a hell of a guy, and women didn't typically hate him at first sight. And Nick never stuck around long enough to give them time to change their opinions.

"Your house is big," she said when they turned a corner and moved down the wide hallway.

"I'm a big guy," he told her with a wink. She frowned. He stopped at the guest bedroom but didn't want her to leave yet so he blocked the entrance as he searched his brain for something to say.

"Why don't you tell me what we're going to be doing?" he finally asked.

It took her a moment to adjust to his change of subject, then her face lit up, and he could see he'd gone in the right direction this time. If he spoke about work, maybe she'd open up. He knew *he* loved talking about his job.

"I'm an RN, with a specialty in orthopedics. I decided to move into physical therapy because I'm intrigued by the idea of fixing, through manipulation, what most people think is impossible to mend via surgery. I've studied your injuries, and you've done really well with most of your body, but I've been told you aren't taking proper care of your knee," she told him.

"I've been doing what the doc has told me," he pointed out.

She sent him a wry glance. "I don't think so. I know the doctor told you to use your crutches sparingly until you've had therapy. Your uncle said you don't go to the chair often enough. If you try to do this on your own, it can lead to permanent injury. For me to do my job properly, you're going to have to trust *and* listen to me. If you aren't willing to do those two things, then there's really no point at all in my being here," she said with a stern expression.

Nick laughed, and that made her eyes narrow on him. He held up his hand. It had been a while since he'd laughed. It felt pretty damn good, he had to admit.

"I will do anything you want of me, Doll," he promised.

"It's Chloe," she pointed out.

"I like Doll better," he said with a waggle of his brows. She sighed in frustration. The woman was far too easy to rile up, which only made Nick want to do it more and more. It might be boredom, it might be lust, but whatever it was, he was glad his therapy would take time—and to think, just that morning he'd been pissed about it.

"I don't care, that's not my name," she pointed out.

"Gotcha," he said. "You'll get used to it, though."

Her cheeks were growing a very appealing shade of pink in her frustration. He decided he liked the color a lot. He bet her entire body blushed with excitement when she was turned on. He most definitely was going to have to see that for himself—and he didn't want to wait too long. It had been months since he'd been with a woman, and he was more than ready.

"Look, Nick, I'm not some doe-eyed young intern. I'm a professional and I've helped NFL athletes so they didn't have to retire, hockey players get back on the ice, given baseball players many extra years, and other professional athletes," she told him. He opened his mouth to speak, and she held up a hand. "Not only have I helped many men like you who don't think they need my help, but then are always incredibly appreciative when they get to continue their careers, but I've also

26

worked with other doctors, nurses, and professionals who need to be on their feet all day. You're very lucky to have me here doing this for you. I would appreciate you giving me the respect I've earned."

Damn, he liked her sass. He was seriously going to enjoy their time together. Nick was sure this would be one therapist he'd have no desire whatsoever to chase away. He wouldn't mind chasing her to his bedroom, but he'd save that for another day.

"I have the utmost respect for you, but you have to realize, too, that I'm not your typical patient. I like to push myself, and I don't want kid gloves while doing it. I'm only going to get better if I don't cry every time something hurts a little," he told her.

"I'm the one who will tell you how far you can take it. We need to get that very clear right now or this relationship isn't going to work."

"Relationship? I like the sound of that," he said.

"*Professional* relationship, Mr. Armstrong," she reprimanded. He laughed again, and she scowled at him.

"I'm up for any type of pairing you have in mind," he told her.

For a brief moment, Nick thought back to the week before when he'd been uninterested in dating or sleeping with any women. How quickly his mind could be changed, he thought with a crooked smile.

It hadn't been that he'd been uninterested. He realized he'd been waiting for that spark he'd needed to ignite a full-blown fire. Nick felt more himself while the two of them faced off in his hallway than he had in months. Even before the accident, he'd been feeling restless, uneasy, like he was missing something.

Maybe all along he'd been waiting for this particular woman to step into his life. She'd soon learn that when given an inch, it didn't take long for Nick to go a yard. And it felt damn good to know that, even if his leg wasn't working properly, at least his libido was. He'd take all the wins he possibly could right now.

Their gazes locked together, and he saw fear in her eyes. It wasn't fear of him, he was sure of that. Chloe was afraid of the scorching attraction between the two of them, a smoldering burning that no amount of water was going to be able to put out.

Nick also knew when it was time to relent for a while. He moved back a bit and pushed open her bedroom door. The two of them stood in the hallway as she looked inside with an unreadable expression.

"Get settled in, and then we'll continue our discussion," Nick said as he scooted back, leaving her bag in the doorway and allowing her access to the room. He stayed close enough that she would have no way of getting past him without brushing against his leg, but she tried anyway—and failed.

Grabbing her bag, she pushed it inside, then turned and looked at him one last time before wordlessly shutting the door without saying anything else. Only then did he turn around to head back to the main part of the house, a big grin on his face. Let the healing begin.

CHAPTER THREE

The morning light was shining in Chloe's window far too early for her liking. Normally she was very much a morning person, but on this day, she knew she was going to have to spend it with Nick, and she also knew he wasn't going to make it easy on her. No matter how much she tried to keep a professional distance, she had an inkling that the man had no idea what that concept even meant.

It was six in the morning, and she only had an hour to herself before the long day began. She jumped from bed, put on her jogging clothes, and crept from her bedroom, grateful when she didn't see any signs of Nick being up and about.

Stepping from the house, she stretched her sleepy muscles, then began a slow jog through the trails surrounding Nick's property. It was an exploratory run to empty out her mind and wash sleep away. She wasn't trying to set any records.

But this morning Chloe wasn't finding the peace she so desperately needed as she moved through the lush foliage of the forest surrounding Nick's property. Her mind was uneasy as she thought about what she was supposed to be doing.

Nick had been the pilot of the helicopter that had crashed—giving her brother a burial at sea that he'd been too young to have. His body hadn't been recovered, and the pain she felt from his loss still ate at her.

When Chloe's father had found out she'd been hired to be Nick's therapist, the man had flown into a rage, trapping her against the wall as his spit spattered her face, making that terror she'd felt as a child come back to the surface.

After his rant had ended—taking nearly an hour—he'd then gotten a look in his eyes that had scared her far worse than his rage. It had been cunning and calculating. He'd given her a stare that told her she'd best not disappoint him. Her father had said they could use this opportunity to dig up the evidence on Nick Armstrong the judge would need to send his ass to prison.

Nick was already guilty in her father's eyes. They just had to make sure he wasn't going to somehow get out of it. Chloe didn't trust her father, but another crewman had stepped forward to say he'd seen Nick drinking the night he'd flown that helicopter out into the storm. If that was the case, then Nick was guilty of his crew's demise—and he should pay for their deaths.

Three good people had lost their lives while Nick had lived. Hadn't she once heard that many drunk drivers survived because they were too wasted to tense up during an accident? It seemed to be the case with Nick.

But Chloe didn't like to go into any situation blind, so she'd done her homework on the Armstrong family, had studied everything she'd been able to get her hands on—especially pertaining to Nick. She hadn't found anything to back up her father's convictions.

Guilt ate through Chloe. Guilt at losing her brother and not doing everything in her power to avenge his death, guilt at lying to a patient—even if that patient was guilty of murder, guilt at plotting the demise of a man—even if that man was *not* guilty of murder, guilt at doubting her father.

Chloe was torn. She hated that she felt attracted to this man who was supposed to be her enemy, and she hated that she had ulterior motives and that her oath to "do no harm" as a medical professional felt like a lie. She had to treat him as any other patient, had to leave him able to walk—even if he were doing so behind bars.

Chloe was so deep in thought, she nearly tripped over a branch when her phone rang, yanking her back to the present. Normally, she would ignore a call while she was exercising, as it cut off the music that helped motivate her to keep on moving, but that ring tone was her best friend, and Chloe needed to speak with her.

She answered just before the call was sent to voice mail. There was a pause on the other end of the line, and then Chloe had to quickly push the button on her ear set when her best friend's voice boomed over the line.

"It's a good thing you answered, because I was getting ready to hang up, which means I would have called back over and over and over again," Dakota said.

Dakota and Chloe had met in elementary school and had been best friends from the very first moment they'd found out they shared a love of chocolate. Chloe had been shy and afraid, thanks in large part to her unaffectionate father. Dakota had been full of life. Against all odds, the two of them had sparked an immediate bond that hadn't broken in all the years they'd known each other.

Chloe credited her sanity to Dakota. Without having her friend around, Chloe wasn't sure what she would do most days. Dakota had gotten her through the best and worst of times, and the two had even stuck together through college.

"I'm running," Chloe told her, but her steps faltered, and then she began moving slowly along the path she'd been on. She suddenly wasn't in a hurry to return to the house. She needed to speak to her friend more than she needed to get Nick's therapy started.

"Pssh, you are gorgeous and don't need to run every stinking day," Dakota told her.

"Says the woman every other woman hates," Chloe reminded her.

"Whatever. You have to say that since you're my bestie and therefore responsible for stroking my ego."

"Your ego doesn't need to be stroked, Dakota," Chloe pointed out.

"Ah, darling, we've had this conversation before. Every woman needs her ego stroked," Dakota countered. "Among other things," she added with a giggle. Chloe sighed and the silence was piercing for several moments.

"What's wrong? I know that sigh," Dakota said, her voice instantly understanding. It brought tears to Chloe's eyes.

"I'm on a job, and I fear it's going to be a hard one," Chloe admitted.

"The patient is gonna have a hard-on?" Dakota said with too much innocence.

Her friend's wit did the job, and Chloe smiled though Dakota couldn't see the gesture. "If you were here, he most certainly would," she said.

"Someday you are going to see yourself for who you truly are," Dakota said with irritation.

"I look in a mirror every morning," Chloe said.

"But you don't *see* what's gazing back."

"Now it's my turn to tell you that you *have* to say that," Chloe said.

"I cannot tell a lie. You know that's my most debilitating fault," Dakota reminded her.

"But you can if you believe it hard enough."

"I might have to make a trip to see you so I can slap some sense into that calculating brain of yours," Dakota threatened.

"I might have to tick you off so you do just that if it means I get to see you," Chloe said.

There was silence again for a moment. "Do you need me, Chloe?" The question was serious.

"Always, but no, I'm just feeling sorry for myself," Chloe assured her.

"If you do, you know I'll drop everything and be right there," Dakota told her.

"I know that, too."

By the time Chloe hung up, she felt a smidge better, but as she walked up to the house, her nerves came back tenfold. She thought about running some more, but she was already late.

She had a nice gleam of sweat coating her as she walked into the house and made it to her luxurious bedroom. If there was any benefit to the job she was currently doing, it was that she had an exquisite bedroom with an even better bathroom. She would love to take a nice hour-long bath, but maybe she could do that later in the evening.

As much as she'd like to cause the conceited man some much needed pain, she had taken an oath to help the injured. She would attack him in legal ways that wouldn't cost her the job she loved so much.

Taking a quick shower, she changed into her unflattering scrubs and headed to the kitchen with no time to spare. She wasn't much of a morning eater, but she found some apple-cinnamon muffins and munched on one, washing it down with a glass of ice-cold milk. She already felt better.

Now she was wondering where Nick was, though. She'd told him they would begin at seven. He could at least give her the courtesy of being there on time—even if she wasn't.

Deciding she'd wait for him in the gym, she moved through the house, looking for the private gym that Sherman Armstrong had assured her Nick had. She found the doors to his private gym wide open. She stood there in the doorway, finding her breath stalling as she glanced in at the shirtless man as he pulled down a lateral bar, his shoulders and arms bulging with the effort, a nice sheen of sweat coating his naturally tan skin.

The only word that came to mind was magnificent. He was truly a beautiful man. If she didn't know he'd been in a helicopter crash—one that had caused the deaths of three other people—she would have no clue he had sustained any injuries.

Grunting, he pulled the bar a few more times, all without knowing she was watching him. She enjoyed the private moment a little too much. If she gave into these odd feelings of desire she'd been feeling for Nick, she would be compromising not only herself but also her family—especially her brother. This man could be the reason she would never again sit across the table from Pat, never see his smile, never feel reassured by the one man who had never let her down.

Finally, the weight bar snapped down, which also startled her into movement. "I see you've gotten started without me," she told him as she entered the room, trying not to stare at the rigid muscles of his back.

"I'm an early riser," he said, shifting in his seat to see her.

She moved over to him and knelt down. She was completely professional as she examined the knee brace he wore. It allowed him to move the leg, while taking pressure off the shattered patella. The skin was a healthy color, and the surgeon had done an excellent job to keep the scarring to a minimum.

"We're going to work on light exercises today so I can see what you can do. I want to stretch the leg out really good first, though," she told him.

"You can do whatever you want to me, doc," he said with a smile.

"I'm not your doctor," she informed him.

"You have a doctorate. That makes you a doctor," he pointed out.

She smiled at him. "Some people who earn the credentials insist on the title. I'm not one of them," she said.

Their eyes connected and she felt warmth creeping through her veins. She wiped the smile away and reminded herself he was just another guy who she had vowed to help. She had also promised to take him down. Her ethics were fighting within her.

"Where do you want me?" he asked, turning in his seat while she was still kneeling by him. This put her between his legs, her face entirely too close to the part of his body she didn't want to be thinking about.

"I'm going to have you lie on the mats over there where I can stretch your muscles. I'm sure you haven't been doing it," she said, her voice a bit too breathless.

His smiled widened. He knew the effect he had on women—had on her—and he enjoyed it. She would just have to prove to him she wasn't a typical female, grateful for a crumb of his attention.

Chloe helped him up, and he limped over to the mats. Though she was sure he could get down on his own, he was all hands as he shifted to the floor and laid on his back. Wearing only basketball shorts, shoes, and the knee brace, entirely too much of his skin was on display.

She noticed a scar across his stomach that she wondered about. If he were just any client, she might ask him. But she had to remember this was Nick Armstrong, and the less she knew about him on a personal level, the better for her sanity.

"Some of this is going to really hurt, but you have to trust me that I'm doing my job correctly. If it becomes pain instead of simple soreness, you have to tell me. I don't know exactly where you're at right now."

"Got it, doc."

"Lift your injured leg up."

She didn't assist him as he did this. She wanted to see what strength he had in the muscle. It had been a while since he'd been able to do much with it. His teeth gritted as he lifted the leg into the air, and the movement was obviously uncomfortable for him. The muscle truly was weak.

"Okay, I'm going to grab your foot. The brace will keep your leg straight, and I'm going to push it toward your head. When I tell you, I want you to push back to me, and then I will have you release the muscle. Let's see how far of a stretch we can get," she said.

Nick nodded as she gripped his foot, then he gave her a wink. "I should know a little bit more about you before we get so intimate."

"I warned you last night to knock off the flirting, Nick," she said before resting his foot on her shoulder and stepping a bit more into him. The movement caused the muscle to stretch, and he frowned.

"Damn, what are you doing?" he asked with a grunt.

"I'm testing your flexibility," she told him.

"Or punishing me," he countered.

She chuckled. "I'll be sure to tell you *when* I'm punishing you," she said.

"Mmm, kinky. I like it."

She pushed her weight a bit more toward him, stretching the hamstring. That wiped the smile off his smug face.

"Okay, now push against me," she said as she kept one hand on his foot, the other on the outside of his thigh. Her breasts were being crushed by the weight of his solid calf muscle, but she tried to ignore how intimate stretching could be. She tried not to think about how much their bodies were touching.

But she was breaking out in just as much sweat as he was. And not from exertion. The growing attraction she felt toward this man was seriously messing with her head. She had to get it together, and quickly, before she really did do something that would cost her the job she loved. And the respect she held for herself.

They pushed and pulled for a while longer, Chloe pushing aside the unfamiliar stirrings he was causing in the pit of her stomach. The more she did, the more Nick's forehead broke out in sweat. He continued to make small jokes, but the longer the stretching went on, the quieter he became.

"Okay, now we're going to test your hips," she said.

His eyes flashed to hers. "I assure you, my hips weren't injured in the accident at all," he told her.

The remark made her glance down between his legs, and she jerked her gaze away to meet his eyes again. He winked at her. Chloe let out her breath, telling herself she had to keep it together.

"We're going to take the leg across your body slowly," she said. Then she pushed his leg across the other one, bringing her closer to him. He winced, but as she worked with him, she got him to release the muscles. When she next looked at his eyes, he was smiling at her again.

"I might need you to stretch out my arms in the same manner," he said, his voice husky.

"You can keep on wishing that," she told him.

They finished the stretching and Chloe was impressed, though she didn't want to admit that to the man. He was cocky enough without her telling him she was impressed with what excellent shape he was in.

"I think you can expect a full recovery if you do what I say and we work on more stretching along with the exercises. I don't want you working the leg at all until we stretch. There are some you can do on your own, but for the first couple weeks, let me work with you and chart the progress."

"Anything you say, doc," he replied.

Chloe dropped his leg gently back to the ground and took a step back. She turned away from him as she sighed. This truly was going to be a long six weeks. Maybe she could shorten the time frame. He was a capable man. The sooner she got him healthy, the sooner she'd be able to push him from her life.

Nick climbed back to a standing position. It took him far longer than she figured it normally would. But he got up without asking for help. When she turned to look at him, she did notice that his pride had hurt him.

"Come over and sit down, Nick," she said, indicating a chair. She handed him the crutches, and he used them to move over to the chair. He sat down slowly.

She once again kneeled in front of him. She'd better get used to it. She was going to be in close quarters with him for quite some time. If she didn't suck it up, it was going to be unbearable.

"I'm going to cup the back of your foot. I want you to lift your leg ten times."

She showed him the movement she wanted and they began. The morning was slow and laborious, but she had to give it to the guy—he didn't complain once. He did everything she asked of him, making sweat pour off him in droves as he gritted his teeth, but by the end of their second hour there was no doubt he'd impressed her.

She'd had patients who'd quit after the first five minutes. It wasn't easy stuff she was putting them through. When she was finished with the morning session, she handed him a towel and smiled. She couldn't help but feel respect for the man who was working so hard to improve himself when most would have quit by now. Her turbulent emotions were all over the place, and they weren't welcome in the least.

"You've done excellent, Nick," she said, having to give him some praise.

"I'm weak," he told her as he blew out his breath. "I don't like it."

"You aren't used to not being able to do whatever you want, are you?"

"No, not at all," he grumbled.

"Well, suck it up. You're one of the lucky ones who actually gets to walk away from this. Don't waste time feeling sorry for yourself."

His head whipped up at her words. She expected to see anger in his eyes, but she saw humor instead. That threw her off balance.

"Don't hold back, doc," he said with a laugh.

"It's not my job to hold back. It's my job to tell the truth and to get you where you're supposed to be."

"Maybe it's my job to get you to loosen up a little bit," he countered.

She rolled her eyes at him. "Not everything's a joke, Nick," she warned.

"Who says I'm joking?"

He gave her an intense look that had her squirming as she stood there facing him.

"Nick . . ." she said in a warning tone.

"Look, doc, I want you to push me hard, but at the same time, have a little fun. I don't like being down physically or emotionally," he said.

She smiled. "I guarantee you, I have no problem pushing you hard. I can do without the fun."

"I have a feeling I'm going to be hard around you a lot."

"Quit acting like a child," she snapped.

"It's not my fault," he said, holding up his hands.

"Don't you dare say it's mine," she said.

"What do you expect when you look the way you do?" His eyes took her in from head to toe, which made her shift on her feet again.

"I'm perfectly presentable in my scrubs," she told him.

"Doc, you could be wearing a potato sack and still look good."

"Look, I have respect for my patients and what they've gone through and what I'm about to put them through. That's why I'm here—to help, not to put up with your crap."

"You know what, doc, I have a good feeling about this. I tend to listen to my gut, and what it's telling me right now is that you know your stuff. I'm willing to follow your rules as long as you're willing to acknowledge that you don't know me and what I'm capable of. You have to be flexible."

"I always adjust to my clients' needs. Don't think you're any different than anyone else I've ever had to deal with," she pointed out.

"All righty then. I guess this is you putting me in my place," he said with another chuckle.

"I find I have to do that a lot with hotheads like you," she said.

Nick's smile grew until it looked like his cheeks might hurt he was smiling so big. Chloe leaned back, concerned. He appeared as if he'd gone mad, either that, or he was enjoying himself too much.

"Baby, I guarantee you, I'm hotter than any of your past clients," he said, his voice dripping with sex. She despised herself a little when her eyes latched onto his lips and she licked her own in lust.

"Nick . . ." The warning was clear in her tone as she headed for the gym doors.

"I can't wait to see your uniform for the pool," he called out after her. She stopped for a moment, but then resumed walking. She wasn't going to dignify that with a response.

Chloe knew with zero doubt that being in the water together was going to try the very little patience she had left. If only she didn't find him so damn attractive. She was sure that was temporary insanity and the feelings would soon pass.

She certainly hoped that was the case. She turned to face him.

"Can you behave for even five seconds?" she asked. He smiled.

"I promise to be the ideal patient. You'll never want to leave here," he told her.

"I *guarantee* you, I'll want to leave," she countered.

"We'll see about that."

"Look, Nick, I'm not trying to be rude, but I don't date my patients. I'm here to do a job, to learn about you, and to fix you," she said. "And now I'm the one in need of a break. Have some lunch and we'll do water exercises in the afternoon. I want you to ice the knee in the meantime," she told him as she continued leaving.

Day one wasn't even over yet and she was ready to run for the hills.

CHAPTER FOUR

Nick beat Chloe down to the pool and easily slid into the warm water. He wasn't going to tell her that this had been his main source of therapy over the past month. He was Coast Guard, and he knew how to handle himself in any body of water. To be out of it for too long was like taking a piece of his soul.

Once in the pool, there was no pressure on his knee, and he could float for hours. He swam more slowly now than he had, but that would eventually get better as well. He was definitely favoring his right knee, but he had no doubt that, before long, he would be in the best shape of his life. He wouldn't quit pushing himself until he got there.

Though she didn't make a sound, Nick knew the moment Chloe was inside the warm room. He could practically feel her as the water lapped around him and she entered the pool. He desperately wanted to turn and see what she was wearing, but he had all afternoon to take in her appearance. The anticipation was half the fun.

"You shouldn't get in here without someone in the room. Your muscles are weak and you could get a cramp," Chloe scolded him as she waded through the waist-high water to where he floated.

Only then did Nick turn. She was wearing a one-piece suit that hugged her curvaceous breasts. He couldn't see her lower half well.

The water distorted it. He would enjoy that pleasure when she got out of the pool—or when he lifted her to the side so he could trail his lips down her legs.

"I'm a Coast Guard pilot, doc, I think I know how to handle the water," he said, while gazing at her chest.

"My eyes are up here, Nick," she said with warning.

He *really* loved when she got that proper edge to her voice. It was a turn-on unlike anything else. He couldn't wait until he had the doctor unraveling in his arms. She was so tightly wound, it was likely she'd go up in flames the minute she let go.

"I know where *everything* on you is located," he said, but he lifted his head and met the heat of her gaze.

"Does this attitude of yours ever get you where you want to be?" she asked, startling him.

"I don't know what you mean," he said, being careful now. She had a look in her eyes that he didn't at all trust.

"All the innuendoes and flirting? Do women actually respond to it?" She was keeping a good five feet of distance between them that he desperately wanted to close.

"Yeah," he admitted.

"Well, let me assure you that it doesn't work on me. I'm here to do a job, not to sleep with you, not to flirt with you, and not to pretend to swoon over you. Keep your dirty thoughts to yourself and your . . ." She paused and looked at the water lapping at his waist. "And keep your other parts in your pants."

He smiled as he gazed at her. Even though her swimsuit was what most would consider modest, he found it even more sexy *because* of what it was hiding. He wanted to peel it away and see what she didn't want him to notice.

"Can't say the word, doc?" he mocked her.

Her eyes flared as she gazed at him. "I can say all sorts of words. I'm actually educated, unlike most of the women you date, I'm sure."

"So we're dating now?" he asked, only choosing to focus on the end of her sentence.

All of a sudden her arm lifted, and a surge of water hit him in the face. When he wiped it away, the shocked expression she wore was priceless. The doc had lost her temper and had acted without thinking. That was progress.

"I don't think that was too professional, doc," he told her as he took a step nearer.

She immediately began backing up. "I'm sorry about that. It was a reaction," she said, the warning clear in her eyes.

"Too late for apologies. Just remember you started this." He moved closer, closing the distance between them.

"I don't want to play," she warned. She turned to flee, and that's when he propelled himself.

Nick grabbed the back of her suit and tugged, then wrapped his arms around her. With his good leg, he kicked himself off the floor of the pool and launched them both into the air.

Chloe screamed as they began going back down, but the momentum was too much. She couldn't get away. Her cry was drowned out when they both went underwater. Nick didn't release his hold on her as they rose above the surface for air.

She was spluttering as he spun her around so she was facing him. Her nipples were hard, poking through the material of her black bathing suit, and he relished the feel of them pressing against his naked chest.

Without thinking twice, one hand wound in her wet hair and he held her in place as he closed the distance between them, taking a taste of her sweet pink lips. It was even better than he'd imagined it would be.

This therapy stuff wasn't bad at all, he thought again as he began losing control, tugging on her hair to get better access to her mouth. She struggled against him for a moment and then melted as her lips responded to his touch.

He was thick and hard and wanted their clothes out of the way. Nick reached into the water and grabbed her leg, wrapping it around his back as he felt the soft curve of her ass. He grew even harder as he pulled her center tightly to him and pressed up so she could feel exactly how turned on he was.

Moving them through the water, he reached the wall and pressed her against it as he devoured her mouth. There was no resistance as he swept his tongue inside and explored the velvet of her tongue.

She moaned against him, and he felt the small circle of her hips as she tried to seek relief for herself. She wanted him as much as he wanted her. She was just a hell of a lot more resistant to admitting that.

"I want you so damn bad," Nick said as he wrenched his lips from hers and trailed his mouth along her jaw to her soft neck, where he sucked the skin.

Her fingers moved to his hair as she held him in place. Nick slipped his fingers beneath the band of her swimsuit and touched the soft skin of her ass, groaning at how good it felt.

"Let's go to my room." Though Nick wasn't opposed to making love in the pool, it wasn't his favorite place.

His words made her stiffen, and he groaned inwardly. He shouldn't have said anything. He should have just pulled her swimsuit away and given her what she was too afraid to admit she wanted.

She began struggling against him, and this time he released her. Nick was more than willing to seduce her, but he would never force a woman. She took several steps away from him, her cheeks flushed, her body trembling.

"There's nothing wrong with wanting each other," he told her as he moved back toward her.

"That shouldn't have happened," she said as her fingers lifted and traced her very kissed lips.

"Yes, it should have. We want each other," he said.

Each step he took forward, she took two back until she reached the stairs of the pool, which she quickly ascended, giving him a spectacular view of her glorious body. She had curves in all the right places, her breasts full and firm, her hips wide and graspable, her legs lean with muscles running through them.

"Therapy is over for the day," she said as she grabbed a towel and wrapped it around her, closing off his view.

"We didn't even get started," he told her as he reached the stairs.

She practically ran to the door before she turned back around.

"If that happens again, I'm leaving," she warned. There was a bit of panic in her eyes at the thought, and Nick knew then she needed this job. It was the leverage he desperately had to have.

"I'm a patient man, Chloe, but trust me, it *will* happen again, and it *will* be because you can't keep your hands off me," he told her.

She scoffed at him before running out the door. Nick smiled as he jumped back into the water and began swimming, hoping his arousal would eventually die. She wasn't going far . . . he could let her escape for now.

In one day, this woman had swept into his home and brought him back to life. He wasn't willing to let her run away until he explored what he was feeling a hell of a lot more. He liked Chloe Reynolds—he really liked her.

CHAPTER FIVE

Chloe knew she had to pull it together. She couldn't allow what had happened with Nick in the pool the day before to happen again. Not only was Chloe a professional, but she couldn't forget Nick was also the enemy.

It had only been a couple days of her being around the man, and already the lines of right and wrong had blurred so badly she wasn't sure they could be repainted. When her father had demanded she be on his side, she'd hesitated—a first for her. Fear of her father had always made her do his bidding without pause.

So what was different now? Though she didn't want to say aloud the answer, the difference was Nick. From the second she'd looked into the man's eyes—and then fallen into his lap—she'd felt a connection she hadn't felt with another man.

How could he be the devil if he inspired loyalty within her? She couldn't help but to remember how her father had always told her about people in angel's clothing while the devil resided within their souls. Was she such a fool that she didn't know the difference? Maybe.

As Chloe turned a corner while jogging, she saw a magnificent view of the bay. She went down a trail that led her to a dock. Immediately

Chloe was enchanted. Her feet slowed as she stepped onto the dock, finding a beautiful gazebo on the end.

Shedding her shoes, she hung her legs over the edge, the icy water giving sweet relief to her feet. She was sure the water was only this cold because the day had yet to heat it up.

Leaning back, she closed her eyes and felt peace wash over her. That was, until her phone rang. This wasn't a welcome tone. There weren't a whole lot of contacts on her Android, and each one had its own ringtone.

Her eyes snapped back open, and she thought about ignoring the call, but she knew that would only lead to worse repercussions. She either took the call and faced her father now, or he would bully her until she did.

Pressing the button on her ear set, she said a meek hello.

"Why haven't you given me an update?" her father's voice snapped into her abused eardrum.

"I just arrived a couple days ago, sir," she said. He wasn't dad, daddy, or even father. He was sir, and if she was stupid enough to forget that, she would certainly pay for it when she next saw him.

"I expect nightly reports," he snapped as if speaking to a soldier who was showing disrespect for an officer.

"I can't risk calling you daily. If Nick overhears, I will be kicked out of the house," she said.

Though Chloe did fear exactly that happening, it wasn't the biggest reason she didn't want to speak to her father nightly. She dreaded each time they spoke, hated it even more when it was in person.

Her father kept tabs on her because she was his property. He reminded her, and had reminded her brother often, that they wouldn't exist if it weren't for him. Because she knew that was the truth, she did feel loyalty to him—but felt no love.

"You will do what you're told." There wasn't an *or* in that sentence. He had no doubt she would fall into line.

"Yes, sir," she said. Her resentment was building by the moment. It was a new feeling for Chloe, one she didn't quite comprehend.

"What have you found out so far?" he asked.

"I've only been here for two days," she said again.

"Don't you talk back to me," he snapped. "Two days is plenty of time to find evidence."

"I was just getting settled in and working on therapy. I haven't found anything yet," she told him.

"What?" he yelled, making her wince as she turned her phone volume down a couple more clicks. "You are doing *therapy* on the man?"

"That's why I'm here, sir. If I don't do the therapy, he certainly won't allow me to stay in the home," she pointed out.

"I don't like this. You better not help him," her father pointed out.

"I can't purposely try to impede his therapy," she said, the exasperation coming through in her voice, though she was trying to tamp it down.

"I might need to pay you a visit. It seems you are forgetting where your loyalty belongs," he threatened.

A shudder passed through Chloe. The last thing she wanted was another lesson from her father about respect. Those sessions normally ended with bruises she had to work hard to cover up. If people truly knew what a monster he was, she feared he would have nothing else to lose and therefore wouldn't need to hold back.

"I will keep you updated, sir. I'm sorry I haven't been doing that," she said, hoping the panic in her voice wasn't coming through as loudly as she felt it was.

He was silent for several heartbeats, and Chloe could practically feel the smug satisfaction coming through the line.

"Very well. I expect to hear from you tomorrow," he told her.

"Yes, sir," she said. She just wanted the call to end.

Finally, it did. He didn't bother saying good-bye. He just hung up. She wasn't worth the time for him to waste words on. Chloe didn't care.

With a heavy heart, she pulled her feet out of the water and dried them as best she could before slipping her shoes and socks back on. She was too worn out to begin jogging again, so she simply made her way back up to the house.

It was a new day, and she wasn't going to let her father ruin it for her. She had enough stress to deal with—and a patient she had to keep at arm's length. At least she couldn't say her life was dull.

CHAPTER SIX

When a person was flying over the ocean with sixty-knot winds and raging seas, time stopped having any meaning. You weren't going to rescue anyone if your helicopter had no chance of making it back to land because you'd been foolish enough to run out of fuel.

But when a person was held up at home due to an injury, time began to have a whole other meaning. Nick had never been one to glance frequently at a clock, not even in his downtime. But since the wreck, as a day turned into two, and then a week, and then a month and longer, Nick found that time seemed to be the one constant he was aware of.

He was still confident in his ability to get Chloe into his bed—and very soon—but he must not be making the smoothest of moves on her. After the fiasco in the pool, she hadn't come out of her room, not even when he'd knocked on the door. He hadn't exactly known what he was going to say, but he wasn't too worried about it. Nick had never had problems before with knowing exactly what to say.

She couldn't avoid him for long. When she did emerge, he would be sure to give her his full brigade of flirting, attention, and focus. If she could still avoid him, then he'd have to figure out something new.

His moves had always been legendary, but if she could resist, the world would have something seriously wrong within its sphere.

Patience wasn't a virtue Nick possessed, so as he waited for her to show up for their morning session, he found himself glancing at the clock, wanting to know exactly what she was doing and how soon they would be together.

All this obsessing over a woman was strange and a bit disturbing. He knew this, but he couldn't seem to do anything about it. He also knew he wouldn't be stopping it anytime soon. His brothers would have a heyday at how he was behaving if they could see it. Luckily, they weren't around.

But the one definitive was that Nick wasn't going to lose this mission. He wasn't the type of guy who accepted defeat, even when all the cards were in favor of the opponent. And right now, Chloe was most certainly his opponent—he was the predator and he would strike.

Nick had to admit, if only to himself, that he sort of liked the effort he was having to put into this one-sided relationship. It was a challenge, and he was a sucker for a woman he couldn't obtain. Of course, that hadn't been the case for him with that one girl in basic training. No matter how hard he'd chased after her, he hadn't gotten her to give him the time of day. He still wouldn't have accepted defeat then if she hadn't been sent to another country. Even then, he'd been tempted to chase her down, show up at her base with roses, and see if it made a difference. Eventually, with the distance, he'd simply lost interest. He wondered if that would be the case with Chloe. He somehow doubted it.

He refused to accept the same results from her. She was attracted to him, as her kiss the night before had clearly shown him. She was just hella good at containing how she felt. He simply had to get her to let down her guard long enough for him to sneak past her defenses. Nick had every confidence he'd be able to do just that.

The smooth steps of Chloe walking on his tile floor alerted him she was drawing near. Much to his surprise, his heart rate picked up as he leaned against the kitchen counter and waited for her to turn the corner. When she did and looked up, their eyes connected and he felt it all the way to the soles of his feet. That kind of connection wasn't often felt by two people, and to ignore it would be foolish. Nick so badly wanted to push himself from the counter and walk to her, pull her into his arms, and take her pink lips, which were open the slightest bit as she gazed back at him.

Soon. He was now determined even more than before to heal as quickly as possible. He didn't enjoy his limitations. They didn't allow him to do what he wanted as soon as an idea popped into his mind.

"Good morning," he said, his voice a low drawl. He enjoyed the flash of heat that instantly sparked in her eyes. Nick wondered why she was fighting this so badly.

"Morning," she answered after a long pause. Her voice was crisp, and it looked almost as if her feet were weighted down as she took her first step closer to him. She picked up her pace and passed right on by as she moved to the coffeepot and poured herself a hot cup.

Nick watched her slip a bagel into the toaster, all while avoiding looking at him. Her stubbornness made him smile. Maybe he had to rethink his entire philosophy on who he was attracted to. Stubborn, smart, and prickly was looking pretty damn good to him since meeting Chloe.

"What's on the agenda today, doc?" he asked her.

"Stretching, then a few hours in the pool," she told him.

"Mmmm." He didn't add more, and only then did she look up with narrowed eyes. She set her cup down, ignoring the bagel when it popped up. Placing her hands on her hips, she gave him a stern gaze.

"I'm going to make this perfectly clear. You stepped so far over the line yesterday, if it had been a cliff, you'd be crushed on the rocks below. I am used to men trying to prove their manliness after an injury, flirting and coming on to me. If you think I'm impressed, you're very much mistaken. What *would* impress me would be you admitting you've been injured, and then allowing me to help you without all the macho posturing. Do we understand each other?"

Nick was completely taken aback by her speech, and he was stunned to realize she was somewhat right. Not completely, of course, but somewhat. He was unbelievably attracted to her, and he was pushing hard to get her into his bed, but maybe he was wrong in how he was going about it. It had been a long time since his hand had been slapped for misbehavior, but Chloe had done it pretty damn impressively.

"I think we understand each other quite well," Nick said with a genuine smile. His change in attitude seemed to knock her off-kilter. He noticed her fingers trembling when she picked up the cup and took a sip of her cooling coffee before setting it back down again. In silence, she grabbed her bagel, slathered on cream cheese, and took it, and her coffee, to the breakfast bar.

"I'll let you finish your breakfast while I get warmed up," Nick told her.

Chloe gave him a sharp look before finishing the bite she'd been chewing. "Don't do anything until I get in there. It will only be a couple minutes."

As Nick walked away, he thought about what a contradiction she truly was. She obviously took her job very seriously because she didn't want him hurt. And it was more than clear she was attracted to him, but she wanted him to know there was a line she wasn't going to cross without one hell of a battle.

It must be hard to walk around as uptight as she was, he thought with a chuckle as he slowly moved through his large house. If she even had an inkling of his thoughts, he had a feeling she'd kick his ass. Nick was adding *strong women* to his list of "types" he found attractive from the opposite sex.

Pausing as he pulled the lateral bar down, Nick enjoyed the burn as he held it for several seconds before releasing it back up. He completed his set, then leaned back, knowing Chloe was in the room with him.

When he turned, this time he *expected* the zap of electricity that passed through him. He kept his gaze trained on her, saw the awareness in her, and felt power in their connection. What he didn't understand was her reasoning in holding back. If he could comprehend that, then maybe he'd give her some breathing room.

"What is your secret, Chloe?" he asked, surprising them both. Her eyes widened for the tiniest moment before she blanked her expression. Her lips turned up, but there was no amusement in the expression.

"I'm an open book, Nick," she said. She kept her distance.

Nick had no doubt she was lying to him. He didn't know why, though. And what was even more shocking was that it didn't affect how he was feeling. Shifting on the bench, he decided to watch her actions and expressions rather than focusing on her words.

Chloe's lips moved as she said something, but he had no idea what she'd just said. She moved a little closer and her floral scent wrapped around him, fine-tuning even more of his senses. Sight, smell, touch. Who needed sound? Not him, unless it was her moans filling the air.

His mind took him back to the pool, to the feel of her lips against his, how they'd been so pliant, soft, and flavorful. He had never fantasized about a kiss before, never replayed it over and over again in his mind, had never become hard from fantasizing about where else he'd like to kiss one particular woman.

His imagination continued on as he pictured running his fingers through her silky hair, and then down her smooth shoulders, over her plump breasts and down to her hot center. How was he going to work so closely with her day after day without living out his fantasy? He wasn't sure he'd accomplish the task.

"Did you even hear what I said?" Chloe snapped. Then her expression became concerned as she moved even closer to him, prolonging his torture of her nearness. "Are you okay, Nick?"

"What?" he asked, almost in a trance.

"Nick, I'm worried. Are you having a seizure? Stroke?" She bent down and reached out to him, but she didn't touch. It was the most beautiful agony he'd ever endured.

Nick felt like stone as he pinned her to the spot with the intensity of his gaze. The connection between them was so real—but he'd always been open with his feelings. Maybe he was misreading the situation. Nick didn't even know anymore.

"I'm feeling a bit hot," he said honestly. "But I'm not having a stroke or anything else."

"Are you being real right now?" she asked. The concern was genuine on her part. It was just another reason he respected this woman.

"Yes, but I'm not ill," he told her with a sigh.

A look of understanding crossed between them. Nick was surprised when she didn't back off. But there was a look in her eyes he didn't know how to interpret. There was determination, sadness, and a hint of desire. She was fighting it, but there was more reasoning behind it than she wanted him to know about.

"Nick," she began with a sigh. He thought about interrupting her, but he waited for her to finish, though the pause seemed to draw out for an endless amount of time. "I'm not a fool. I won't lie and say I'm not attracted to you. But nothing can come of it."

Now it was his turn to pause. She didn't say anything more.

"Why? I don't get it, Chloe. We're both adults, and we like each other. What's wrong with doing something about it? Is it because you don't see me as a whole man?"

He said it with a smile, but underneath his forced expression, he felt an ounce of insecurity. He couldn't move how he'd once moved, and he couldn't pick her up in his arms and carry her off to his bedroom. Maybe she was slightly repulsed.

Chloe instantly reached out, touching his cheek as a sheen of tears entered her eyes. She blinked them back.

"Never would you be considered anything other than a whole man, Nick. You are the epitome of sexiness," she said with a slight smile.

"Prove it," he told her, his grin returning.

"You are also hopeless. Can we please just focus on your recovery?" she asked, almost sounding desperate.

The softness in her touch and expression in her eyes gave him hope of something more happening between them. It gave him the strength to push through this. Maybe if he focused on his recovery, the rest would fall into place.

"Okay, doc, we can do it your way for now," he said.

"For now," she agreed.

It was a start.

CHAPTER SEVEN

Their morning routine was down pat. Chloe would get up, do her jog while exploring the beautiful land Nick lived on. Then they met in the kitchen where they shared coffee and had something to eat. Then they spent hours in the gym and the pool.

He hadn't quit flirting with her, but the intensity of it had diminished. It was more fun, almost innocent. And she was enjoying it far too much. She was still speaking to her father, but not daily, and she found herself not wanting to tell him anything—not that there was much to share.

No matter how she looked at the situation, she couldn't see Nick as the monster her father said he was. She knew people could be good at deception, but the man worked hard, smiled often through the pain, and had a kind word to say to anyone stepping through his front door. How could he have done anything to put people who relied on him in danger? The pieces just weren't adding up.

Chloe was exhausted from having her guard up all the time and fighting the attraction she felt toward the man. She wasn't sure she'd be able to endure this task until the end—unless she told her father to go to hell and focused strictly on Nick's recovery.

As appealing as that sounded, she'd never once before disobeyed her dad. If she were to do it now, the consequences wouldn't be worth the lack of stress in her life. She was torn, and it most likely wouldn't get better anytime soon.

Sitting on the back patio, Chloe heard the door open, and her breath hitched as she felt Nick draw closer to her. She wanted to turn and watch him, but at the same time, she didn't need for him to realize how attuned she was to his every move around her.

"Why aren't you in your swimsuit, doc?" he asked. He was close, no more than a foot behind her. Though she was sitting and he was on his feet, she still felt as if his hot breath was cascading down her neck.

"We're doing something different this afternoon," she told him.

"I'm officially intrigued," he said.

With a lot of effort, he slid down, wincing only a bit as he took too much weight on his leg before his butt reached the seat.

"I wouldn't get too excited. I'm gonna make you hurt," she warned him. Finally, she turned her head and felt the impact of his gaze. She wished it didn't still affect her so much, but if anything, the attraction had only grown stronger in the past few weeks. He still made her world spin a little bit faster each time she got lost in his eyes.

"Ah, doc, you hurt me all the time," he said with a smile. There was truth behind his statement, though, which made her wince.

"Yeah, my job isn't always appreciated," she said. There were times after working several weeks or months with a client where she had to take some much needed time off. Getting a patient back to full health, or thereabouts, meant hurting them along the way. There was nothing she could do about it, but it still made her feel bad.

"It's appreciated more than you could ever know," he said with sincerity as he reached out and laid his hand on her thigh. The spark of heat that gesture caused to rush through her made her clench her teeth together.

Maybe it had just been too long since she'd allowed herself to let go—to get lost in a man's embrace. That had to be all this was about. The alternative was too crazy to even think about.

Chloe almost wished Nick would grow tired of her distancing herself and give up on her. If that were really the case, though, she wouldn't feel the pang that thought caused her. Maybe Chloe was going crazy—on the way to becoming like her father—mean and bitter, with too much time on her hands to be a happy part of normal society.

Whatever was going on, she had best pull it together. Shifting in her chair, she managed to knock Nick's hand off her leg as she stood. Strangely, she felt a loss of warmth at the removal.

"We're going to practice some stairs," she told him.

Already she'd set up the equipment she needed in the yard. It was a beautiful summer day, and she couldn't force herself to go inside the hot gym with him. Maybe the fresh air would clear up her muddled brain.

It was doubtful.

Nick didn't give her any arguments—as usual—just pushed through the new brutal tasks. And he earned even more of her respect.

CHAPTER EIGHT

Each day for Nick was exactly the same as the next as he rose, worked out, got a break, worked out some more, then without Chloe's knowledge, pushed himself even harder when she wasn't there.

He hadn't wanted to rely on the wheelchair, and now it had been a week since he'd felt enough pain that he'd had to resort to using it. From the moment Chloe had come to his house, he'd also been determined to give up the crutches—and although that had only been at his home a few days, and he went to bed exhausted each night, he'd put those away as well.

It was all because of Chloe. Sure, he pushed himself as well, but he had no doubt if she hadn't come along, he'd have injured himself further. He'd known he was being a fool, but he'd also been consumed with sorrow at losing his crew, and anger at being weak. He'd felt he'd had something to prove. Nick didn't feel that way any longer.

It was because of Chloe and her faith in him, in the way she made him look at the world so differently. There were still things about her she was keeping from him, but he didn't think it could be anything that would change how he felt about her. Instead of his feelings tapering off, they were only growing stronger.

He knew a lot of his appreciation was due to her help—especially with him walking without the aid of crutches, even if it were far shorter distances than he would like—but it was more than that as well. When she entered the room, he wanted to be a better person. Before she'd stepped into his life, he hadn't even known he'd needed to change anything about himself.

Was it possible he was growing up? That thought made Nick smile. According to his mother and favorite uncle, Sherman, he sure as hell needed to. Maybe he'd keep these newfound thoughts to himself so he wouldn't have to deal with their smug looks. Still, he was acknowledging his own faults. A few months ago, he'd had no faults—at least according to himself.

His coat on, he waited for Chloe to enter the room. When she did, she eyed him with suspicion before moving to the coffeepot and pouring herself a cup.

"Are you planning on skipping out on therapy?" she asked.

"Yep," he told her with a grin.

"My time is valuable, Nick. If you don't want my help . . ." She trailed off as she shrugged.

"I have to tell you I love it when you get that little scowl on your brow and your lips pucker. It's adorable," he said. That made the scowl deepen.

"I'm not trying to be adorable," she said, the word sounding like a curse. "I'm trying to do a job."

"Well, we're taking the day off. I want to go down to the base."

"Base? What base?" she asked. The scowl disappeared.

"My Coast Guard base," he said. He reached for his truck keys. "Why?"

"Because it's my second home, and I miss it," he said simply. "Now hurry and finish up with your breakfast so we can go."

"I didn't offer to go with you," she pointed out.

"But you're my doc, and you have to ensure I get there safely or you'll be responsible for a delay in my recovery," he said, not afraid to use emotional blackmail to get her to do what he wanted.

"That's low, Nick," she told him with an eye roll. "And a lot of BS."

He laughed. "Okay, let's just say I want your company," he admitted.

"Maybe I don't want yours," she told him, not looking him in the eyes.

"Come on," he said with a chuckle. "I'm a hell of a great guy to be around."

Her lips tilted up before she covered them with the cup of coffee. He had won this little battle. He could see it.

"Fine. I'll come with you, but only because I don't want you behind the wheel of a vehicle right now."

"Good enough for me," he told her. He then had to wait impatiently while she slowly ate her bagel and then went to change out of her scrubs. He was almost sad to see them go. The doc looked damn good in them.

He changed his mind when she met him by the front door, wearing a pair of tight jeans and a fitted blouse. She was so naturally beautiful she didn't even need makeup, though she wore a minimal amount. How had Nick ever thought the window dressing was the most important thing about a woman? Maybe it was because he hadn't yet met Chloe.

They slowly moved from his house, Nick taking his time to get down the stairs. He wasn't ruining his outing by slipping and falling. Then he wouldn't be going anywhere but bed. Of course, if Chloe were in it with him, that would be a much more fun afternoon.

When they made it to his truck, she stopped in her tracks and turned to shoot him a disbelieving glance. He smiled at her before looking at the old Ford truck.

"You don't actually think I'm driving that thing, do you?" she said.

"Of course I do. She's a classic," he defended as he reached out and ran his hand over her flawless hood.

"Yeah, a classic for sure," she said before she took his arm and began leading him away from his beloved truck to her small car. He was now the one to pause.

"Seriously?" he questioned. "You want me to turn myself into a pretzel trying to get into this thing?"

"This is a perfectly nice Volkswagen Jetta. It saves the environment and doesn't pollute the air with a loud engine or emissions," she pointed out.

"And it's a death trap on wheels. Hell, if a bicyclist hits us in this thing, we're done for," he told her.

"I happen to know it's one of the safest compact cars on the market," she countered.

"There's a lot of things I do for women, but this has to take the cake," he muttered as he moved to the passenger side of the car and opened up the matchbox-size door. It took him two attempts to bend down far enough to get inside, and then he fell into his seat with absolutely no grace.

Getting out of the thing was going to be even more of a problem. He was almost sweating as he adjusted himself and reached for the seat belt. He turned in time to see Chloe trying to hide a chuckle.

"Don't think I haven't noticed how much you're enjoying my misery," he told her.

She turned his way and gave him a brilliant smile that took his breath away. Damn, if he had known he was going to get that sort of reaction from her, he would have made an even bigger fool of himself. It was well worth it.

"You're such a baby, Nick," she said as she chuckled. He grinned back at her, and suddenly the laughter died down.

They were a heck of a lot closer together in her car than they would have been in his truck, which gave him some appreciation for the small vehicle. Nick desperately wanted to lean over and taste her lips. Her breath hitched, and he had a feeling he could get away with it.

But then he had no doubt she would regret it immediately, and their field trip would be over. So with a lot of reluctance, he resisted the urge to pull her across the short space between them. When she licked her lower lip, Nick's body pulsed, and he cursed the distance she put between them.

"I need the address," she told him, her voice husky. Nick wanted to groan. Instead he gave her the information for them to get on the road, and he tried to relax in the tight space of the car with her perfume saturating the air.

Though it took a lot of effort, Nick managed to make small talk while they took a ferry ride and rode into the city and made their way to the Coast Guard base Nick had been serving at for the past eight years. Chloe was tense for the first part of the drive, but she loosened up along the way. Nick was careful not to touch her, though that was difficult in the small space. He'd never been so relieved to pull up to his base as he was when they reached the guard unit.

Nick showed his ID card, and they were allowed inside. That familiar feeling of euphoria filled him as they drew closer to the base of operations. His leg twitched, and without thinking, he reached down and touched it. He wanted to fly, wanted to serve. He didn't want to admit he wasn't ready.

Nick led Chloe to a parking space and then was even more frustrated when he needed Chloe's help to get out of the car. Her kindness in trying not to be obvious about it was nearly his undoing.

"It will get easier, Nick," she promised him when he finally managed to get to his feet.

"Logically, I know this, but I don't do well with limitations," he admitted.

"You're doing much better than most of my clients would be at this point," she told him.

"I appreciate the words, but they're just that. This injury isn't going to continue to beat me down," he grumbled. Chloe didn't respond, and he realized he was being an ass. "Sorry," he added.

"You don't need to apologize, Nick. Why don't you tell me what a normal day is like for you here?" she said.

"Are you trying to get my mind off my pathetic situation?" he asked with a laugh before slinging an arm around her shoulders.

"You're touching me again," she pointed out.

"You should be used to it by now," he told her, not removing his arm. She laughed as he led her inside the large building. More progress, he thought.

"So are you going to tell me what you do here, or do you just stand around looking pretty?" she asked as they moved farther inside the building where Nick could hear the familiar chatter of crew members.

"You think I'm pretty?" he said, waggling his eyebrows at her.

"You know you're pretty," she said with a roll of her eyes.

"Ah, now I'm blushing." She glared at him. "Fine. It's not all that exciting," he told her. "I've been at this station for eight years. Usually, a pilot moves every four years, but since I've gone up through the ranks quickly, I've been able to stay here close to my family, which is important to me. I have done some time up in Kodiak, which is a whole other ball game. When I'm looking for excitement, I love to go there."

"What's the difference?" she asked.

"Extreme weather, for one thing," he told her.

"You'll have to tell me of some of your experiences there," she insisted.

"I can't divulge it all to you at one time," he said. "That way you'll stick around longer."

"I'm here for as long as it takes to do the job," she said.

"Spoilsport," he said. They moved closer to the command center, and Nick felt a stirring deep inside. He wanted to be on duty. "This is killing me a little. I miss work," he admitted.

"I know it's hard, but you'll be back soon. You're already making great progress," she assured him.

"Most days it's uneventful. I work about eight twenty-four-hour shifts a month. We're not awake that whole time, but we have to be ready to launch within thirty minutes of a call, so we're always on alert," he said.

"That's sort of scary . . . that you're flying in bad weather right after waking up," she pointed out.

"We're used to it," he assured her. "I usually get about thirty hours a month flying time with different missions."

"What are the missions?" There seemed to be something more behind her questions, but Nick was taking it all in and someday soon he would have it figured out. For now, he was happy to just answer.

"Some are training missions, scouting flights, rescues. It just depends."

She was about to say something else when his captain spotted him and grinned, walking over to the two of them.

"What are you doing down here, Nick?" he asked as he stepped up and shook Nick's hand.

"I can't get enough of this place. You know that, Cap," Nick said.

"I'd enjoy the time off if I were you," Captain William McCormack said.

"I've never been good on my ass," Nick said.

Both men laughed. Nick glanced down and saw a look in Chloe's eyes he didn't understand. She seemed confused. He was about to ask her about it, but she turned away from him, shutting him out.

With his captain there, he couldn't ask her about it right then. He was determined to get to the bottom of it later.

"I was going to give Chloe a tour of the base, maybe take her out on a boat ride," Nick said. Chloe looked back up, excitement lighting her eyes. It had been a last-minute idea, but apparently it had been a great one.

"The boys are getting ready to go out on a practice run. I think we could get you two on board," William said. Chloe practically bounced on her feet next to him.

There was more than one way to impress the girl, he thought. He should have thought about wowing her sooner with his Coast Guard suaveness. Maybe he'd gotten knocked in the head a bit harder than he'd originally thought. But now, more than ever before, he was determined to break through the good doc's defenses.

They moved through the base, and Nick felt sweet anticipation in the air.

CHAPTER NINE

Chloe was almost as giddy as a child as Nick helped her zip up in an official Coast Guard wet suit. Though it was a practice run, they took it seriously and wore full gear. She grinned at Nick as the two approached the large boat they'd be going out on. Nick was sore, she could see it by the way he was favoring his good leg.

"We can go back, you know," she said, trying not to show the disappointment in her tone.

"Are you afraid?" he asked with a wink. His hand lingered near her neck and a tremor washed through her. Nick looked so damn good in a wet suit that she was sad to see it covered by the large life vest that he placed over it.

"Not at all, but I'm your therapist, and I can see you're hurting," she said.

"I promise to sit while on the boat," he assured her.

Chloe was too excited about going out on the water to fight him any further. She knew she should, but as they reached the boat and she looked at the beautiful red-and-white vessel, she assured herself she'd done her best to stop him.

"Welcome aboard," a man said as he held out his hand to assist her.

"Thanks so much for letting me come along," she said, trying to contain her excitement.

"Your first time?" he asked, grinning.

"Back off, Jed, she's mine," Nick said with a scowl.

"It's not every day we get such a pretty passenger. Doesn't hurt to try," the young man said before he laughed. He then led them to the front of the boat.

"What was that?" she asked Nick when the young man left them.

"You have to realize that the crew are a bunch of horndogs. You're going to be flirted with left and right," he told her, his frown still in place.

"You're exaggerating," she said. "And I don't *belong* to anyone," she told him. There was no way she was allowing him to get away with that one.

"We'll see," he said. The frown fell away, though, as he reached out and took her hand. She tugged against him, but after a moment, gave up. She liked how her hand felt in his a bit too much. She pushed down the feelings of betrayal to her family.

For this moment, she could have an enjoyable time. She knew she needed to be asking questions, trying to find information on Nick, but the bottom line seemed to be that all the men seemed to like and respect him. He also held the regard of his captain and the other people at the base. Everyone had seemed happy to see him. It appeared she was the only one, at this point, that knew an investigation was under way. She also knew he'd soon be getting served. Would that change how people were going to react to him? Would it make a difference to him? She wasn't sure.

They moved out into the water, and the wind whipped through Chloe's hair as she enjoyed the calm waters and the conversation between the men. She was trying to think of questions she should be asking him, but she didn't want the moment ruined.

The radio began to crackle, and Chloe heard official-sounding chatter that had all the men onboard coming to attention. Nick stiffened beside her, and Chloe glanced up in concern.

"What's going on?" she asked.

"It appears the training has just gotten aborted. A 911 call just came in from a recreational boat caught aground in a low tide," he told her.

"That doesn't sound too bad," she said.

"No. But the sea is unpredictable, and things can change on a dime. We're rerouting to the location to help. It's probably nothing, but a lot of people who own boats don't know the first thing about safety. If someone gets knocked out or panics, they can get swept out to sea," he said. "We take it all seriously."

"I'm sorry." He was so anxious. This was another clue that just didn't add up. Nick did not seem like a man who would be careless about the safety of his men.

"I want to help," he said with a frustrated sigh as he gripped his sore leg.

"You will again," she said before cringing. If her father gained the right evidence on him, he wouldn't be helping anyone ever again. He'd be locked up behind bars. That somehow seemed wrong to her. How many heroes were truly out there in the world? Chloe would guess the number was surprisingly small.

The Coast Guard boat sped through the water, and Chloe remained where she was with her eyes glued to the area. Finally, she saw the small boat, half submerged with what appeared to be two adults and two children on deck. They were waving their arms frantically as the water tugged against the craft, seeming determined to spill it over.

"We can't get in there. The water's too shallow. Those rocks are too close to them, and I'm afraid they're going to get hurt if we don't get them out soon," one of the men said.

"Call the helicopter in. We'll stay here," the captain told them before picking up a megaphone and calling out to the frantic people of their plan.

Chloe couldn't tell if they were happy or not about the situation, but as their tiny boat drew closer to the rocks, their panic seemed to escalate. It seemed forever before she heard the engine of the helicopter overhead as it drew closer.

Everything happened with such precision. Chloe was utterly fascinated. A man was lowered from the helicopter that hovered high above the wrecked boat. He dropped down on the deck, and the two young children reached for him, wrapping their arms around his legs. It looked to Chloe like he smiled at them before kneeling and saying something she assumed was reassuring.

A small dog jumped up against the Coast Guard's leg, and he reached down and scratched its head while he spoke to the parents. The boat shifted and the woman fell down. The Coast Guard quickly assisted her up before waving his hands at the chopper above him, giving them a signal.

A basket began lowering from the chopper, the wind tugging on it, but it made a smooth descent. The kids cowered behind their parents' legs as Chloe watched the event continue to unfold.

One of the children and the family dog got in the basket, and it slowly ascended back into the helicopter. Chloe found herself holding her breath until it reached the safety of the chopper. Once they secured the child and dog, the basket lowered again and the smaller child and mother went up next.

They took the father last, and then the Coast Guard rescuer ascended. Chloe watched as the chopper flew away. She turned back in time to see a wave hit and the boat get shattered against the nearby rocks.

"That was too close," she whispered to Nick.

"Sometimes it's a matter of seconds whether a person lives or dies," he told her somberly.

"How do you do this so calmly?" she asked.

"It's my job. If I panic, it does no one any good," he told her. He seemed even more tense as his gaze followed the chopper until it was out of sight.

"You really miss flying," she said. She almost felt sad for him.

"Yeah, more than you know," he said before turning his gaze away from the sky. "It just feels good to be out there, to save lives."

"Why a helicopter and not a boat?" she asked.

The boat they were on turned and began heading back to the base. The training session was cancelled entirely as the sea was picking up turbulence. They wanted to get her and Nick back to the base.

"I went to flight school and knew from the first time I took a helicopter up in the air that that was all I wanted to do. There's no way I would be happy sitting on my ass day after day. And though I love boating, the rush I get from flying is incomparable," he told her.

"What made you choose the Coast Guard instead of something else like the Army or even a civilian job?" she asked.

"My oldest brother chose to fly for an airline, which didn't last long," he said. "He's too much of a control freak, and though he loves to fly, he soon had to own his own company so he could have the best of both worlds. My other brother, Maverick, flies for the Marines, and I wanted to do something different. I wanted to help people instead of try to destroy them or cart them around," he said with a shrug. "Flying is in our blood. My dad and uncle both flew. For my uncle, it was as much a passion as it is for my brothers and me. For my dad, it was more of a hobby."

"Was the job hard to learn?" she asked. These weren't the questions she should be asking him. She should be trying to delve into that night her brother had died, but this was what she wanted to know, even if she didn't understand why.

"Yes and no. There is a lot you have to remember to protect your crew. Each flight has two pilots, and it takes us both. Weather is extreme. It might be beautiful one moment and low visibility the next. Washington gets a lot of fog and a lot of unpredictable storms. Most people don't check a weather update before heading out to sea. It's not that they're stupid, it's just that they're inexperienced. I think there should be far stricter boating laws, but that's just my opinion. My brother always tells me if I want to get into the politics of it, then I should run for office."

"Have you thought about doing that?" she asked, surprised.

"Not a chance in hell," he said. "Can you imagine me in a monkey suit?" He grinned at her.

"Yes, I can, actually," she said, almost able to envision it. He would look mighty fine in a three-piece suit.

"What is your favorite thing about being a pilot?"

He hesitated as he looked out at the water. She liked that he was considering the question. "I suppose part of it is knowing I have a skill that most people don't. I can fly a helicopter through the worst of weather and reach someone who is otherwise unreachable, and therefore save their life. I'm not doing it alone and we don't always win, but when we do, it's a euphoric feeling unlike anything else," he admitted.

"I've heard pilots have God complexes," she said with a laugh.

"You've heard right," he told her with a wink. All of this should make her distance herself even further from him, but it was making her have respect instead. He seemed so honest with his answers. She was growing more and more confused.

"Is there anything you don't like about being a Coast Guard pilot?" she asked.

"Nope. Nothing," he told her.

"Will you ever do anything else?" What would it do to him if he weren't able to do the job, she wanted to ask, but she feared that would lead to suspicion on his part.

"Definitely no. This is more than a job, it's a calling. I'll be here until I retire, and I won't retire without kicking and screaming. The new kids will come in, and I'll be an old crotchety man," he said with a laugh.

"I somehow can't picture that," she told him as the boat docked at the base and she stood up.

"With the way I'm walking now, it's easier than ever before to picture it," he said with a laugh that didn't have any merriment in it.

After a long bout of good-byes, they made it back to Chloe's car. She was silent on the return trip to his house. The day had given her far more questions than answers, and she was even more confused than she'd been on the first day she'd arrived.

She feared it was only going to get more difficult the longer she was with this charismatic man.

CHAPTER TEN

After their trip to the Coast Guard base Nick had thought things might change with Chloe. He'd felt her opening up to him, but after their return, he'd watched her retreat again. Several days passed with him trying to speak intimately with her. She avoided conversation with him. That look in her eyes of concern and confusion seemed to grow day by day. He was determined to find out why.

The woman was incredibly good at avoiding his questions and his advances. Tonight, if she was able to resist his charm, he might be left with no choice but to throw in the towel and accept defeat.

The sun was several hours from setting. After their late-morning session, she'd told him to rest up for a walk they'd take later. He'd been too amped to rest, but at least it had given him time to get done what he'd wanted. With a favor called in to his brother Coop, he had a picnic waiting down on the dock. He was going to give the woman a night of romance.

Waiting by the back door with her jacket on his arm, he once again glanced at his watch. She was taking her time getting there, he thought, but she was well worth the anticipation of her arrival. He was sitting on the back of the couch because he needed to maintain all the energy he could in his weaker knee. He had much more pleasant activities planned for him and Chloe than a simple walk.

When the door to her room shut, the click sent a shot of adrenaline through him. It was showtime, and Nick planned on it being an all-night event. Chloe entered the room with her typical aloof smile in place, and Nick responded by grinning at her.

He was satisfied when her steps faltered for just a second before she approached.

"How's the knee feeling? We worked it hard today," she said. She kept her distance. He held out the coat, giving her no choice but to move closer. She did so with hesitation.

"It feels good enough for a walk," he told her. She tried to grab the coat, but he held it open. She sighed and gave him a look, then turned around and let him slip it on her.

He caressed her shoulders for a moment too long to be appropriate and felt her stiffen beneath his touch. She was worried she'd cave in to him—that was why she went overboard on trying to maintain proper distance. Nick didn't mind that at all. It just proved to him that she wanted him even if she didn't like feeling that way.

"We'd better get going. I don't want you moving too fast since this is the first trip outside. I want you to watch where you're going and to take it easy. If you're thinking about trying to impress me, the way to do it is by acknowledging the injury and doing what I ask."

"I love when you talk to me in that doctor voice," he told her, unable to tear his gaze from her face. She rolled her eyes. He wanted to grab her and haul her in for a kiss. He stopped himself, but just barely.

They walked outside, and he gripped the railing to step down the stairs. She kept her eyes on him, but maintained a couple feet of distance as they reached the path that would lead them on a trail to the dock. She tried to take him in another direction, but he moved where he wanted to go. It was about six or seven minutes to the dock moving at the slower pace he was forced to travel.

She kept silent the first couple of minutes, and Nick purposely stumbled, drawing her immediately to his side. Her arm came around him, and he had to fight the satisfied smile from appearing on his lips. Now he had her where he wanted her. She tried to pull away once he was steady, but he kept his arm around her and held on tight.

"I better hold onto you so I don't trip," he said, almost choking on the words. But to get her attention he had to seem vulnerable. He could do that if it meant her sidled up beside him. The feel of her pressed against his side was pure heaven.

The stiffness in her body slowly evaporated as the two of them continued moving down the trail. He was watching the ground carefully, something he'd never had to do before. But he didn't want to ruin the night he had planned by stumbling over some root or rock on the ground. If he landed on his knee, pain would radiate through him and making love to her on the nicely set up dock would be the last thing he'd be thinking of. Okay, maybe not the last thing, but it would be knocked down several rungs on the ladder.

"I don't want to push this too far, Nick," she warned when he kept moving steadily forward.

"I have a surprise for you. It's not much farther," he told her.

She stiffened again in his arms, and he could feel her looking up at him. He stopped and gazed into her eyes while giving her his most seductive grin.

"What sort of surprise?" she asked.

"You'll have to keep walking to find out," he told her, tugging to get them moving again.

She kept her feet planted. "I don't want anything. I'm here to do a job, remember?" she said, her voice back to the stern schoolteacher one she preferred.

"Too bad. You call the shots all day long. It's my turn," he said.

This time he exerted more force, and she was pushed into moving. She grumbled something he didn't quite manage to hear, and he had to hold back laughter. Though he wouldn't go so far as to call Chloe predictable, he would definitely say she was stubborn. If something wasn't her idea, she tended to veto it. She'd have to learn to bend as long as she was in his life.

That thought sent an unwanted pang through him. He wasn't sure how much time he had left with Chloe. He had no doubt she would be ready to run out the door without looking back the second he was pronounced good enough to be on his own. He didn't think he wanted that to happen. Nick enjoyed being with this woman. This was his chance to see if he wanted to maybe date her after all the physical therapy stuff was finished.

Nick didn't normally enter into long-term commitments, but for this woman he might consider it. He could almost visualize the unbearable teasing he would have to take from his brothers if that were to happen. But Chloe was a one-of-a-kind woman. She might be worth the good-natured ribbing.

When they rounded the bend, Chloe once again stopped and Nick looked up. His brother had done well. The dock had a beautiful gazebo built on the end of it, and Cooper had hung a lantern that was glowing softly. On the ground was a thick blanket and a basket he was sure held excellent food. There was a bucket beside it with a bottle of wine chilling.

It was a warm summer evening, but even that didn't matter. Nick had known from the moment he'd bought the property that he would spend a lot of time at the end of the dock, fishing, soul-searching, sitting back playing guitar, whatever he wanted. He preferred being outdoors. He didn't love being cold, though, so he'd installed a gas fire pit that did a great job keeping the gazebo area nice and warm. Flames flickered in it, adding to the entire atmosphere.

"What's going on, Nick?" Chloe asked. She didn't seem anxious to get down to the place.

"I thought we could have dinner down here by the water," he told her.

"How did you manage to get this all set up?" she asked. He couldn't tell by her tone if she was pleased or not. She should be—it was damn creative, if he did say so himself.

"I called my brother earlier and had him do it for me. Soon, I'll be moving around a lot better and can do it all on my own," he said. It still bothered him that he was depending on other people to do the simplest of things for him. Nick didn't like asking for help. He was the one who was normally being called for assistance.

"This is a bit much, don't you think?" she said, but he saw the beginnings of a smile on her lips. That gave him hope.

"Not at all. When I'm my normal self, I eat down here all the time," he said. That was honest at least. "I've missed being here." The hint of vulnerability he allowed to touch his voice changed her mind. She was beginning to cave.

"With low lighting, wine, and a blanket?" she said with a touch of sarcasm.

"Well, I wanted to make sure you were comfortable," he said. He tugged on her and was grateful when she fell in step with him.

"What am I going to do with you?" she said, but a soft chuckle escaped, and the sound was music to his ears.

"I can give you a few suggestions," he told her with a wide smile.

Normally, at this point was when she pulled away from him. This time, though, she simply laughed, which encouraged him greatly. Damn! He should have tried the romance route a hell of a lot sooner.

"Sit down, Romeo," she told him when they reached his perfect setting.

Getting up and down was still a chore for Nick, especially with the brace giving him only limited movement. There was no graceful way for him to slide onto his butt. Bending his good knee, he went down, and then slowly shifted until he managed to get all the way down. He was more than a bit disgusted with himself when he found his breathing strained from the effort.

"Join me," he said, holding out his hand.

She looked back up the dock, and he nearly panicked when he realized she could rush away and there'd be nothing he could do about it. He couldn't catch her yet—soon, but not yet.

With a sigh, she sat across from him and lifted the lid to the picnic basket. Nick hoped his brother had done what he'd asked and not tried to be funny. Chloe pulled out fried chicken, fruit, salad, crackers, cheese, and olives. She looked at him and smiled again.

"I approve," she said. Her compliment had him practically glowing. How far he'd sunk into the pits of what he'd once considered hell. He'd never been so worried about impressing a woman before. He didn't appreciate that he cared right now.

"I've learned a thing or two about you the past few weeks," he assured her.

She raised her eyebrows and looked at him with skepticism. "Really?" The word was drawn out, and she was letting him know she doubted he was speaking the truth.

"I pay attention, doc," he said, accepting the plate she handed him with a little bit of everything on it.

"Prove it," she told him.

Nick's heart raced as she picked up some cheese and a piece of fruit and popped them into her mouth. This was a test. He was sure of it. And never in his life had he been so worried he wasn't going to pass.

But Nick had been through hell and back in his job, and he'd never run away from a challenge. He would ace this one—and then he'd have Chloe exactly where he wanted her—in his arms and in his bed.

CHAPTER ELEVEN

Chloe knew she shouldn't have accepted the third glass of wine when Nick offered to top her off. But she was on her best behavior every single moment she was around the man, and it felt good to let her guard down, to laugh and enjoy his stories. It felt good to forget for a single moment who she was and who he was.

She wasn't so foolish as to think this would change anything between them, but to have a single night off without her father's voice in her head—without analyzing every move Nick made—wasn't asking too much of herself. So she did accept the refill, and she leaned back against one of the posts on the gazebo as she picked at her chicken and laughed at yet another story Nick was telling her from his days at the Coast Guard base.

". . . After the itching powder incident, our captain had to ban all practical jokes. About ten of us were going around shifting a hell of a lot as a part of our bodies burned that we'd rather were in perfect health," he finished.

"I have never understood how guys think it's so funny to hurt each other," she told him, but she'd been laughing right along with him, nullifying her words.

"It's not that we want to hurt each other. We just want to get the upper hand," he said.

"And were there any winners in this practical joke campaign?" she asked pointedly.

"If I had to declare a winner, I would say it was me. Johnson had to shave his head to get the glue out of his hair. That was genius," Nick said proudly.

She looked at him as if he was insane. That only made him laugh all the more. "Come on, give me some credit. It took me a while to find the right glue and to get it in his shampoo bottle without him knowing it."

"You are terrible. And it really isn't fair because he won't be able to get his revenge with the captain's ruling," she pointed out.

"Nah, after a few months, the captain will forget all about it, and then the games will begin again," he told her with a chuckle.

"Don't you think it's time to grow up at some point?" she asked.

"I've never understood that exactly," he said, sounding almost serious.

"Understood what?" she asked.

"Growing up," he said. "Just because we turn a certain age, does that mean our entire personalities should change?" He waited as if expecting an answer.

"Well, we can't be kids forever," she told him. Though there were a lot of days she would love to have no responsibilities, to be free like a child. Why had she rushed to grow older? She didn't really know.

"Why not? Why can't we have fun and embrace life? Why is it so important to change into a new person just because the number of candles on your birthday cake has increased each year?"

He was serious as he said this. The questions surprised her. She wasn't sure what the correct answers were. Everyone said you had to grow up. It might not be an actual law, but it was just what people did.

"Well, I guess it's because if adults ran around acting like children the world would be in chaos," she said.

"How so?" he asked.

"What do you mean by that?" He was really pushing this point. She wasn't sure what to think about that.

"Do you honestly think the world would have half as many problems if people didn't take themselves so seriously?"

"What are you talking about?" she asked with exasperation.

"Okay, here's an example. When you are in grade school and you want to make a friend, what do you do?"

"I don't understand," she said.

He sighed as if he were talking to a child. "It's a simple question. Think back to your elementary days and tell me specifically what you did to make friends."

She thought for a moment. It had been a long time since she'd been in school. But he seemed to want a genuine answer.

"I guess I shared my toys," she began before she smiled. "And my mom used to put a treat in my lunch every day, usually something coated in chocolate. I met my best friend, Dakota, that way. I would sneak it into class with me, and when we were supposed to be having quiet reading time, I would pull it out and give her half," Chloe told him.

"Were you stressed that the teacher might catch you?" he asked.

She laughed. "No. As a matter of fact, she might have known what we were doing, but she never called us on it. We weren't hurting anyone," she pointed out.

"That's my point, exactly. You made friends by sharing your treats, by helping a friend with homework, or by playing at recess. You didn't have to put on airs, didn't have to try to be someone you weren't. You were yourself and you drew people to you. Why can't it be that simple now?" he pushed.

"Because we have to grow up," she said with a huff.

"But why?"

"I want to know why you're pushing this," she said, her voice growing more agitated.

"Because I've been told since I was young that I needed to grow up, that I needed to take on responsibility and act like an adult. But why can't I have the best of both worlds? What's wrong with playing baseball in the rain and getting coated in mud? What's wrong with having an epic Nerf battle with my friends and family? What's wrong with sharing my candy with a pretty girl?"

As he finished his little speech, he pulled out a box of chocolates that had been hidden. She immediately smiled and reached for them. They were the creamy fruit-filled chocolates that were a secret vice of hers. She had no idea how he had figured that out.

"There's nothing wrong with playing," she reluctantly admitted. "But we do have responsibilities as adults—to have a job, pay bills, follow the law," she said, moving closer to him to reach the chocolates. He was holding them just out of reach, and she was growing more frustrated by the second.

It took her several moments before she realized she'd made a point about breaking the law and hadn't immediately thought of him during the sentence. That took her back. Maybe it was the wine, maybe it was his company, and maybe it was his persistence, but from the beginning of all of this, she'd had her doubts he'd been responsible for killing her brother. Now that she knew him better, it seemed impossible. There was still a small part of her that held him responsible, but there was a bigger part that couldn't see him ever doing anything that would endanger someone he cared about. Afraid of what she was feeling and thinking, she scowled at him as she tuned back in to what he was saying.

"We have those same responsibilities as children," he pointed out.

"We don't have *jobs* in grade school," she said. She didn't realize how close she was getting to him in her attempt to get to the chocolate.

"Yes, we do. We have chores. We have homework we have to get in on time, and we have bedtimes and curfews. We get older and those things are given different names, but we still have to adhere to the rules. But as a child we also have recess, movie nights, and sleepovers. All I'm saying is, it's okay to be young forever. I can live by the rules, but the day I have to grow up is the day I give up on life."

His words hit her hard. She'd grown up in an incredibly strict household where if she didn't listen to her father, she would be punished—and punishment was a spanking by a paddle that had left bruises on her. She'd learned quickly that either you obeyed the head of the household or you paid the price. What if her life had been different growing up? Would she be an entirely changed woman?

"Do you live by the rules?" she asked him, trying desperately to focus on the original task she'd been browbeat into accomplishing when she'd taken the job as his therapist.

He smiled. "Of course I do," he said with nonchalance.

"Always?" she pushed.

Nick's smiled faded as he analyzed her expression. She was too tipsy to mask anything she was feeling, making this a really bad time to be asking him any sort of questions, but she also couldn't seem to stop.

"What are you getting at?" he finally asked. "This seems like a pointed question."

"I've just heard that pilots are reckless and have a God complex. I wonder if you're the same way—that because you fly a rescue chopper that maybe you might think the job rules don't apply to you."

Nick's mouth set firmly and his eyes narrowed in a way she'd yet to see from him. She might have pushed him too far. A tremble quivered through her. And almost as quickly as his frown had appeared, Nick wiped it from his expression.

"I think you're getting close to me, and it's scaring you, so you're trying to cause a fight by questioning my honor," he said before his lips turned up again. "Not gonna work. The night has been too perfect so far to allow that to happen."

Strangely, Chloe let out a relieved breath. She didn't want their perfect night to get away from them. She pushed away her father's voice that was a constant sound in her ear. She didn't want to hate Nick tonight.

"Okay, I concede," she said, practically sitting on top of him. She hadn't even realized she'd still been reaching for the chocolates, even throughout their small spat. He finally released the box to her. She ripped off the lid and pulled one out, popping it into her mouth and savoring the sweet tang it left on her tongue. The last of her tension drained away as she chewed.

"I don't think you do. I think you were just trying to get the candy so you're agreeing with me," he said. "Now that you have the treat, are you going to change your mind?" It was a good question. She should say yes, but she was too content to do that.

She chuckled. "Maybe it was that, too," she admitted.

"Then you must be punished."

Before she realized what was happening, Nick had her pinned beneath him on the blanket. He straddled her waist and gripped her hands over her head. The box of chocolates tipped over, spilling out on the blanket. She gasped at the injustice of wasted candy.

"Stop it right now, Nick," she said as she tried to break free.

"I don't think so," he said, a wicked smile lighting up his face. It took her breath away. Though he'd been talking about being young forever, the thoughts she was feeling with his warm body holding her down were anything but childish.

"I'm warning you that if you don't let me go within the next few seconds, I'm going to have to hurt you," she said, trying to sound stern.

With his free hand, he moved to her waist and she inhaled sharply. His touch against her skin was enough to drive her mad. She'd managed to keep her distance from him for the past couple weeks, but tonight she'd let down her guard. That hadn't been smart. But for the life of her she couldn't exactly figure out why that was.

Just when she thought he was about to caress her, his fingers dug into her side. Within seconds, squeals of laughter were escaping her throat as he tickled her.

"What are you doing?" she gasped in between squeals as she tried to buck him off her. Nick was stronger than he'd been when she'd first arrived. If he didn't release her, there was no way she was going anywhere.

"I'm trying to help you find your inner child," he told her.

He laughed with her as the torture continued, his fingers finding every sensitive place on her body. She squirmed beneath him, but he showed no mercy. Finally, when she couldn't breathe anymore, he relented.

"Do you admit it's more fun to never grow up?" he asked.

"No," she said. He reached toward her again. "I mean, yes, yes," she yelled.

He laughed and backed up, allowing her to scramble away from him. Chloe wouldn't admit it to him, but she couldn't remember the last time she'd laughed that hard. He might just have a point with what he'd been saying. Then again, it might also be that she'd consumed too much wine.

"We really should get back," she told him. Though she hated to see the night end, it was late and they had a busy day of therapy starting in the morning.

"Want to have a sleepover?" he asked with a wink. She stood up quickly and smiled down at him.

"I don't think so," she said, but there wasn't any bite to her words. "How deep is this water?" she asked as she looked out at the calm blackness.

"Deep enough for fishing and swimming," he said. She could see he was struggling to get to his feet without showing her it caused him pain.

"I should test it out before I leave," she said. She turned away to give him the privacy he deserved. He didn't say anything as he stood, but she was sure he appreciated the gesture. He walked over and stood next to her at the edge of the dock.

"It's cold, but refreshing," he told her. He grabbed her arm and tipped her like he was going to push her in. She squealed and reacted fast, stepping back and shoving.

In horror, Chloe watched Nick lose his balance as he favored his injured knee. She was too slow when she reached for him, and almost in slow motion, he tumbled over the side of the dock, a loud splash telling her the moment he hit the water. She was too stunned to move as she watched him pop back up, his eyes wide, his teeth clenched. A shiver raced through him.

"Okay, it's a bit more than cold," he said, his teeth chattering.

"I'm so sorry," she said, horrified by what she'd done. "Is your leg okay?" If she'd caused him further injury, she would never forgive herself.

"I can't feel it so I'm assuming it's fine," he said as he came closer to the dock.

"You shouldn't have pushed me. I just reacted," she scolded him.

"Good to know." He then grinned at her. "Want to join me? Now that I'm used to the water, a night swim seems like an excellent idea."

"Um, no way," she said. "I was thinking about a swim in the middle of the day when it's nice and hot out."

He gave her a grin that she was beginning to realize meant trouble. She took a step back. Suddenly his face changed, and he looked injured and weak.

"I don't think I can get out on my own," he said, sounding forlorn.

"Oh, don't be a baby. I see you get out of the pool all the time," she said. He started to sink.

"Nick . . . Nick!" Screaming as his head went under, she dropped to her knees and reached out for him.

That was her first and last mistake. Like a shot, he jumped back up and grabbed her hand. It didn't take much before he had her flying through the air, landing in the water right next to him.

Spluttering as she surfaced, Chloe was seriously worried her limbs might break off.

"This is freezing," she said in a chatter, the words drawn out in her agony. "Not swimmable even *when* it's hot out."

Nick tugged her into his arms, and that's when she realized the water only came up to their chests. He'd been faking it the whole time to get her to the edge of the dock so he could have his revenge. If she believed in payback, he'd be in serious trouble. But unlike him, she was an adult and didn't stoop to such measures.

She tried to pull away, but he yanked her into his arms, wrapping himself around her tightly, pressing her body to his chest. Unbelievably, it was warm. Instead of trying to pull away, she pressed closer to him.

"Our date can't end without a kiss," he said. He didn't give her time to think, simply bent his head and took her breath away.

The kiss was consuming as he traced her lips before pushing inside her mouth and taking possession of her. He reached down and clasped her butt, tugging her against his body. She was shocked when she felt his thickness pressing into her. With the temperature of the water, she wouldn't have thought he'd be able to grow excited.

He devoured her mouth and she fell into him, forgetting all the reasons why they shouldn't be kissing, touching, groping each other.

One hand gripped her hair, and he pulled her more tightly to him, taking possession of her mouth. She forgot about the cold water enveloping them, and simply allowed herself to get lost in his embrace. But when a shiver wracked her body, he pulled back, reluctance written all over his face.

"I picked the wrong time to start this," he said, his fingers caressing her cheek. "As soon as we climb from this water, you'll put your wall back up and run away."

She wanted to lean forward, connect their lips again, and prove him wrong. But he was right. Tugging against his hold, she almost regretted it when he released her. No matter how much she might want to take his advice and be a kid, that wasn't who she was.

The heat of his kiss stayed with her as she exited the water and stepped up on the dock. But the moment the wind touched her wet skin, she shivered uncontrollably. Nick quickly joined her and grabbed the blanket, draping it over her shoulders.

"You need this," she said, but she couldn't push it off her. He turned off the fire and lanterns and left the rest of their picnic for them to get another day.

"How about you share it with me, since you *did* push me in?" he suggested. He didn't just make her do it, though. He was letting the choice be hers. She should just give the blanket to him, but she didn't want to let it go.

Not looking him in the eyes, she opened one arm, and he climbed in beside her before slipping his arm around her back and tugging on his end of the blanket with his other hand. They walked slowly back to the house without saying another word.

When he stayed next to her while she moved to her bedroom door, she thought of a million things she wanted to say to him. Had he been drinking the night he'd flown her brother out into a storm? Did he feel regrets? Did he have so much money he thought he could do whatever he wanted? She wanted to ask him flat out if he'd killed her brother.

But she asked nothing. Instead, she dropped the blanket, turned the knob on her bedroom door, and slipped inside. She regretted her decision the rest of the night as she lay in bed alone and aching. She finally did drift off to sleep, but then her dreams were filled with Nick, and the two of them were certainly not acting like children.

When her phone rang first thing in the morning and she saw it was her father calling, she let it go to voice mail. Yes, she knew she would face his wrath for that sin against him, but she didn't care. Her emotions were too unsettled, and she couldn't try to figure them out enough to take a call from her father.

If Chloe didn't pull herself together fast, it might just be her being the one locked up instead of Nick. As it was, he had a good case against her professional ethics for what she planned on doing. He had a right to his privacy just as he had a right to fair medical treatment.

Chloe wanted to give up on all of this. But she couldn't exactly do that. So instead, she buried the problems again—just as she'd been doing for the past couple weeks. Maybe someday it would all be buried so deep, there would be no chance of someone coming along and digging it back up.

CHAPTER TWELVE

Nick was absolutely positive that he was going to die. He was sure of it. Even in the ocean with no way of knowing whether he would be rescued he hadn't feared death like he did at this particular moment. His life was flashing before his eyes, and he only hoped the suffering would stop and it would happen quickly.

Leaning his head against the wall of the shower, he turned the water to cold and began counting. He reached a hundred, then five hundred, then a thousand. His body was turning blue, and only then did the swelling in his aching shaft begin to go down.

He would love to be able to say that Chloe was a tease, but he knew that wasn't the case. She had made it more than clear she didn't want a relationship—and he *supposed* that meant sex was off the table. His body just wasn't getting that particular message. He wished with all his might that she would change her mind, but the woman was sticking to her guns, and he was living in a constant state of arousal.

The other night he'd even tried to please himself. That hadn't worked out too well for him. He wanted *her* hands and mouth on him. He wanted to be slipping deep within her folds. He wanted her wrapped around him. And it seemed nothing else was going to do but exactly that.

Until she decided to give in to the desire surrounding them both, his life was in danger. He wondered if he could explain that to her in a way she would sympathize with. He somehow doubted it, though it seemed perfectly reasonable to him.

Climbing from the shower, he toweled off, his hardness only partially deflated. Putting on a pair of underwear was painful, and the sweats that went on next felt way too constricting. But Nick had been in aroused states before. He would get through it—or maybe not, he thought with a grimace as he stepped into the kitchen and found Chloe with her back to him, her perfume lingering in the air.

Maybe her entire goal was to off him? That seemed to make a lot of sense actually. No normal woman would resist her desires so completely. He was sure of it. Just the sight and smell of her had his body pulsing painfully. He had visions of walking up behind her, ripping off her sexy scrubs, and thrusting deep inside her until she was screaming his name.

Those thoughts weren't helping his current predicament in the least. He groaned low in his throat, and she must have heard the sound because she spun around and searched his face.

"How are you feeling this evening?" she asked as she sipped on a glass of milk. She had her evening ritual, he had his, but often they shared a drink before they each headed off to bed so it gave them an excuse to talk over the therapy they'd accomplished earlier.

He scowled at her, which she seemed offended by. "Like shit," he said. He took the cup she held out to him with a bit more force than necessary, but he didn't feel like apologizing. She sure wasn't sympathetic to *his* plight.

"Is it your knee?"

"Think higher," he snapped.

"Your ribs?" She truly did sound concerned. He should give her a break. He was in too bad a mood to do that.

"Lower," he grumbled.

Her eyes searched over his body, which made him pulse even harder. He heard her gasp, and he nearly smiled. He was sure nothing was hidden from her view, as hard as he was. He leaned against the counter and sipped his juice and let her take in his condition.

"Oh, well, I . . . um . . ." She stopped trying to speak and turned away from him.

Nick's mood improved, but barely.

"Is there a problem, doc?" he asked. If he was in pain, then she might as well know it was her inflicting it.

"No, not at all. We had a long day today, and tomorrow it will be even harder," she said, her cheeks flushing at her choice of words, though she tried to pretend she hadn't slipped. She tried adding an extra edge of sternness to her tone, but her voice was coming out too husky for her to manage it.

"I certainly have a problem that I'm pretty sure only *you* can fix," he said.

She whipped around and glared at him. Her eyes remained on his face, no longer searching for injuries. He snickered before taking another sip of juice. Damn, he wanted her.

"It appears as if the current problem you're having is no concern of mine," she said tartly.

"Believe me, doc, my situation is all about you," he said. Without even caring, he reached down and squeezed himself, trying to relieve some of the pressure. It didn't help.

Her gaze snapped downward at his bold movement before going back to his face. The withering look she sent him should have melted him on the spot.

"You're a pig," she told him.

"I want you," he replied.

"Well . . . find someone else."

They glared at each other for several moments before he boxed her in against the counter. "Is that really what you want, doc? Do you want me to go find some other woman and kiss her like this?" he asked before leaning down and sucking on her neck. She gasped but didn't push him away. "Or like this?" His teeth nipped her skin before his tongue came out and soothed the spot.

Next he pressed his body to hers, letting her feel his thickness pushing against her stomach. "Do you want me to slide inside another woman, make her scream my name over and over again?" he whispered in her ear before his tongue traced it. She shuddered in his arms.

"I don't care," she said in a little pant that betrayed her words.

"I think you're lying. I think you want me to take you hard and fast, and then slow and long. I think you want to taste my lips while I'm thrusting inside your tight, wet body. I think you dream about me and wake up aching. I think you want this as badly as I do, but you're too afraid to admit it," he challenged her.

Leaning back, he looked into her smoky eyes before he groaned and leaned forward, pressing his lips to hers. Reaching behind her, he squeezed her ass as he lifted her to her toes and pressed himself against her sweet center. He wanted their clothes gone, he wanted to do this right.

"Nick," she sighed. He wasn't sure if it was a protest or not, but unless she pushed him away, he wasn't going anywhere.

With a low growl, he grabbed her hips and lifted her to the counter before slipping inside her open thighs. He tugged her forward and rubbed himself against her covered core. It was almost enough to make him explode in his pants.

Hell, that would give him enough relief to last at least a few hours. Might be worth it just to not have to feel the constant throbbing. One hand holding her against him, he buried the other in her hair, ripping out her rubber band and inhaling the sweet scent of her shampoo as it drifted over him.

He nibbled on her bottom lip before deepening the kiss, before diving inside her mouth like he wanted to dive into her hot center.

"Just say yes," he practically begged. She whimpered in his arms as she pressed against him.

"Nick," she said, his name coming out a moan.

"Let me love you," he demanded before kissing her lips again. He took her hand from his hip and slowly slid it beneath the waistband of his sweats. Her fingers caressed his skin as he prodded her hand toward his thickness. He released his hold on her and nearly shouted with joy when she didn't pull it from his pants.

He slipped his fingers inside her shirt and quickly unclasped her bra, his fingers tracing her hard nipples. She moaned against his lips, and he greedily drank the sound. She flexed her fingers around his girth, and he was a bit worried he'd never make it inside her. He might come in his pants he was so damn turned on. The slightest of touches from her had him falling over the edge, getting closer and closer to paradise.

"Nick . . ." This time the sound came out almost like a protest. No! They needed this, both of them needed this more than they needed oxygen. She had to admit that or he feared he truly would die.

"Just let me love you," he pleaded. He pulled back to look into her eyes. "We both want it. There's nothing wrong with taking what we need."

She looked unsure so he kissed her again, a long, slow kiss. She squeezed his thickness and he dripped on her fingers. She ran her thumb over his head, and he wanted to tear open her scrubs.

"Please," he begged. Never had Nick begged a woman, but he was more than willing to do so now. He would get down on his knees if she wanted him to. He needed to worship her body.

Her eyes glazed over as he waited for her answer. She pulled her fingers away and cupped his cheek. "We really shouldn't," she said, but to him it sounded like she was conceding.

"But we will," he told her. He didn't want to make it a question.

"Yes, Nick . . ." He felt utter joy at her words, and just as he was getting ready to respond . . . they were interrupted by the doorbell.

Chloe's eyes widened as her head whipped in the direction of the front door. She tried to break free of him.

"I don't give a damn who it is. They can get the hell off my property," Nick said, unwilling to release her.

"Nick, please, I don't want someone to walk in and see me like this," she pled.

Her fingers ripped away from his aching member, and he wanted to cry. Nick couldn't remember the last time he'd actually shed a tear, but right here, right now, in this moment, he thought he could actually cry.

"They will go away," he told her, pulling her close to him so she wouldn't forget how good they felt pressed tightly together.

The bell rang again and several curse words escaped Nick's mouth. "Don't move unless it's to take off those damn sexy pants. I'll be right back," he told her.

Whirling on his feet, he spun toward the front door, fury radiating through him. Whoever was out there would surely regret the interruption. He was just about to reach heaven, and there was no reason on earth that he should be interrupted.

Yanking open the front door, Nick was sure he must look like a wild man. His hair was messed, his clothes wrinkled, and his scowl big. He glared at the two military officers standing in front of him. One of them was Paul Holland, an attorney working for JAG. They'd played ball together every weekend for years, until his injury at least, but he'd never before shown up at Nick's place without telling him he was coming first. And certainly not with another man standing next to him who Nick didn't know.

"Hi, Nick, sorry for interrupting your evening, but we need to talk."

"What in the hell about?" Nick's words came out crisp, but his anger was turning to confusion.

"Sorry. I'm not myself," Nick said when Paul raised a brow.

"I understand. You've been through a lot," Paul told him. "We really need to talk, though. I'm here as a friend—as a possible attorney if you want me."

"Why would I need an attorney?" Nick asked. His confusion dimmed the passion he'd been feeling and completely washed away the anger. He heard noises behind him, but he somehow doubted it was Chloe removing her pants and spreading herself open for him on the kitchen counter. He let out a sigh. Another opportunity missed. He feared another one wouldn't come as soon as he'd need it to.

"You're being investigated," Paul told him.

The final bits of Nick's desire died away as he stared at his longtime friend. "What in the hell are you talking about?"

"Can I come in?" Paul asked. The man standing with him looked at Nick with sympathy, but he didn't say a word. Nick decided he needed to know whatever it was they were talking about so he opened his door. He might as well get it over with.

The two men followed him into his kitchen, which, as he'd suspected, Chloe had vacated. He handed them coffee cups, and then they all moved to the table.

"Paul, you can't hit me with something like this and then leave me hanging as we get comfortable," Nick said.

"There's a witness who has come forward saying you were drinking the night of the helicopter crash." Paul said the words calmly and with disbelief, but it still took several heartbeats before Nick truly understood what his friend had just said to him. He shook his head as he looked from Paul to the stranger and then back to his friend.

"Please explain," Nick finally said.

"Look, Nick, I don't know if you've made an enemy or what the hell is going on, but I do know your file came across my desk. A respected member of the Coast Guard is swearing under oath he saw you drinking before you went out on the water the night of the crash. The JAG offices decided the case was worth looking into. I came out here to warn you, which I shouldn't have done, but you very well could be getting served. There's a good chance it'll go to trial," Paul told him.

"I hear what you're saying, but I don't understand," Nick told him as he hung his head. "Who would say such a thing?"

"I can't name the person at this time, Nick, but he has no strikes against him. He's considered a credible source."

"Paul, you know I would never drink while on the job," Nick said. He was angry he even needed to say it.

"I know that, Nick, your team knows it, your captain knows it. But not everyone at the JAG offices knows you. They have no choice but to investigate. You're going to need an attorney. People died," Paul finished quietly.

"Do you think I don't remember my team dying?" he suddenly shouted. "Trust me, I remember that horrible moment every fucking day!" Fury rushed through him. The guilt he felt at being the only survivor had nearly destroyed him. Now his ethics were being questioned? He felt as if he were spinning out of control.

"Nick, you don't need to explain this to me. I know you," Paul said in what Nick decided was his calm attorney tone. Nick was pissed it was being used on him. "But if you officially hire me, we can get started on this and nip it in the bud before things get out of control."

Nick sat back quietly as he thought about what Paul was saying to him. Did he really need an attorney? He'd done nothing wrong. Shaking his head, he realized that didn't matter. The law wasn't in any way black and white, and if there was someone out there wanting to get him, his hiding his head in the sand wasn't going to make the matter go away. He needed to have a plan of action, and he needed to have it now.

"Yes, I'll hire you," Nick said, his voice much calmer.

"Good," Paul told him. "This is Brandon, my assistant. He's going to take notes. We need to start with the entire shift you worked. I hope you have time."

"I'll make the time," Nick told him.

Nick had no idea where Chloe had slipped off to, and he should be worried about her overhearing what was going on, but though there were still questions he had about her, his gut told him to trust her. He relied heavily on his gut in his line of work, so he was choosing to listen to it now.

After getting more coffee, Nick sat at the table and let out a sigh. He didn't want to relive this memory again. It was too painful. Paul looked at him and gave him a reassuring smile.

"I know this is hard, but the smallest of details really do matter," Paul said.

Nick began. "It was a call like any other, but visibility was low. We had to speak as a team and decide if we were going out. Of course, we agreed and headed to sea."

Paul took notes as Nick spoke, and though Nick knew he needed to do this, he still somehow felt violated by the act. It was ridiculous, but he was sharing one of the worst moments in his life, and every word he spoke was being analyzed. It was an invasion he resented.

"The sea was really pitching a fit as we reached the boat—"

"Start sooner," Paul told him. "From when you got the call."

Nick was growing more frustrated, but it wasn't Paul's fault, and he tried desperately not to take it out on the man.

"We were out on the cutter for routine ops. Gail, Pat, John, and I were sitting down having a cup of coffee and giving each other bullshit like normal. It was a typical evening. The sun was just beginning to set. Everything was calm, but we knew there was a storm in the distance."

"Good. I know this sucks, Nick, but the smallest details matter," Paul assured him.

"Sitting on our asses drinking coffee matters?" Nick snapped. He wasn't bothering to apologize this time.

"Yes, it matters," Paul said, not taking offense.

"Fine," Nick said. "I got a bit restless, so I got up and went outside to look at the sea and think for a minute. I saw lightning in the distance, but it had to be at least forty miles out. I knew there would be someone caught in the storm, though. I could feel it."

"Yeah, you seem to have a knack for that," Paul said.

"Gail joined me, then dragged me over to help her with some gear. We talked about nothing important," he said.

"What did you talk about?"

"Who the hell knows?" Nick snapped.

"Detail, Nick," Paul said again, speaking to Nick as if he were a child.

Nick thought back. "We talked about the storm, about the power of Mother Nature. Crap like that."

"Good, okay."

"I finished helping her and walked over to the landing pad. The feeling in my gut was intensifying so I moved to the bridge to listen for any activity coming over the wire. I wasn't there long when a call came in."

"What was the call?" Paul asked.

"It was a Mayday. The *Southern Belle* was in trouble, taking on water. The seas were churning, and the boat was rapidly going down."

"Good, Nick," Paul told him. "You have an excellent memory."

"It was the single worst moment of my life. I remember it like it was yesterday," Nick told him. His anger had drained, and now, he was filled with sorrow.

"I know. I wish I could say this was the last time you'll have to recount the story, but it most likely isn't," Paul told him.

"Seaman Harper was just a kid, barely out of boot camp, but he kept it together well. He jumped into action, and though his voice was shaking, he replied and took down notes. The *Belle* crew was growing more and more panicked as they relayed their location and the number of people on board," Nick continued.

"What came next?" Paul asked.

"The captain was there. He was calm as usual. He told me to get the crew and save the ship's people," Nick said. "Then he slapped the alarm to get the crew into motion."

Nick took a drink of coffee as he tried to take the emotion out of his voice. He needed to quit allowing the story to affect him and simply explain it.

"I made my way down to the changing room and finished suiting up. My adrenaline was pumping as it always does before a flight. My crew was already good to go, and we immediately got situated in the *Jayhawk*."

"So there were four of you?" Paul asked.

"Yes, Gail, my copilot; John, our paramedic and mechanic; and Pat, our rescue swimmer. We were a great team," Nick said, unable to keep the hitch from his voice this time.

"You had a lot of successful rescues before the crash," Paul agreed.

"Yeah, it doesn't matter how many rescues when all I can think about is the loss," Nick admitted.

"Okay, keep going," Paul told him.

Nick was wrecked. He didn't want to get into the next part. This was what he desperately wanted to forget. But he wasn't allowed that luxury.

"We did our preflight check, woke up the *Jayhawk*, and I checked in with the ship's crew before we lifted off."

"Everyone was fine?" Paul said.

"Yes, we wouldn't have lifted off if we weren't," he said. "Gail called in for departure, and once we had clearance, we lifted off."

"Were there any problems?" Paul asked.

"No. Liftoff was smooth. We headed out toward the troubled boat. All of us could see the storm growing in force as we got farther away from the cutter."

"How long were you out there?"

"It took about ten minutes until we spotted a strobe beacon and a bright yellow raft. Their ship had gone down that quickly. The sea was whipping them around."

Paul took more notes, and Nick used the opportunity to take in a deep breath.

"I got us into position and John hooked up to be lowered down. We knew we had to move fast. The harshness of the storm was escalating."

"What does that mean, Nick?"

"It means if it grew much worse we weren't going to be able to help anyone," Nick said.

"So why didn't you turn back at that point?" Paul asked.

"Because we wanted to rescue them. All of us agreed to get them out of the water," Nick said. "It was hard controlling the chopper, and the waves were rising higher and higher. I was watching the status of the storm as Gail kept an eye on John while he was lowered."

"Then what?"

"We got three of the stranded men out of the raft and into the *Jayhawk*. The fourth was on his way up. It was looking like a success," Nick said, his words quiet. "We were so damn close."

"So what went wrong?" Paul asked.

"Our captain called in, and we told him we were bringing the final man up and then would be heading home. We called in for medics."

"How was the rest of the crew handling the stress?"

"Like the pros they are . . . were," Nick corrected. He still couldn't believe they were actually gone. It didn't make sense to him. "The last man got up, and John gave us the thumbs-up to go home. I turned us back in the right direction, but the lightning was right on top of us. The wind kept picking up as we tried to outrun the worst of the storm. I had never seen such a beautiful sight as the *Orca* when we returned, even though we saw her getting pounded by the waves."

"Must have been a bumpy landing," Paul said.

"Yeah, landing was a challenge, but we set her down, and all of us breathed a sigh of relief," Nick told him.

"The medics ran out and took the rescued men off. That's when one of the guys told us they were missing their captain." If only they hadn't

103

left a man behind, his crew would still be alive. *If only* . . . Those words had gone through Nick's head a thousand times.

"Wasn't the storm too severe for flight at this point?" Paul questioned.

"It was bad, but not impossible. Gail and I looked at each other, and there was no question of us going back out. We had to at least try to find the captain," Nick said.

"Did you ask Pat and John if they wanted to go?" Paul questioned.

"I didn't have to say the words. I turned and looked at them, and they both nodded. If they had shaken their heads it would have been a no-go. We all agree or we don't go out," Nick said. "Gail called control and told them we were heading back out to sea."

"There was zero hesitation?" Paul pushed.

Nick glared at him. "Yes, there was hesitation, but we decided we weren't going to leave a man behind—not if we didn't have to," Nick insisted. "The storm was so much worse, the skies black, the waves high and dangerous. We saw pieces of the *Southern Belle* and did a sweep of the area as the wind pushed us around. There was no sign of the captain."

Paul didn't ask a question this time. He just waited. Nick appreciated that. This was the worst part of the story.

"The alarm sounded and I checked to find our fuel was low. Gail said we had to go back. She didn't want to leave a man behind any more than the rest of us did, but us crashing into the ocean wouldn't help save him." Nick's tone was void now.

"I turned the chopper around, and that's when it all went wrong. A bolt of lightning struck us. I held on to the controls, and felt I was fighting a losing battle, but I was in no way ready to give up."

"Did you speak to the crew at all during this struggle?" Paul asked.

"What does it matter?" Nick asked. "My adrenaline was pumping so high at that point, I can't believe I remember any of it."

"I know, but again, the smallest details are important."

"We slid sideways, heading for a wave. The sliding cargo door came open, swinging wildly half open, half shut. I told Gail we had to pull up. I put the throttle to the max, making the turbine engines scream. I can still hear the sound. We began to lift, but it was too late. A wave crashed into the side of us, filling the *Jayhawk* with seawater, then the door slammed shut, keeping it inside. We now weighed far too much," he said. "I couldn't get her to pull up."

Nick hadn't felt the cold, hadn't felt anything but a desire to get them out of the situation.

"Gail called in a Mayday, telling the captain we were now left with no choice but to jump from the chopper. She was so damn brave. She turned to me and asked if I was ready before repeating it to our guys in the back."

"So you aborted?"

"We were so close, but you have to know this all happens so damn fast," Nick said, running his fingers through his hair.

"Before we could even blink, another wave crashed over us and took us down into the water. We lost communication with each other as we were taken below the water."

"Do you remember what happened next?"

"I'll never forget. The windshield shattered, and we were going down. The lights dimmed, then went out as we continued to sink."

"What next?"

"I woke up on the surface, and my crew was gone." Nick was finished. He couldn't take any more of this. He hung his head and fought the emotional pain that was pulling him under as harshly as the sea had.

"I think that's good for now, Nick," Paul said.

Nick didn't have anything left. Paul and Brandon thanked him, gathered their notes, and left the house. Nick wearily walked to his den where he went straight to the bottle of bourbon he had at his corner bar. He might not have been drinking on shift, but he was sure as hell going to drink now.

He poured himself a double and downed it before refilling the crystal glass. He was on his third when he heard movement in the room. His emotions were raw, and he was too bitter to be with anyone, but as Chloe stepped forward, he found himself nearly dropping to his knees in his need for her to come to him.

Their eyes locked together, and Nick found himself even more lost than he had been before. She was either going to be his undoing, or she was going to be the one to help him lift up the pieces of his broken life. He really wasn't sure which direction the two of them were headed. He closed his eyes, unable to watch as she made her decision.

CHAPTER THIRTEEN

Chloe stood frozen in the doorway to the den as she watched Nick falling apart. She'd been listening as he'd spoken to the two men. Confusion swirled within her. Was he truly that good of an actor or was he innocent?

Everything she'd been told had made her believe he was the reason that helicopter had gone down—was the reason her brother had died, his body never recovered. She'd had a plan when coming to Nick's place. Her excuse for getting in had been to help him recover, but she'd been wanting to catch him in his lies.

Now, she wasn't so sure. Pain filled her at the loss of her brother, but what if it truly had been an accident? What if Nick was innocent? She just didn't know anymore. Could a man fake the pain he was obviously going through as he stood there nearly shaking at what he'd just had to relive?

He'd been so emphatic when talking with his friend. If she were on a jury, she would have a hard time not believing him. Chloe wasn't sure what was the truth and what the lies were anymore.

She found herself stepping closer to him, knowing full well she didn't have all the answers. But she knew that no matter what happened, she took her job seriously. Even though her objective all along had been to find something to incriminate him, she had still planned on healing his injury. She wouldn't risk her job. She'd told herself she wanted him healthy when he went to prison. But it went beyond that.

She'd been hating herself for feeling so attracted to him. But if he truly was innocent, then the unusually strong emotions she'd been dealing with weren't so wrong. She wished she weren't as confused as she was. She should retreat, but Chloe found herself moving closer to him instead.

"Are you okay, Nick?" She was surprised by the question. What she should do is run for the hills, or the ocean, or anywhere but closer to him. She should let him have his pity party—whether it was deserved or not. But instead she was moving closer still. She couldn't seem to stop her forward momentum.

"No." The one word was almost curt. His eyes flashed open, and the look he gave her sent a shudder through her. She wasn't sure if it was fear or desire—maybe a little bit of both. One thing she knew was that she should get the hell out of there . . . and do it fast.

"I'm sorry. I should leave you alone then," she said.

Chloe hadn't ever been hunting. Her family hadn't done it either, but she imagined as she looked at Nick, and the light he got in his eyes, that it was the same look any predator had when it spied its prey. She took another step back.

"We have some unfinished business, doc," he said, his tone changing abruptly. He moved toward her.

She slowly began backing away, her eyes shifting to the door, wondering at her chances of escape. He was moving quicker these days, but she might still be able to get the jump on him. With that look in his eyes, she wasn't so sure, though.

"You know what, we're both pretty tired. I think any, uh . . . business we might have would best be discussed in the morning." She took another step back. He slammed down the remainder of his alcohol and took another step toward her.

"Aren't you the one always saying that things shouldn't be put off, that you have to tough it out even if you don't want to?" he pointed out. His words made her eyes narrow at him.

He was so calm, but the light in his eyes was agitated. She knew when to stay and fight and when to retreat, and at this moment, it was best to call it a day before the tidal wave hit. He didn't even try to hide the fact that he was ogling her body, taking extra time on her breasts, her hips, the crease between her legs. She felt as if she were standing there completely naked. She didn't like the feeling.

Her legs clenched together as heat flooded her. She should hate this man, not be turned on by him, especially by nothing more than a look. But that look reminded her of what had happened only a few hours before, of how it had felt to have him standing between her thighs while his mouth did wicked things against her skin.

"I heard some of what you were talking about earlier," she told him. His gaze narrowed a bit more. She took another step back. "I'm really sorry. I'm sure you need time to process it all." Her words came out in a rush. She was becoming more nervous and confused by the second. He'd been bold in the weeks she'd been there, but there was an entirely new light in his eyes—one she didn't trust at all.

With each step he took closer to her, she felt her heart race a bit faster, her skin tremble a little more. The hungry look in his eyes was making her core tight and hot, and she wasn't sure what to think about it. She wanted him, that was definite. But she also knew she shouldn't be having those feelings.

Chloe knew beyond a doubt that she would regret sleeping with the man—regret it deep in her soul. It would be a betrayal to her family—to herself. She had to get control over this situation and get the hell away from him fast. Even with this knowledge, she wasn't trying to run fast enough. He was taking two steps forward with every one of her retreating moves. She didn't think she wanted to be captured, but that's what it seemed like.

Nick's eyes never leaving hers, he lifted his fingers, his movements slow and deliberate. He undid the top button of his shirt, then the next . . . and the next. She was mesmerized by the widening view of skin he was showing. She trembled as she continued moving backward while he advanced, his shirt slowly coming open.

"What are you doing?" she asked, her voice shaky. Her tongue came out and moistened her dry lips, her legs stopped wanting to work.

"I've had a *really* bad day, and I'm getting more comfortable," he said as the last of his buttons came undone and he moved to his cuffs, undoing those before he shrugged out of the shirt and dropped it, the light material floating to the floor.

She watched the movement, completely mesmerized. Then her eyes shot back upward, landed on his solid chest, and refused to budge from that delicious sight. She'd seen him several times without his shirt, and she'd seen fire burn in his eyes before, but not like this. There was hunger in the air. Nick was taking aim, and she was his target. She knew if she refused him, of course, he'd let her go. She just wasn't sure she had the willpower anymore to do what she should.

Chloe continued moving backward, the gap between them only a couple of feet now. She hadn't even realized she'd been moving down the hallway until she found herself at her bedroom door. The thought of the large bed on the other side of the solid wood sent a rush of wetness to her panties.

Her fingers shook as she lifted her hand to the knob and turned it, the door squeaking open. But she just stood there, gazing at the man following her.

"I'm sorry you've had a bad day," she whispered, her voice deep and husky. Her eyes caught the flex of every muscle as he approached. She was surprised she didn't sink down to the ground in utter submission. "I'm going to turn in now."

She stepped into the room and pressed her hand against the door. A very small piece of her knew she should thrust it closed, but she'd barely pushed it a few inches before he stepped forward, stopping her from shutting him out. One word, or maybe a few, and she knew he would go away. Why couldn't she say the words?

"I want to keep talking," he told her as his eyes raked over her, making her visibly quiver.

"I don't think that's a good idea right now," she said. He was too close to her, and she gave up on shutting the door, deciding pulling back farther was the safer method. It seemed the best option. "I'm exhausted and I should sleep." The words were a lie. Sleep would be impossible given how she was currently feeling.

He called her on it.

"You aren't tired, Chloe—you aren't tired at all. You're aching, and you're fighting it. You want me as badly as I want you, but you're afraid to admit it. Let's help each other tonight—no games, no lies, no threats. We want each other, and there's nothing wrong with it. Just admit how much you want me," he demanded.

He was so close she could feel heat radiating off his body. She wanted to reach out and touch him, but she knew if she did, it would be all over. She wanted to lie down on her bed and let him take her to the sweetest recesses of heaven.

She didn't feel ready for that—and *really* not ready with this particular man. It was a mistake, her mind was shouting at her, but her body knew exactly what it wanted.

He closed the gap between them, and slowly, achingly, his arms reached out. His hands slipped over her hips and cupped her behind her back as he pulled her forward. He didn't move quickly, giving her plenty of time to protest. The words wouldn't exit her mouth. She was afraid if she spoke, it would be to beg him to kiss her, love her, take the ache away.

He leaned down and pressed light kisses to the corner of her mouth, and her body trembled, but then he pulled back, his eyes burning, his arms shaking with the restraint he was using. It only made her want him that much more. She wanted to lean forward and take his mouth, but she wasn't sure quite how to do it.

Her reservations were quickly disappearing. She was trying to tell herself it was just sex—only sex. But when was sex just sex? For other people it might be that way, but not for her. She equated sex with love—with intimacy. She couldn't do it with the enemy. But even telling herself this, she wasn't pulling away. They were in a standoff, her bed only two feet away, his body hard and unyielding.

"Do you still want to *talk*, Chloe?" he asked as he licked her bottom lip. She opened to him, but he didn't dive inside her mouth. "Or do you want something else?"

It was a taunt, and she knew it. It was a challenge. He could walk away from her, she was sure of it. Was that what she wanted him to do? The thought of him seeking satisfaction with another woman after she'd been the one to bring him to this state of arousal made her stomach sick.

"Nick . . ." She wasn't sure what she was planning on saying, but his name came out as a deep sigh. She ached for him.

He tugged her against him, all of her softness pressed against his hardness, and the feeling was absolute euphoria. She could stand there like that with him for hours or days—get lost in his embrace.

A moan escaped her tight throat before she could hold it back, and he rewarded her by leaning down and running his tongue up her throat. Then he kissed her softly again. She didn't want softness anymore. She wanted hard and scorching.

Her breasts ached where they pressed against his solid chest. Her stomach trembled where his arousal pushed against it. She wanted to shed her clothes and feel all of his hardness pressing into her soft curves.

One of his hands drifted down and curved around her butt, squeezing her as he lifted her higher so his thickness could be pressed against her aching core. She was so tightly pressed against him, if there weren't clothes in the way, he would be slipping inside her. She closed her eyes and sighed at the beauty of it.

Clenching her fists together to keep from reaching for him, Chloe struggled with what to do. If he moved the slightest bit, put any more pressure on her body, she might come from just that. Maybe then her mind would clear and she would return to her senses. She wiggled against him and moaned at how good it felt.

She was wrong, though. That just made the ache deepen. It did nothing to satisfy the cravings he was creating within her. She wanted him. Could she admit it? It seemed he wanted her to say the words. She wasn't sure she could do that either.

Lifting her leg up, he slid between her thighs, mounting the pressure ever higher. They were in a dance that could go on for a lifetime.

"We've been here before, Chloe. You want me, but you're afraid to admit it. As soon as you let down your guard, as soon as you tell me how much you want this, I'm going to slide my mouth over every single inch of you. I'm going to strip off your clothes and make you come over and over again. I'm going to slide inside your tight, wet body and make you scream my name. All you have to do is let go—admit this is right between us. Let me take the pain away for both of us. Tell me you want me," he demanded.

He spoke against her ear, his tongue tracing the lobe before he bent and sucked on her neck while his hips pushed forward in circular motions, rubbing against her wet heat. She whimpered in his arms as she strained against him, feeling his hardness pulse against her body. It could all be hers with just a few simple words.

She buried her head against his chest, and her lips traced over his nipple, her tongue sliding out to take a taste. He gasped in pleasure as his hips thrust forward. She was on fire.

Reaching out, he tangled his fingers in her hair and pulled her face back so she had no choice but to look into his flaming eyes. He kissed her a bit harder this time, still holding himself back, though.

He spoke while his lips were still against hers. "What do you want, Chloe? Your body is telling me exactly what it needs. But you have to say the words."

She licked her lips again, her tongue caressing his mouth at the same time. She groaned at the taste of him, wanting him to devour her. Opening her lips, she invited him in, but still he didn't take the bait.

She didn't want to say the words, didn't want to admit how badly she needed this. That would be a betrayal to herself. If she simply gave in, then she could tell herself it was in the heat of the moment, couldn't she? But if she voiced her wants, there was no taking them back.

Nick reached between her thighs and caressed her heat, pressing upward so his fingers were touching her exactly where she wanted. He squeezed his fingers and she whimpered again. Shifting, she tried to put him where she needed him, but he wasn't doing what she needed. There were too many clothes in the way.

"My stubborn little doc," he said with a sigh. "Don't you realize that as soon as you voice your wants, I'm going to lay you back on this bed and strip your clothes away? I'm going to sink so deep inside you, you won't know where you end and I begin. We're wasting these precious moments on your internal battle—moments I could be taking you to the highest reaches of pleasure. Give in to me, darling, and I promise you'll have no regrets."

Chloe shook her head, and he stepped back from her. Panic zipped through her entire body. Was he going to leave her like this? She wouldn't be able to handle it. She looked up, met his eyes, and saw triumph in his expression. She let out a breath as she clenched her fingers together.

He began to undo his pants, and her gaze zeroed in on the new flesh he was showing—on the part of his body she hadn't yet been able to gaze upon. She'd felt him so many times, but she hadn't yet gotten to see his perfection. She had no doubt he would be perfect. How could he not be? Every inch of his skin was flawless—even the scars only added to his overall appeal.

Within seconds, he was standing a couple feet away—naked. His beautiful erection was hard and thick, standing up, making her mouth water with her need to touch him—taste him—have him sink within her. He was even more perfect than she could have ever imagined.

As she gazed at his stunning thickness, it pulsed, a bead of moisture escaping from the tip, making her want to drop to her knees and taste his essence. She quivered uncontrollably as she stood there gazing upon him.

"I'm all yours, Chloe," he told her as he reached down and wrapped his fingers around himself, stroking up and down as she gazed at his magnificence. "I want your fingers and mouth on me. I want to be buried inside you. As soon as you tell me you want it, too, we will make explosions happen together."

He stepped forward again, and she didn't even think about retreating. He easily pulled her into his arms, and she sighed at how good it felt to have him naked against her. The fight within her was lost. She reached for him, moaning as her fingers wrapped around his solidness.

"Yes, Nick," she said, her words barely audible as she pressed her body against his burning heat.

"What?" he asked, pushing his thickness against her palm as he moved his lips to her neck and sucked hard. She could feel him losing control, and she reveled in knowing it was her doing it to him.

"Yes, Nick, I want you," she said.

The words freed her. She nearly cried in her euphoria at knowing he would be sinking inside her, that he would make them one. She couldn't have regrets. This was too perfect to not want it.

He didn't hesitate. He gripped her shirt and thrust it over her head before undoing her pants and shoving them down her legs. Her underthings went away in seconds, and then she was before him—naked, hot, wet, and needy.

"Make me come, Nick, please make me come," she said in a sob as she pushed against him, seeking relief. His fingers trailed across her naked back until they gripped her butt and pulled her tightly against him. He spread her thighs, and his thickness slipped between them, rubbing on the outside of her core.

She squirmed against him, trying to get him to push inside her, but he was punishing them both, pressing their bodies together without entering her. She reached behind him and tugged on his head, needing to kiss him. This teasing had gone on for far too long.

A switch flipped inside Nick, and he growled before gripping her ass and lifting her up. She wrapped her legs around him as he moved his hips, his erection rubbing against her and spreading her wetness. She tried to shift, tried to bring him inside her, but he continued moving in slow circles, rubbing every inch of her sensitive flesh without diving inside where she wanted him most.

She tugged on his hair, and he leaned forward, his lips finally taking hers the way she needed him to. He owned her mouth, his tongue slipping inside, his lips urgent as he possessed her. She clung tightly to him, her ankles locked together behind his back, her fingers yanking at his hair as she tried to get ever closer to him.

Chloe was completely consumed by Nick, and she didn't mind getting lost in him, didn't mind the way his fingers squeezed her flesh so hard there would be bruises. He groaned into her mouth and sipped at her. He easily slid along the outside of her folds, her heat soaked wet in her excitement.

"I didn't want this to be so fast," he groaned. "But you're so damn beautiful, so ready for me." He bit her lip, causing her pain, but even that was perfect. "I need to be inside you." The words came out almost as an apology.

"Then take me," she encouraged him. He'd teased her long enough. She wanted him to fill her. "I'm protected." She knew his medical files, and she wasn't worried about him.

That was all it took for him to let go of his final bit of self-control. He moved forward and pressed her into the wall. The coolness against her back and the heat at her chest were even more stimulating. She wiggled in his arms. He pulled back just enough to position himself at the heart of her opening.

His mouth clamped down on hers as he slid his head inside before pausing. She wiggled against him, needing him to push forward. He wrenched his mouth away and trailed kisses down her neck.

"You are so damn hot and tight," he groaned before biting into her shoulder.

She shuddered at his words. She was falling apart in his arms, and he was no more than a couple inches inside her.

Gripping her hips tightly, he looked up. Her eyes were mere slits, but she could see the ardor in his. He was nearly out of control. With a feral cry, he surged forward, burying himself deep within her heat.

Their cries rang through the air as Chloe nearly shattered from the fullness of him inside her. She wanted more. She clawed at his back, and he bit harder on her shoulder—anchoring himself down as he pulled back and then surged forward again.

She was glowing from the inside out, her body damp with heat, her insides burning up. The tightening in her core grew and grew until she was whimpering with the need to explode. His groans accompanied hers as he picked up the pace, moving steadily in and out of her, faster and faster as they clung to each other.

He thrust inside her again, pushing her into the wall, and she let go, her body flexing over and over as she screamed out her pleasure. He sped up as he drew out her orgasm, his grunts reverberating through her. And then she felt him shudder, felt the hot spurts of his pleasure coat her insides. She came again, squeezing him even harder. He groaned as his body stiffened, pressing her against the wall.

They both shook as they came down from the incredible pleasure. She sagged into him, her body spent, her legs locked tightly around him, shivering with the release of the built-up pressure.

Nick finally moved them over to her bed and sat down, their bodies still connected. She clung tightly to him, not quite willing to let him go. She knew she would need to soon, but for now she wanted to enjoy the pleasure of him inside her, of their bodies so tightly joined.

She didn't want to think of anything other than being right where she was. It was perfect in so many ways. He laid back, her on top of him, and she closed her eyes. Exhaustion filled her, and she let go, feeling content.

CHAPTER FOURTEEN

Nick stretched in bed, taking a few moments to realize where he was. The sun was sneaking through the cracks in the blinds, and from the low intensity, it was early in the morning. He didn't need to glance at a clock to figure that out.

Chloe slept soundly next to him, her body well loved and exhausted. He'd fallen asleep with her after their intense lovemaking, only to wake a few hours later and take her again. The stress of the day before had evaporated while in her arms, and he wanted to do it again and again.

Since being with her, she was all he thought about. Nick wasn't sure if that was a good thing or not. He'd always enjoyed sex, but this was different. He felt a connection with this woman he didn't normally feel when he made love. When he was finished, he'd never felt the need to hold a woman close, to caress her soft skin. Once his body was sated, he wanted to be on his way.

But not with Chloe. With her, he wanted to touch her, run his fingers over her delicate skin, memorize every inch of her. And he wanted to slide within her slick heat over and over again—get lost within her.

As she slept peacefully beside him, he was drawn to her, couldn't take his gaze away. Sure, she was beautiful, her light eyes now closed in sleep, her fair skin creamy and soft, her hair that of an angel's. She took his breath away.

But there was so much more to her than just her looks. She was feisty and strong, determined and stubborn. She challenged him in a way that he enjoyed, and she made him burn like no other woman had ever come close to making him feel.

The last couple of weeks had been packed with frustration and joy and a need to make her smile. His every thought was being consumed by this one woman, and he couldn't even find it within himself to care about that.

One moment she would be serious and stern with him. The next she would be laughing and making him smile. She praised him when he pushed himself, and she made him want to be a better person. She was tearing his world apart. When the pieces came back together, he knew he would be a new man. The strange thing was, he didn't have any regrets about that.

When he'd first met her, he'd instantly wanted her, but whether that was to prove his manliness to himself or whether it was to win a conquest, he wasn't sure. What he did know, beyond a shadow of a doubt, was that he didn't feel that way anymore. He'd taken her several times, and it still wasn't enough. He had a feeling he would never get enough of her—in or out of the bedroom.

Mumbled words escaped her sweet pink lips, and he stilled his fingers on her smooth stomach. She stretched, her hand reaching forward, and he smiled. Was she seeking him out even in her sleep? A frown line puckered between her brows, when she came up with empty air and she stirred a bit more as her body shifted toward the warmth of his skin. She mumbled a few more words and then fell back asleep.

He grinned at the sight. He was going to choose to believe she wanted him, needed him as much as he needed her. They were drawn to each other even in the deepest recesses of their minds. He wondered if he did the same movements when he was dead to the world. He wouldn't be at all surprised if he did.

Nick lay there with her for about a half hour before the need to get up for the day was too overwhelming. With reluctance, he left her side and went back to his own room where he grabbed clothes and took a hot shower. Closing his eyes while the steaming spray jetted over him had him going hard all over again as he pictured her fingers replacing the water, her lips trailing down his stomach and then taking him deep within her mouth.

Snapping his eyes open, he had to push those thoughts away. That was going to lead him to rush back to her room and wake her up before she had a decent amount of sleep. They had plans for the day, although she wasn't aware of them. He was sure he could get her on board, though.

Dragging himself from his room, he tried to do some work in his office, but his thoughts continued to stray to Chloe in her nice warm bed all alone. How easy it would be for him to slip inside her room and take her for a leisurely morning of lovemaking. His brothers could wait on him.

That thought made him smile. Now he understood why his siblings were so often late for events. They couldn't keep their hands off their wives. He'd envied them the smallest bit, and then he'd kicked himself for feeling that way. With Chloe in his life, he was beginning to understand their reluctance to leave the bedroom. Once would never be enough.

Nick managed to let Chloe sleep for a couple more hours, and then he decided he wanted her awake with him. She was normally a morning person. He hadn't missed how she snuck out of the house to go running each day. He only regretted his knee still wasn't strong enough for him to go out there with her. Soon, he'd be back to normal health and he would enjoy running the island with her as the sun was rising over the hills.

He could picture doing a lot of activities with Chloe if he really thought about it. He would love to take her up in his private plane, land in a field that was out in the middle of nowhere, and make love to her below the wings with nothing around them but the animals and sun. He enjoyed her company, and he had a whole lot of ideas of what they could do to make their time together even more enjoyable.

Lying down on the bed—on top of the covers to prevent too much temptation—Nick leaned over Chloe and kissed her lips softly. She stirred, her eyes fluttering as she began to wake up. Then she tensed.

He frowned as he looked into her widening eyes. She was trying to retreat. He had no doubt about it. Her body stiffened, and she looked wildly around the room while lifting a hand up to cover her mouth.

"Not quite the reaction I was seeking," he said as he pulled down the covers, exposing her breasts, and ran his hand over them. Her nipples instantly hardened, and her breath rushed out. He leaned forward and tried to push her fingers away.

"No," she mumbled beneath her fingers.

He frowned. "Why not? I kissed just about every part of your body last night," he reminded her.

"For one thing, I have morning breath . . ." She stopped speaking and he continued massaging her breasts. Her breath was coming out faster and he could feel her heartbeat accelerating.

"I woke you up twice in the middle of the night, and you didn't complain about breath then," he reminded her.

"Nick, this is moving too fast," she said, but the words ended on a moan as he tweaked her nipple. She wanted him even if she didn't want to want to.

"You weren't worried about that last night," he told her. Since she wouldn't let him have access to her lips, he leaned over and took one tasty nipple into his mouth. Her back arched off the bed before slowly going back down. Then she grabbed his head and pulled him away.

He looked into her eyes and saw the desire there, but he also saw fear. That he didn't understand. What could she possibly be afraid of? There was no possibility of her being embarrassed. She had a fantastic body, and he'd taken his time studying every single inch of her skin.

"I didn't *force* you to have sex with me last night," he reminded her.

"I know you didn't. I wanted to make love. It's just that I don't normally move so quickly," she said. Her breath was coming out in pants. And he was working himself up as much as he was arousing her.

"It's too late to take it back," he pointed out.

She sighed as she yanked on the covers. Much to his disappointment, she covered up her luscious breasts and then scooted up and leaned against the headboard, hugging her knees and the blanket to her chest.

"I understand that, but just because we had sex last night doesn't mean it's now an open invitation. I have a job to do here," she told him.

His eyes narrowed as he studied her. "What kind of game are you playing?" he asked. He'd rarely been around for the morning-after chat, and he wasn't loving how this one was going.

"I'm not playing a game. We both were worked up last night. We had sex. Can we forget about it and go back to normal now?"

Nick was stunned into silence. He'd been making plans all morning, and she wanted to pretend like nothing had happened. His ego was taking a major hit.

"Or I could keep you in this bed all day so you forget about anything other than having sex with me," he told her, liking his idea a whole lot more than hers.

Her eyes widened and he could see her breathing deepen. She still wanted him. What he didn't understand was why she would try so hard to fight it. Maybe it was a mystery he had to figure out before he went completely insane. It would probably be smarter for him if he just let it go, but Nick wasn't the type of man to back down. But this wasn't the time to get too much into the conversation. When they finished the discussion, he wanted to make sure there were no possibilities of an interruption.

"Get dressed. We have company coming over."

He stood up and walked to her bedroom door. He was angry, but he wasn't sure if he was more frustrated with her or himself.

"Nick," she called out. He stopped but didn't turn. "I'm sorry, okay."

He didn't respond. He just walked out the door. Nick went straight to his gym and pushed himself as hard as he could before his leg began to give out on him. Normally when he was angry, he could run hard for a good ten miles, and that would wear him out enough to push the rage away. With the knee injury, he didn't have that luxury. That just riled him up all the more.

When he came back to the living room, he found Chloe fully dressed, her eyes following him, slightly rounded as if she were afraid to speak. That irritated him all the more. He liked how they acted around each other. He didn't want her to be some meek little mouse too afraid to stand up to him.

Yes, they'd had sex. That didn't have to change the entire dynamic of their relationship. If anything, it should make it that much better. He moved past her and heard her slight intake of breath. He wanted to grab her, push her down onto the couch, and make her scream with pleasure. He wanted her to admit how badly she still needed him.

He didn't get it. Yes, she was beautiful. So were millions of other ladies in the world. Yes, she stimulated him, but again, many other women did the same. He wasn't fascinated with all of them. So what was it about her that had him breaking all his normal rules? Why couldn't he just push her aside and forget about what had happened?

Maybe it was the unknown. Maybe he wanted to unwrap her, figure out exactly why she acted the way she did—what her secrets were. She wasn't the usual type he went after, so what was it that made her so special? He might find that it was nothing. He probably would see, after a short while, that she was just like every other woman on the planet and his interest would wane. He didn't believe his muddled ramblings, but it helped him try to work through it.

Neither of them spoke as they drank their morning coffees, both of them in their own heads. Nick wasn't quiet by nature, but the tense silence in the room was suffocating. He wanted to break the silence, but he also didn't want to be the first one to do so. It was a battle of wills, he decided.

His doorbell rang, and Nick nearly let out a breath of relief. He didn't think he'd be able to sit there too much longer without either strangling her or pulling her onto his lap to straddle him. If this was a prediction of the days to come, he was in for some serious trouble.

"Who's here?" she asked as he got up.

"My brothers," he told her.

He didn't wait for her reaction, but instead went to the front door and opened it. Cooper and Stormy were there alongside Mav and Lindsey. They all wore smiles. A baby cried from a car seat, and Lindsey's belly was about a mile out there.

"I'd give you a hug, Lins, but I don't think I can get past all that stomach," Nick said, his mood instantly lighting up as his family entered his home.

"Don't make me kick your ass," Mav growled as he leaned in behind his wife to kiss her cheek. "You are absolutely stunning," he told her.

"Nick, you better give me a hug anyway otherwise you might hurt my feelings," Lindsey said with a pout.

He carefully put his arms around her and gave her the barest of squeezes. He was terrified of breaking her. He really cared for Lindsey, and he was very aware of the horror she'd gone through several years ago. He took extra care when he touched her, but especially now that she was pregnant. "You *are* stunning, you know that right?" he said to make up for his joke.

"I'm a bloated whale, but I'll take all the compliments I can get," she said as she patted his cheek and stepped past him.

"You guys are late. I was going to start the food without you," Nick told his brothers before he leaned over them and pulled Stormy into his arms, squeezing her a lot harder than he had Lindsey.

"Ha, *you* cook the meal. That's entertaining," Mav said. Nick scowled at him.

"Some of us have children to take care of before we're allowed to leave the house. We should have made you come over to our place," Stormy told him.

"Yeah, what she said," Coop added with a smile.

"Pathetic. You are both so pathetic since you've gotten married," Nick said to his brothers, but he laughed. He actually enjoyed how happy they were. He wasn't going to voice that thought out loud, though.

Stormy's attention was caught by something behind him, and Nick knew Chloe had entered the room. She was most likely trying to sneak back to her bedroom before the crowd entered the house. Nick smiled again. She'd have a hell of a time doing that with his sisters-in-law there. They loved to talk, and a pretty woman residing in his house was way too juicy for them to miss.

"Hi," Stormy said as she brushed past Nick. "I'm Stormy Armstrong, and this man over here is Cooper, my husband. The terror standing by him is our three-year-old son, Aaron, and the wailing infant is our month-old daughter, Addie."

Stormy patiently waited for Chloe to speak. All eyes turned in her direction, and Nick watched as a becoming shade of pink infused her cheeks.

"Um . . . I'm Chloe Reynolds, Nick's physical therapist." She seemed unsure how she wanted to introduce herself. Just to make it slightly more awkward for her, Nick sidled up to her side and stood far too close for a client-patient relationship. She stepped aside slowly and he followed her.

The tension flowing through the woman could be felt by all, but his family didn't point it out. That wasn't their style unless they were trying to embarrass someone. They'd have to get to know Chloe a heck of a lot better for that to happen.

Lindsey moved forward and introduced her and Mav, and then the girls dragged Chloe along with them into the kitchen. She tried to make a polite excuse, but the women weren't having any of it, just as Nick had predicted. He sure did love his family.

"Let's leave the ladies to chat so you can show us the new boat," Mav said.

Nick found himself reluctant to leave Chloe alone with the girls. He knew they were excellent at interrogating people, and he wondered what Chloe might say about him. Never before had he even cared. But for some reason the idea of her trashing him to the two women who had married his brothers brought a frown to his face.

He was torn about what he should do.

"Don't worry, Nick, the ladies will still be here when we get back," Coop said with a laugh. That comment got him moving. He didn't want to seem like he was hung up too much on Chloe.

They made their way down to the dock where his newest toy was tied up. He hadn't been able to take her out since the injury, but he would get her on the water soon enough.

"Damn, she's a beauty, even if I do prefer to be in the air rather than on the water," Mav said with a whistle as he took in the thirty-foot fishing boat with all the bells and whistles. It had a nice cabin below so Nick and a girl could head out to sea for a few days and not have to worry about interruptions.

Right now, the only woman he wanted to take anywhere was Chloe, and he didn't see her jumping up and down with joy at the thought of being lost at sea with him. But there was something about being on the water with no chance of anyone interrupting a couple that made it that much more appealing. Why did he want this woman all to himself so much?

The brothers climbed on board, and Nick pulled out some beers he had chilling in the fridge. They sat down and enjoyed the view of the gently lapping water.

"How's therapy going?" Maverick asked.

He inwardly winced. It had been going pretty great the night before. "It's moving a lot slower than I would like, but I'm able to be on my feet quite a bit longer before the ache sets in. Chloe thinks I'll be golden in a few more weeks if I don't try to 'push it,' as she says," he explained with a laugh.

There really wasn't a joke when it came to his injuries, but he had to laugh it off or he got angry. Nick didn't like being immobile, even partially so. Thinking of that brought to mind yesterday's visit from Paul. Should he share his legal complications with his brothers? He was reluctant to do so, but he didn't understand why.

"Listen to the hot therapist, for sure," Coop told him with a grin.

"You have a wife. You don't need to be looking at Chloe," he warned his brother.

That had both Maverick and Cooper laughing at him. He should have kept his mouth shut. He was far too easy to read at the moment.

"Now you know what you put us through every time you flirt with our wives," Coop said before slapping him on the back. Nick had to smile.

"Okay, it might be a bit annoying, but Chloe and I aren't exactly in a relationship," he said.

"Seems like that might be something you want to change," Mav pointed out.

"No, I have too much going on right now." He sighed before he looked at his brothers. They waited, knowing him well enough to understand he needed to form his thoughts before he spoke.

Then he told them about the visit from the attorney. Their eyes narrowed as he went through the charges pending against him. He didn't know why he'd hesitated to tell them. Of course they were going to have his back. Why had there been a small percentage of his brain that had worried they might believe the worst? If he told them he'd even wondered about their loyalty, they'd be pissed enough to kick his ass right off the boat for a cold bath in the seawater.

"We'll get through this, no problem," Mav said. "I have some well-connected contacts. I'm going to make a few calls."

"Whoever is out to get you will learn quickly not to mess with one of the Armstrongs," Cooper added.

"I'm not worried about it," Nick told them. "I'm just a little pissed that someone would lie like this. I wanted to put the crash behind me, and the accusations make everything—the accident, the death of my team, my injuries—surface once more. Anyone who knows me knows there's no way I would put my crew in danger." His words rose in volume as he slammed his fist down on the table in front of him.

"Of course you wouldn't," Mav quickly agreed.

"When you have what we have, we're bound to make enemies. You can't let it bring you down," Cooper pointed out.

"Have you ever been accused of something that could land you in prison?" Nick asked.

"No. But I wouldn't be surprised if it happened someday," Cooper said in all seriousness.

"We'll get through this, bro. Coop and I are going to be at your side every step of the way," Mav said again as he clapped his shoulder.

"I know and I appreciate it." He sighed before looking down. "I have to tell Mom and Uncle Sherman. I'm really not looking forward to that conversation."

"You can't put it off too long. If you do, they're going to be furious with you," Coop warned.

"I know, I know. I just found out yesterday. I've barely even had time to process it yet," Nick told him.

"We'll go to them together," Mav said.

"Thanks. I'm glad I didn't wait to tell you," he said. They both nodded. "However, I don't want to discuss it any further today. I just want to enjoy a nice barbecue visiting with my family," Nick insisted.

Mav laughed. "I think I can smell food all the way down here. The ladies must be cooking." Nick appreciated the instant change in subject.

"Then we'd better get our butts up there. If we're sneaky enough, we can get our fill before anyone else arrives."

"Are you expecting more company?" Coop asked.

"With the way your wives cook, the entire island might show up," Nick warned.

"Before we go anywhere, you have some serious explaining to do," Mav said.

"What more do I need to explain?" Nick was confused.

"You're avoiding talking about the hot PT, and it's obvious there are some serious sparks going on between you two," he said.

"Not that you can see anything in your marriage-induced love coma, but it would be none of your business if anything were going on," Nick told him.

"That means there's definitely something to tell," Coop said with a laugh.

Nick glared at them both. Had he been this annoying when they'd begun to fall for a woman? That thought stopped him in his tracks. Was he actually falling for Chloe, or was it just about sex and the chase? He wasn't really sure.

"Nothing at all to tell," Nick said with a grumble.

"I didn't know if I'd ever see the day," Coop said, looking at Nick as if studying him beneath a microscope.

"I'm gonna kick both your asses if you don't shut up," Nick threatened.

"Dang, I think you're protesting far too much," Coop said.

"She's hot, obviously," Nick told them. Maybe that would shut his brothers up. But his words only made the gleam in their eyes brighten.

"Maybe Mom will be getting another wedding soon," Mav said with a chuckle. His brother ducked just in time to avoid the flying beer bottle aimed at his head. That only made Mav laugh harder.

Nick needed to see Chloe again, but he wasn't going to admit that, especially now. He was way too confused. He didn't like it.

"Let's find food," he muttered.

His brothers laughed, but they relented. Then all of them walked back up to the house. Nick was moving much better than he had when Chloe had first arrived, but still not at peak performance. His brothers were slowing their usual pace so he wouldn't strain himself keeping up. He didn't say anything, but he appreciated what they were doing. Nick didn't like to feel weak, and he didn't like to ask people to modify their normal routines for him. All the brothers felt the same way. It was a matter of pride, and if the Armstrong men knew about anything, it was pride. They had it in spades.

They reached the house laughing as Mav entertained them with a tale of his last boxing adventure. The moment they stepped through the back door and entered the kitchen, though, their talking stopped and their stomachs instantly growled. The women were cooking, and it smelled delicious.

Mav walked over to Lindsey and wrapped his arms around her waist, his hands cupping her burgeoning stomach. "It's smells good, Sugar."

"Flattery is going to get you everywhere," she told him with a beaming smile. She turned around and leaned forward to kiss him before she frowned. "My stomach really is getting huge," she pouted.

"You are the most beautiful pregnant woman on the planet. No other holds a candle to you," he assured her. His words brightened her face immensely.

Nick glanced over at Chloe and noticed the yearning in her eyes as she watched the couple hold one another. He was willing to do that for her, so he didn't understand why she wouldn't accept it. As if she could feel his eyes on her, she turned and the pink in her cheeks deepened. He smiled at her as he winked.

She turned away, and he suddenly felt the need to chase her. Maybe the fun was only just beginning. She'd been a challenge from day one. Why should that stop just because they'd already made it to bed together? He couldn't see a reason.

"Okay, you're making me want to do naughty things with my husband with all this kissing and sweet talk," Stormy said as she sidled up to Cooper and gave him a sweet kiss. He reached down and squeezed her ass, making her squeal as she swatted at him.

"And you're all making me want to vomit," Nick told them.

"If you don't like the show, then you're free to leave," Mav said with a wink.

"It's my house, ass," Nick said, but his eyes went to Chloe again. He wouldn't mind walking over to her and taking her into his arms, showing his brothers how a real man kissed the woman he desired.

As if she could read his thoughts, she looked away, suddenly finding the hem of her shirt fascinating. He took that as encouragement. She was more affected by him than she would ever admit. It was taking an immense amount of control to hold himself back.

Something had switched in Nick's brain that he didn't quite understand yet. He'd always been afraid to settle down with only one woman, but when he looked at Chloe he couldn't imagine not having her around. Was his family still enough? Or did he need a relationship with a woman like his brothers did? He wasn't sure anymore.

"You boys are completely hopeless," Lindsey told them. "But that's why we adore you so dang much. But if you don't leave us alone . . ."

Mav and Coop muttered, but they released their wives and Coop grabbed Nick's arm, suggesting they go watch the game.

Nick said, "My beer is gone. I need another. Anyone else?" The brothers followed Nick to his den, but he was no longer in a visiting mood. His head was too filled with conflicting thoughts.

In the middle of his brothers' arguing about the Mariners game, he got up and left. The last couple of days had just been too much for him. It soon had to get better, he assured himself.

CHAPTER FIFTEEN

Chloe desperately wanted to leave the kitchen, but she was at least grateful the women had kicked the men out. She was standing there feeling not only like a fifth wheel, but missing those times with her brother when they had laughed like this. In addition, seeing the close relationship between Nick's brothers and their wives was sending an extra pang through her heart.

She'd always assumed she'd grow up, get away from her family, and maybe start her own—do it the right way. She wouldn't marry a controlling man, wouldn't be with someone who didn't allow her to make her own choices. But as life had gotten away from her, more time passed. She was now twenty-eight and focused on her career.

She didn't have the time or the inclination to find Mr. Right. And if she *were* looking, Nick Armstrong wouldn't be that man. He was so . . . so . . . hell, she couldn't think of the word. It wasn't that he was controlling exactly. He was definitely confident, but he didn't try to do it *only* his way. He respected her during therapy sessions. Sure, he teased her a lot and flirted like the devil, but he listened to what she was saying.

And in the bedroom—oh, holy hell, in the bedroom—the man was certainly in charge in there. But *that* she didn't mind. It wasn't as if she had a lot of experience to compare him to, but the man had made her feel things she hadn't even known were possible before being with him.

That had scared her far too much. She hadn't had time to process last night yet, and now she was surrounded by his family, and her mind was whirling. She needed to go for a run, go down to the ocean, do anything other than sit in the room with two happily married women who were practically glowing in their wedded bliss.

"We want a tell-all, Chloe," Stormy said as she continued throwing ingredients together. Chloe had no idea what the two women were cooking, but the men had been correct. The house smelled better than it ever had before.

"What do you mean?" she asked. She knew to be on guard, but she didn't know what they were going to throw at her.

"We're not going to allow you to play coy. We love these Armstrong men, but we also know they can be a real pain in the ass. I wanted to throttle Maverick as much as I wanted to throw him down on a bed and have my wicked way with him," Lindsey said with a chuckle. "Obviously the wicked way route was the one I took," she added as she rubbed her round belly.

Chloe blushed again. "Nothing is going on between us," she said. Her flaming cheeks were giving her away, though, and by the ladies' looks, they knew she was lying.

"You've been here for a bit over two weeks, right?" Stormy said, throwing her off track. Chloe tried to find hidden meaning but couldn't, so she decided to answer honestly.

"Yes, almost three weeks, working on his knee," she said, to remind the women she was a professional.

"And you're sleeping here?" Lindsey questioned, though she obviously knew the answer.

Her cheeks most likely matched the red towel Stormy was drying her hands on. Chloe abhorred how easily her face could be read. If she didn't prepare carefully before telling a fib, there was no chance of her getting away with it. Since she and Nick had just warmed the sheets the night before, and Chloe hadn't known his family was coming over, she wasn't at all prepared. These women were going to eat her alive.

In Chloe's field, she worked with a lot of men. She didn't easily make girlfriends, except for Dakota, who was really more of a sister than a friend. She wasn't used to the gossip circle, and she was becoming more and more uncomfortable by the second.

"I should go and check on the equipment for our session later," Chloe said, thinking of any excuse to get away.

"Not a chance, woman. It's more than clear you're trying to hide something from us. We are masters at getting information," Stormy told her with a wicked smile.

"Well . . . um . . ." She stopped trying to find another reason to get away and slumped onto the stool. She'd offer to help the women, but her hands were trembling so badly, she was more likely to cut off a finger than prepare food.

"You've been here for nearly three weeks, and you're going to tell us nothing at all is going on?" Stormy pushed. Chloe's cheeks stayed heated. "With all the sexual energy flashing between you and Nick, I don't buy it for a moment."

"He could barely keep his eyes off you while we were standing here. That's not like Nick at all. He has always been a flirt, but he's also known to lose attention with the opposite sex pretty dang quickly. I didn't see any of that today. He looked as if he were about to devour you right in front of us," Lindsey told her.

"Yeah, I was getting all hot and bothered just being in the room with the two of you," Stormy added as she fanned her face.

It was more than obvious that she'd better talk or they were going to continue grilling her. She shifted on her seat, feeling increasingly uncomfortable, but also feeling the need to share with someone. Her mouth opened before she could think twice about it.

"Some things might have happened—*very* recently," she said. The girls grinned at her. "But it's *not* going to continue. I'm a professional and I'm only here to get him back into top shape so he can get on with his career. I'll be gone within the month and we won't ever see each other again."

She felt conviction in her words, even if she did feel a pinch of regret at saying them. She wasn't exactly sure how she felt about never seeing Nick again. He wasn't who she'd originally thought him to be, but that was only because she didn't know a lot about him. She enjoyed his company, and *really* enjoyed his touch. But it was so wrong. She had to remember that. Until she knew for sure whether he was guilty of killing her brother, any sympathy or love she felt toward the man was a betrayal of Patrick.

Even as she had those thoughts, though, she looked at his sisters-in-law and wondered how bad a man he could be, how bad the entire family could be, when they inspired such loyalty. The two brothers were married to what seemed to be intelligent, kind, beautiful women. Could they be as evil as she'd been told they were and still have such sweet wives? It was beginning to not make any sense at all.

"You totally want him, don't you?" Stormy said, her attention fully focused on Chloe. "Don't worry, I won't go and tell him. Just be honest with me," she coerced.

"We promise what happens in the girl circle stays in the girl circle," Lindsey said, holding up her hand as if she were under oath. Chloe let out a sigh and couldn't help but smile at the two women as they waited for her response.

"It might have been the best sexual experience I've ever had," she admitted, much to the glee of the two women who smiled huge grins. "But he also drives me insane. He's bossy, and cocky, and flirts nonstop while I'm trying to do my job. If my body would learn to listen to my brain, I wouldn't be in such a mess right now."

Stormy and Lindsey laughed, and Chloe sent them a stern look, which only made them laugh that much harder.

"Okay, okay, sorry, but you've only just met our husbands," Lindsey said in between giggles. "Trust me, that attitude runs through all the Armstrong men. But underneath all their chest-puffing lay truly amazing men who would rather die than let someone they love get hurt."

Her words sent a pang through Chloe's chest. If what she was saying was true, then there was no way Nick could be responsible for the crash that had taken her brother's life. But did Stormy and Lindsey know Nick as well as they were professing to?

"What's wrong?" Lindsey asked, stepping up to her and taking her hand before Chloe knew what she was doing. "We're just giving you a hard time and maybe a little bit of advice. I will tell you that Mav was there for me in my darkest hours. His brothers were right by his side. I would trust those men with this baby I'm carrying, with my own life, with the lives of all the people I love. The boys are a pain in the butt sometimes, but they have hearts the size of Texas. If you're afraid of being hurt, don't be. Nick is a lot of talk and no real bite."

Chloe felt tears come to her eyes, and she shook her head, hoping to send them away. What Lindsey was telling her was straight from the heart. She knew the woman wasn't lying. It was just that Chloe's entire world felt like it was crashing around her. If she didn't have her beliefs, then what was she to do? Was it her family who was wrong? She just didn't know.

"I'm sorry," she said, taking in deep breaths.

"Never feel bad for having a moment," Stormy told her as she walked up on Chloe's other side. "We all have them. In this family, the great thing is we don't have to suffer through them alone. We take care of each other."

A tear escaped and fell down Chloe's cheek. Lindsey quickly grabbed a paper towel and handed it to her. Chloe didn't know what to do with what the women were saying. It was all a lot to take in. And it was Chloe who was supposed to be taking care of her brother the way this family was so determined to take care of each other. But she couldn't do that—not ever again.

"I think the Armstrong brothers are too dang good-looking for the sanity of all women," Chloe said as she attempted to make a joke. Stormy and Lindsey smiled while nodding their heads.

"We'll leave you alone about it, but we're going to give you our numbers. If Nick gets out of hand, you just call us. For that matter, if you just need a woman to speak to, call us and we'll be here for you in a minute," Stormy said.

"Unless I'm in the delivery room," Lindsey added with a smile. "But even if I'm there, you can come talk to me in between contractions."

This made Chloe laugh. "Yeah, I think I'll pass on that one," she told her.

"Might be smart. Stormy was yelling at everyone in sight while she was giving birth. I have a feeling I might be worse than she was," Lindsey said.

"Okay, in my defense, childbirth should be used as a torture device. If men had any idea how much pain was involved, they would never want us to go through with a delivery," Stormy said.

"But then we wouldn't have these wonderful children to raise," Lindsey pointed out.

"Yes, it most certainly is worth it in the end," Stormy said as she looked down at her sleeping daughter.

Chloe followed her stare and gazed at the beautiful baby girl. She was so tiny in her little car seat with blankets tucked around her. There had been a time when Chloe had wanted her own children so badly, she could practically taste it. Now she wasn't so sure. She didn't know what kind of mother she would be, and if she was anything like her own mom, weak and pathetic, she didn't want anything to do with becoming a parent.

Chloe couldn't ever imagine letting anyone beat her children—not even their father. As she watched the love shining on Stormy's face, she felt another pang in her heart. If her own mom had loved her as much as Stormy loved her children, maybe Chloe wouldn't have had to endure the hell she'd been through growing up.

It didn't do her any good to try to imagine how things could have been. That was a waste of her time and emotions. She would never have the answers because she was grown up now. Her life was what it was.

The women stopped grilling her, and she found herself enjoying their company as she stayed and helped them make a mountain load of food while the men socialized elsewhere. She was scared, though, because as she hung around them and laughed and listened to their stories, she found she wanted to be with them even more.

She wanted to be a part of their family. It felt safe and comforting—something she wasn't used to. If she weren't careful, she might find herself wanting something she could never have.

Just as she had that thought, Nick and his brothers walked back into the room. Her eyes met his, and the intensity between them took her breath away. There was a promise shining from his beautiful green depths—a promise that told her she only needed to reach out to get it.

Was she brave enough to do that? She knew she wasn't. Instead of walking to him and allowing herself to explore what was going on between them, she broke the connection of their gaze and instead focused on a spot on the wall.

Nick walked up to her, but she found a reasonable excuse to move—to avoid him. She hated herself a little bit for doing it. But she knew it was the right thing to do. It left her feeling incredibly lonely, though, even in a room full of people.

Chloe knew that was just how her life was destined to be. She'd accepted it long ago. Being with Nick might make that concept a bit harder to accept, but it was the way it had to be. Dreams were for those with the luxury of having a choice.

CHAPTER SIXTEEN

The moment Chloe stepped out of the house with the ladies to join them on the back deck, Nick could practically taste her. They were like two magnets being drawn toward one another, and he had no desire to run away. It had only been about an hour since he'd been in the room with her, but even that seemed too long.

His heart began to race, and everything within him wanted to be with her. He tuned out whatever it was his brother had been saying, and his eyes focused on the beautiful woman with a smile on her face as she carried Stormy's daughter, Addie.

The sight of Chloe with the small infant in her arms sent something burning through his chest. Never before had the sight of a woman and child evoked such a deep yearning in him, but as he took in the smile on her lips, the flush to her cheeks, and the baby cradled protectively in her arms, he wanted to pull them both close to his heart, and block out the rest of the world.

She looked down with awe as the infant cooed at her, and he melted from the inside, turning into a puddle. He couldn't look away from her—couldn't even begin to imagine what he was feeling.

"She's so small, I'm worried I'll hurt her," Chloe said. Stormy laughed as she patted Chloe's arm.

"Trust me, she might be small, but she's a warrior, and she has the lungs to prove it," Stormy assured her. Chloe giggled as she lifted a hand and ran her finger delicately across the top of the bald head.

She was still smiling when she looked up and their eyes met. Her features froze for a moment before she tried to shutter her expression. He still saw the worry residing deep in her telling eyes. It nearly broke him to know he was the cause of her losing that glow she'd been wearing only seconds before.

Moving quickly, he slid up to her, his eyes never leaving her face. His heart was thundering as he reached out and touched her arm. "You look beautiful," he said, his voice filled with awe.

Just being near her, having her within touching distance, soothed his frazzled nerves. He drank her in, pride filling him as she gazed upon him with equal intensity. The rest of the world faded away. It was just the two of them and the tiny baby. He wouldn't mind all of his days being this focused on family.

Nick had no clue that their small circle had drawn the attention of their guests. Their reactions were the furthest thing from his mind.

Chloe might have told him they were moving too quickly. She might have insisted on pulling away from him, but that wasn't what her eyes were saying. She desired him. What Nick didn't fully comprehend was that it was so much more than desire—it was a melding of souls.

Her holding the newborn was sending emotions through him he didn't know how to evaluate, but in his heart he could imagine it was their baby she cuddled close. Having a child with a woman had always been a fear he considered when having sex. He never trusted the woman to be on birth control, never had sex without protection.

But with Chloe, that's exactly what he'd done. He'd trusted her when she'd told him she was protected—he hadn't even hesitated at her words—he'd thrust forward and sealed them together as one.

Was it because he wouldn't be devastated if she were to become pregnant? Nick couldn't imagine he'd be okay with that. He didn't understand this voice in his head telling him she could be the one he never wanted to leave.

She looked like she should have a baby in her arms. She looked like she would be a beautiful mother and wife. Nevertheless, Nick had decided long ago he wouldn't marry. However, seeing his brothers so happy was making him realize it might not be the end of the world.

His thoughts were scaring the crap out him. But even so, he couldn't seem to pull away from Chloe. He tried to assure himself it was only the sex messing with his brain. He tried to think that if they were in a relationship for any length of time, his hormone levels would go back to normal and all the odd thoughts would disperse. But he'd lusted after women before, and never once had he imagined a baby in their arms, let alone imagined the infant to be his.

She'd pulled away from him that morning, and he'd given her space for the entire afternoon—well, the early part of the afternoon. Nick wasn't too good at letting people have their distance if he didn't want to be away from them. Personal boundaries had never been an issue for him.

Without saying another word to the woman who was looking at him with startled eyes, he pulled her close to him. Careful not to jar the baby, and without a thought as to who was watching, he pressed his lips to hers, taking them gently as he became even more mesmerized by her.

She sighed against his mouth, and for that moment it was just the two of them. His brothers and their wives disappeared. He deepened the kiss, and the baby squirmed between them, reminding him they weren't alone. He pulled back instantly, afraid he'd hurt his niece.

His hand came up and caressed her soft head, and he looked into Chloe's eyes. They were slightly glazed as she licked her lips and watched him with confusion and a bit of wonder.

"I'm not good at taking things slowly," he told her.

As he said the words, he felt a spark of anger ignite inside him. She wanted him—liked him—needed him—so why in the hell was she acting like she didn't. His emotions were weighing him down, and he needed to talk to her, needed to understand what it was she was thinking.

Chloe's expression became shuttered as she read the tempestuous emotions flickering across his face. He was turned on, angry, and half out of his mind. She should be slightly worried. The only thing saving her from him dragging her off to be alone was the fact that she was holding his niece.

"You don't get to choose how I want to take things," she told him, firming her shoulders as she looked him in the eyes.

He smiled at her. "I've always loved a challenge, doc. You're making this adventure a lot of fun for me," he told her.

He ran his hand down her arm and his anger disappeared. He couldn't stay upset, not when she was gazing at him in that confused way. He just needed her to admit there was something special between them. He was determined to hear her say those words.

"But I can certainly call you out when you are lying, even if it's to yourself," he told her.

She took in a sharp breath as her eyes narrowed on him. She didn't like him calling her out. Good. If he got her riled up, she wouldn't be so composed, she wouldn't be able to give him standard answers. She'd be a heck of a lot more truthful with him.

"I thought there was nothing going on between the two of you," Stormy said with a chuckle as she joined the conversation.

Nick wanted to tell Stormy to go away. He could see panic setting in for Chloe, though, and he thought it might be best to take the baby before she forgot she was holding her. With gentleness he was used to exerting with his niece and nephew, he slid his hands beneath Addie's warm body and extracted her from Chloe's arms.

Chloe's hands dropped to her sides when she saw the baby was safely cradled against Nick's chest.

"How's my precious girl?" he cooed at the baby. The last of his temper completely drained away. How could he hold on to such an ugly emotion when he held something so innocent in his arms?

"I'm going to take my daughter to safety so the two of you can finish whatever this is in . . . private," Stormy said with a laugh. Nick kissed his niece before handing her over to Stormy. His arms felt unusually empty when the bundle was taken away.

Nick hadn't ever considered being a father, he had to remind himself. That wasn't going to change just because he had some precious moments with his niece and nephew. Then again, when he'd held them before, he hadn't thought he wanted his own. It hadn't been until he'd seen Chloe with a baby in her arms that the ache had spread to his chest and made him feel somehow empty.

Shaking his head, he tried to push away the disturbing thoughts, but now that they were planted, he feared they were going to grow. He had enough problems to deal with without having his paternal clock ticking.

"Come with me. We need to be alone," he told her. She stiffened as his arm went around her. He looked into her eyes, wondering what was going on inside those sweet, deep depths. He had no idea. He wasn't sure how he felt about that.

He had a feeling that the only reason she allowed him to lead her away was because she didn't want to cause a scene in front of his family. Instead of taking her back into the house, he led her down one of the many trails surrounding his property, giving them all the privacy he could ever want.

When they were a safe distance from the place, she stopped moving, making him halt his steps. She turned and gave him a withering glare.

"You shouldn't have kissed me in front of your family like that. I just got done telling the girls earlier that nothing was going on between us," she snapped. He loved when there was fire in her eyes. It made him feel less like a predator.

"You shouldn't have lied to my family then," he said simply. She gasped at him.

"I didn't lie. Just because we slept together last night doesn't mean our entire future has been decided. It certainly doesn't mean I want anything else to happen between us. And I *really* don't want people talking about it," she told him.

Something about her words caught his attention. He looked at her, and her cheeks blushed as she turned away from him.

"Who the hell cares what people are talking about? What's going on is between us. It doesn't matter if other people have an opinion. All that matters is how we feel about one another," he pointed out.

She flinched at his words, and he wondered again what was going on in that brilliant brain of hers. She most certainly was hiding things from him, he just wasn't exactly sure what they were.

"I care what people think about me, Nick. I have a reputation to maintain, and if it gets out that I sleep with my clients, I'm going to draw in the wrong sort of customer," she told him.

There was some truth to her words. He could clearly see that, but there was also something she wasn't saying. He just wasn't sure how he was going to draw it out of her.

"I know who you are, and it doesn't take a genius to figure out you're not that sort of woman, Chloe. However, there is something between us, and I don't want to hide it. I don't do secret affairs," he warned her.

"That's good, because neither do I," she said as she took a step back from him.

"Oh, Chloe, I think you're misunderstanding me," he told her as he stalked her. "I said I don't do *secret* affairs. I am in no way willing to let what we have go."

She needed to fully understand his commitment. They were both in far too deep. If she didn't like him, Nick would let her go with no problem. But she did, and she was fighting it. Why she was, he had no idea.

"You should learn to take no for an answer, Nick. I'm not interested," she said.

For the first time, Nick noticed that when she told a lie, a blush stole over her cheeks. She blushed for other reasons, too, but it was more obvious when she was trying to hide something from him. That was very interesting to know indeed. It meant she wouldn't be able to easily deceive him. He liked the thought of that.

"You weren't saying *no* last night, Chloe. You were begging me to take you each and every time. It wasn't until morning that you put your armor back on. But let me give it to you as black and white as I possibly can. I want you. I am throbbing with the need to take you right here, right now. I can't think of anyone else or do anything without imagining sinking deep within your hot, slick folds. I want to run my tongue over your velvety skin and suck your nipples into my mouth. I want my teeth scraping across your back, leaving my mark on you. I want to take you in the shower, in the bedroom, on the kitchen table—and that's just for starters. I don't think I'll ever get enough of you. By the look in your eyes, I have no doubt you want me just as much. We can play this game of being patient and client all you want, but I have the utmost confidence that you will be mine again. By delaying it, you're only making both of us suffer."

His voice grew huskier the longer he spoke, and her mouth dropped open as her dark tongue came out and dampened her lips. Her chest heaved, and he could clearly see the beaded tips of her nipples. He would bet his life she was hot and wet, and all he'd have to do is pull her pants down and slam inside her with zero resistance.

"That's not what I want," she said, her husky voice in direct contrast with her words.

Nick smiled. He could afford to be affable. He'd get what he wanted, and even though he wasn't normally a patient man, he thought for this woman he could change his ways. His lips turned up in a confident grin as he stood there looking at her. He could practically envision her with no clothes, picture the two of them falling to the ground, her on top of him as she pushed down until he was fully inside her.

Reaching out he grabbed her hand and cupped it over his pulsing arousal. Her eyes practically glowed as she flexed her fingers. She wanted him, and she knew he was ready to give her pleasure. If she was going to force them to wait, then he wanted her suffering as much as he was.

Nick had no doubt she was in misery. Her eyes drifted down his body, and she gazed at her fingers with his large hand over them as she cupped his mass. He was too big, even inside his pants, for her to fully hold. But he was the perfect size to give her what she needed. She was very much aware of that.

"What's it going to be, Chloe?" he asked huskily as his fingers flexed over hers, the pressure both agony and pleasure. He wished she'd just give in to her cravings and undo his pants. He highly doubted that was going to happen.

"I think we need to get back before your siblings send out a search party," she told him.

He backed her into a tree and gripped her leg, opening her thighs and pushing into her as one hand cupped her face and one squeezed her butt.

"Okay, we'll go back. And I promise you this," he said before leaning down and kissing her softly. He was surprised he was able to do so with his hormones raging out of control. He kissed her again, and she sighed against his mouth as he pushed against her.

"What?" she gasped when he moved his lips.

It took him a moment to remember what he'd been saying. "This will be the last time I initiate it, Chloe. The next time is all on you. Just know that every single time you walk into the room with me, I'm going to be hard and ready for you. All you have to do is say the word, and I will make both of us fly."

He ground against her one more time, wanting so badly to remove their clothes and plunge inside her, but knowing she had to come to the decision on her own. If he did it now, she'd just put the wall back up the moment it was over. That didn't help either one of them.

When he pulled back, he could see the worry in her eyes. He could also see that she didn't trust him to keep his word. With a throbbing body, and already regretting his promise to her, he released her and took a few steps back.

He shifted on his feet, trying to find a comfortable way to stand with the aching erection straining against his pants. There was nothing making it better. He untucked his shirt, and hoped the material would cover him enough so his family wouldn't have to see the pathetic condition he was in.

He then turned and walked away, the shocked gasp that came from Chloe's mouth music to his ears. Nick knew he could seduce her, and that was enough to keep his sanity somewhat in place while he waited for her to come to him. He was sure she would. They wanted each other far too badly for her not to.

Nick just prayed he survived the wait.

CHAPTER SEVENTEEN

Chloe's arms were shaking as she pushed down on Nick, her fingers digging into his flesh, a moan escaping his parted lips. She wanted to wipe the moisture from her forehead, but her hands were occupied.

"Yes, Chloe, just like that," he groaned.

Her stomach tightened as her core clenched and heat flooded her entire body. Nick was so firm, so perfectly put together, that touching him was both ecstasy and the ultimate torture.

Chloe's oiled fingers slid down Nick's spine, which elicited another moan. She reached the curve of his well-defined ass and felt the need to pull his shorts down. Her breathing became more erratic, but she held herself together.

"Push there," he said.

Chloe couldn't help but smile as she leaned down, her mouth entirely too close to his ear. "I'm the one in charge here. I know what I'm doing," she said, feeling an odd sense of triumph when a shiver racked his form.

"You can do whatever you want to my body, doc," he said on a long sigh.

Chloe moved down to his leg, and her fingers kneaded the flesh of his thighs. He twitched under her touch, and she used gentle pressure to continue the massage. His moans filled the room, which was growing hotter by the second.

"How does this feel, Nick?" she asked as she rubbed the back of his knee.

"Like heaven," he said.

She wasn't going to last a heck of a lot longer. This was affecting her more and more each time she ran her fingers over his burning flesh. Never before had she rubbed down a client and found herself in total erotic bliss.

"Turn over," she said as she sat back.

Nick didn't hesitate for even a second. Using his good leg, he flipped himself over, and Chloe inhaled sharply when she couldn't help but notice the massive erection he was sporting. Her eyes shot up and looked at him, and the fire burning in his eyes nearly made her come while kneeling at his feet.

"Anything you want," he promised.

Chloe shook her head to try to clear it. Her hands quivered as she placed her fingers on the top of his thigh and began rubbing downward. Her gaze kept straying back to the erection pulsing in his shorts. She wanted to reach out and touch him, run her fingers along his thick length.

He moaned again, and Chloe began to wonder why she wasn't doing something about it. She had no doubt that if she leaned forward and splayed her body atop his, he would clasp her in his arms and take her to a whole other reality.

"Well, looks like therapy is tough business."

Chloe froze, her hands midway down Nick's thigh. Her fingers tightened, and a low rumble escaped Nick's throat again before both of them turned toward the doorway where a woman was standing.

"Dakota?" Chloe shook her head, trying to clear the fog. Was that her best friend leaning in the doorway with a smug grin on her face?

"The one and only. I called your cell phone, and knocked on the door several times to no answer. Now I understand why," she said.

"How did you get in here?" Chloe couldn't focus, which was making this conversation very difficult.

"Nick should have better security. His front door was unlocked, and when I didn't get an answer, I came inside to make sure you weren't being mauled by a grizzly bear. Someone apparently is getting mauled, but it doesn't appear that any pain is being inflicted," Dakota said.

Nick was silent through the entire exchange, and that's when Chloe realized she was still gripping his thigh. As if her hands were on fire, she wrenched her fingers away and leaned back. Nick grinned first at her, and then at Dakota. He sat up as her best friend stepped closer.

"I'm Dakota, nice to meet you," her confident friend said as she joined them and gracefully sat down on the floor.

Nick reached out his hand. "Nick Armstrong. You have terrible timing," he said with a grin.

"I'm known for that," she said with a wink. "Want me to leave so you can continue?"

"Sure," Nick said with a wolfish grin.

"Don't be ridiculous. I was just giving Nick a massage. It's part of his therapy," Chloe said with a scowl directed at both of them. "We were just finishing up anyway."

"I wasn't finished," Nick muttered. But his grin quickly came back. "Apparently I need a cold shower, though … to get the oil off."

"Don't you need a hot shower for that?" Dakota pointed out.

"Cold will be much better in my condition," he said with a wink.

Chloe's cheeks burned as she glanced down at his still hard body. At least it wasn't as obvious while he was sitting. She knew, though, that there was no way Dakota hadn't seen it. The man was magnificent.

"Why don't you go take care of yourself while Chloe and I have a drink," Dakota said as she jumped to her feet and held out a hand to Chloe.

"I have oil on my hands," Chloe said as she pushed herself off the ground. She knew better than to help Nick get up. He was stubborn and prideful, and even though he had no problem taking a massage from her, he didn't like to accept help.

"Have fun, ladies," Nick said as he pushed himself off the ground. This time, Chloe averted her eyes. She was already hot and bothered and didn't want to look at his thickness again and think about running her fingers and tongue over him.

He left the room, and Chloe felt her muscles shaking. That had been one hell of a massage. She and Dakota left the gym and moved through Nick's large house to the kitchen.

"What are you doing here?" Chloe asked.

"That's not a greeting," Dakota told her with a chuckle.

"I'm thrilled to see you, but you didn't say you were coming," Chloe told her as she opened the fridge and pulled out a bottle of white wine.

"I've been worried about you. I thought I would come and check on things, especially since I haven't heard from you in a few days," Dakota said.

"I'm fine. I'm sorry I've been so freakish with my calls to you. There's just been a lot to process in the last few weeks," Chloe admitted.

"Don't you dare apologize to me or I'll be forced to knock you over the head with the biggest stick I can find," Dakota told her. "We don't have much time before Adonis comes in here, so spill your guts."

Chloe smiled. "Yeah, he's pretty damn good-looking," Chloe admitted.

"Something you failed to point out. That man is fine," Dakota said, drawing out the word.

"I'm supposed to hate him," Chloe said.

"You know better than to listen to your piece-of-shit father. Remember what we've always agreed to?" Dakota said.

"Yeah, yeah, we form our own opinions no matter what other people say."

"Exactly!" Dakota exclaimed. "You are smart, Chloe, much smarter than you ever give yourself credit for. And beyond that, you're beautiful, kind, and one hell of a therapist. You don't need your father and you don't need his hateful words filtering through that gorgeous head of yours. If everything inside of you is telling you he's wrong, you need to listen to that. Besides," she added with a leer, "it seemed there were some major sparks in that room during your . . . massage," she added with an evil grin.

"It's just my job," Chloe defended.

"Honey, I want your job," Dakota said before busting up laughing.

"I'm glad you find yourself amusing," Chloe said.

The girls heard footsteps and turned to see a freshly showered Nick strolling into the room. Chloe was relieved to see him covered up in a T-shirt and long pants. His feet were bare, though, and she had to admit she found even his toes sexy. She had serious problems.

"Chloe hasn't told me about you, Dakota," Nick said as he joined them at the breakfast bar and grabbed his own glass of wine.

"That's because she likes to keep me her dirty little secret," Dakota said with a wink.

"I can see why," Nick told her. The two of them smiled at each other, and Chloe felt a rare moment of jealousy.

Dakota was so damn beautiful, and she charmed men without even trying. Chloe assured herself she didn't want a relationship with Nick, but at the same time, she knew it would absolutely kill her to see Dakota and Nick together.

"Dakota can't stay long. We have a long day ahead of us," Chloe suddenly said.

Both of them turned to look at her. Dakota smirked in a knowing way, and Chloe felt like a terrible person. What was she doing?

"I wouldn't want to stop therapy. It looks like a great time," Dakota said before she looked back at Nick.

"It isn't always fun. Chloe likes to push me hard," he told her. *That* had Dakota laughing again.

"Don't be afraid to push her right back," her traitorous best friend said.

"Yeah, time to go," Chloe told her.

"I can take a hint," Dakota said. She left the rest of her wine unfinished as she stood. "I have an appointment anyway." She turned to Nick. "It was a pleasure to meet you."

He held out his hand and the two shook. Some sort of message flashed between them, but Chloe had no idea what it was. Nick was grinning like a loon. Chloe walked her best friend to the door, wanting her to go away before things got out of hand and knowing she'd be missing her the minute Dakota left.

"I'm going to take Saturday off. Can we get together then?" Chloe asked.

"For sure. I found a new hike I want to do," Dakota said. "And then you're going to fill me in on all things Nick Armstrong," she finished.

"Of course I will," Chloe assured her.

The two hugged and Dakota slipped out as quickly as she'd rolled in. When Chloe turned, she found Nick standing there looking at her with an unreadable expression.

"I like your friend," he said.

That tinge of jealousy sparked again. "Everyone likes Dakota. She's amazing," Chloe told him.

"I'm glad to see you have good people around you."

He seemed so genuine while saying it that it took the jealousy away as swiftly as it had come. She had been petty and stupid. For one thing, Nick wasn't hers, and for another, even if he were interested in Dakota, her friend would never do something like that to her. All the messy feelings were her problem and no one else's.

"I've been glad to have her from the first day we met," Chloe said.

Silence surrounded them as he looked at her, making her feel like she was being analyzed—and maybe even coming up short. It was a feeling she was used to, but not one that she liked. Messy feelings. She hated messy feelings.

"I will figure you out," he promised, though it sounded like a threat.

"Good luck with that," she told him. He smiled, and she decided it was a good time to make her exit. "I'll see you in three hours."

Chloe left without another word. She had to have her afternoon breaks from him. It was either that, or she was going to mount the guy. Maybe that wasn't such a bad idea.

CHAPTER EIGHTEEN

Chloe stood outside the door to the pool calming her breathing. She knew he was inside . . . half naked . . . completely delicious. She'd told him she didn't want a relationship. And she didn't, she assured herself. But he *was* a great-looking man who made her laugh as much as he made her grind her teeth. He'd also taken her to the heights of pleasure less than a week earlier. It had been rough working with him since then.

She was 90 percent sure he'd done nothing to cause her brother's death. There was that small inkling of doubt, but it was only because her dad had poisoned her with his toxic words. It had been programed inside her, the seed had been planted, and she was afraid to pull out the roots—afraid of what her life would become knowing that everything in her life was a lie.

But that all led back to how she was feeling about Nick and how much she desired him.

He'd kept his promise, though, about not approaching her again romantically. She told herself this was exactly what she wanted. He'd definitely been hands on during their training sessions, playing on her sympathies for his injury, but he hadn't attempted to kiss her, hadn't touched her inappropriately. And every night when she went to bed, she suffered. There was an ache in her body she'd never before experienced, and it was almost suffocating her.

Chloe had no idea what to do to make it stop. She could quit her job, just take the pay she'd earned so far and walk away, but she was over halfway finished. If she could stick it through, then she would get a very nice bonus—one that she needed desperately to reduce the massive debt her school loans had caused her.

It wasn't as if her mother or father were going to help her. She'd learned a long time ago she was on her own. She'd had her brother, but now she didn't even have him. Her resolve strengthened, she opened the door to the pool, finding him at one end doing his stretches.

There were plusses and minuses to pool work. She couldn't see his body as well underneath the water, but there was a lot of close contact with them both wearing next to nothing. She really wasn't sure which was worse.

At least she had her sturdy one-piece bathing suit on. It didn't come off even remotely as easily as a bikini, which helped remove thoughts of her stripping her clothes away so he could take her against the wall of the warm pool.

"Good afternoon, Nick," she said, making sure her voice was calm and professional.

He looked up and gave her the look that seemed to say he was humoring her. The thing was she loved his crooked smile. He brushed his fingers through his hair, water droplets falling down his toned chest, and she practically panted.

Quickly submerging herself in the water, she went down to her neck so he wouldn't notice her hardened nipples. In a little while, she could blame them on her feeling cold in the pool. Though they'd both know she'd be lying. The room was eighty degrees with the water right about the same. If anything, she normally began sweating by the end of their sessions—whether that was the temperature or the close proximity to Nick, she wasn't 100 percent sure.

"You're running late, doc," he told her as she drew near.

"Sorry, I got caught up in my notes and lost track of time," she told him. The truth was she *had* been taking notes, but then her mind had wandered as it did quite often these days, and she'd been thinking about him for the past hour and what she'd like him to do to her. She certainly wasn't going to tell him any of that.

"Is all your stretching done?" she asked, stopping three feet from him.

"Yep, I went extra deep this time," he told her. His tone was normal, but the twinkle in his eyes assured her he was baiting her. She decided to ignore him.

"Good, then let's get you on the treadmill. You're strong enough that I think we can put it at four," she said, a wicked smile lighting her lips.

Nick didn't say a word as he moved to the underwater treadmill. There were bars on the side of it that he could hold on to for balance, but he never chose to use them. Nick enjoyed pushing it to the maximum when she allowed him to.

"If you feel any pain whatsoever, I need for you to tell me. The water protects you, but you can still get injured," she warned him.

He rolled his eyes, wondering how such a simple task could cause an injury. Sometimes she wanted to smack the man for his ridiculous bravado.

"You might think I'm overreacting, but it's *my* license on the line if you get injured while I'm treating you. If you want to get back in that helicopter and fly again, then you would do well to listen to me," she said, her voice stern, her eyes serious.

"Okay, okay," he said with a laugh as he stood on the machine. "Let's get started *before* my skin looks more like raisins."

She moved over to the control and turned the machine up to two. He looked at her with a brow raised as he began jogging through the water. She slowly increased the speed. When she got to three, she took a breath and went underwater, pressing her hand against his knee.

She often had to touch him, and at first that had led to a lot of sexual comments. Those had lightened in the past week, but the look in his eyes when she would meet them told her more than any words he chose to say.

His muscles felt good and were flexing nicely. She came up for air and moved over to the controls. She kept pushing the speed up, and Nick didn't even breathe heavily as he quickened his pace.

Four might not seem like a high speed to an athlete like Nick, but with the resistance of the water, it wasn't easy to do. Chloe certainly wouldn't admit to it, but she didn't last a heck of a long time at that speed in the water, and she ran six days a week.

Chloe kept an eye on Nick as he faced forward, his stride perfect, his arms pumping. She kept a careful watch on his features to see if he was feeling any pain. He ran for fifteen minutes and didn't even break a sweat. He was stronger—so much stronger than when she'd first arrived.

Chloe realized he wouldn't need her the entire six weeks. There wasn't a heck of a lot more she could do for him that he wouldn't be capable of doing on his own. He was walking without a limp, understood his limits in the gym, knew which stretches to do before any activity, and had all the equipment he could ever hope to have at his disposal.

She might not need to stay past the end of the current week. The thought sent a pang of unease through her. She should be elated she'd be able to leave early, because she would still get paid. She just wouldn't have to deal with Nick Armstrong anymore—or his family. But she liked him. And them.

None of that mattered. She couldn't have a relationship with any of them. It wouldn't work out—it wouldn't be right, even if she never discovered anything nefarious in any of their lives.

"Okay, time to stop," she said. She turned off the machine and had to take a few deep breaths before she could speak again. "I want you to do a cooldown by swimming across the pool and back very slowly, as slowly as you can."

He stepped off the treadmill and looked at her, the expression on his face unreadable. He moved a bit closer before he stopped himself. Chloe didn't even realize she was holding her breath until he let out a sigh, then turned and jumped into the water, slowly swimming away.

She went to the steps to wait for him. She climbed from the pool with him and had him sit down while she examined his leg. Everything was in perfect order. Soon, it wouldn't even be possible to know he'd been injured unless he decided to tell a person.

Chloe told him they were done for the day, and then she walked away. Shutting herself in her room, she hung her head and wondered why she felt so despondent. This was all a good thing. She just had to convince herself of that. More than anything, she had to come to a decision and stick with it instead of faltering so much.

For the next few days, Nick wasn't his usual self with her. Maybe he'd been rejected too many times, maybe he'd lost interest, but as the countdown began for Chloe to leave, she felt a growing sense of unease.

She wasn't sure what she was going to do about it. She knew the best thing would be to let it go, finish her job, and get on with her life. If that's what she would actually do, she wasn't exactly sure. That would be smart, no doubt—but she wasn't always the shrewdest person.

CHAPTER NINETEEN

By day five of Nick and Chloe's standoff—him flirting but never making a move, and her refusing to make any kind of advance—she was exhausted, mentally, physically, and emotionally. The current day had seemed to take forever, but at the same time, it had been incredibly successful. Nick would never be called an easy patient, but he was mending. She wished she could still hate him, but she knew there was so much more to his story than what she'd first thought. Nick wasn't the devil.

But what exactly did that mean? Chloe wasn't sure. One thing she knew for certain was that she couldn't resist him any longer. There was a hunger burning inside her that she'd been fighting for weeks. She didn't want to fight it anymore. The pain of choosing Nick over her family, though, was ripping her in half. Was she telling herself that Nick meant more than her deceased brother? No! She wasn't doing that at all. She was just admitting he wasn't guilty of her brother's death and that she wasn't going to continue letting her father control her.

She moved to the kitchen and put away the leftovers from their dinner. Nick was in his home office doing some work. She had no idea what he did in there for hours on end, but she did know that he succeeded at anything he put his mind to.

Chloe knew she should call it a night, go to the safety of her room, shut the door, and tuck herself into her nice comfortable bed after taking a really long and extra-hot bath. That's what she *should* do.

Instead, she found herself moving through the dark kitchen to the large back window. She spent a lot of time there looking out at the moonlit bay. The view was spectacular and soothing. It calmed her after particularly stressful days.

Turning, Chloe glanced over to Nick's open office door. He was looking down at his computer, giving her time to take a nice perusal of him. The man truly was spectacular. He covered his pain with humor, but she saw what he didn't want her to notice. Maybe that's why she'd gained such a deep measure of respect for him. Even with a frown between his brows, he was impressive.

Something drew Chloe closer to him.

She stood in his doorway for several moments, wondering what in the world she was doing. She tried to walk away, but it just didn't seem to be happening.

"Would you like something to drink before I call it a night?" she asked.

He looked up, flashing her his brilliant smile. Damn, that smile took her breath away. There was that gleam she was very aware of in his eyes that told her all she'd have to do would be to walk up to him and he would take her again and again and again.

Instead of doing just that, she waited for him to answer. The longer the moment stretched, the more she realized she should have just run to her room. It wasn't too late. She began to turn.

"I could use a cup of coffee," he said, his words dripping with sexiness. She knew coffee wasn't what he really craved.

Spinning on her heels, Chloe rushed from the room, finding her fingers trembling when she pulled down the coffee cup. She took her time fixing it the way he liked it before she braved the walk back to his office.

"This is nonsense. It's just a cup of coffee, nothing more," she murmured quietly, then looked around to make sure he wasn't behind her. She didn't need him knowing what she was thinking. That would land her on top of his desk in seconds.

The mere thought of it sent a thrill down her spine. Chloe was in incredibly bad shape at the moment, and it didn't seem to be getting any better, no matter how long she stalled in the kitchen.

Holding the cup tightly in her hands, she braved the walk back to his office. She moved slowly across the large living room to his open door. This time, he wasn't looking down. He watched her approach with a knowing gleam in his eyes. She wished he was wrong in what he was thinking.

As Chloe got closer to him, she noticed he'd unbuttoned the top of his shirt, showing an enticing view of his smooth chest. His sleeves were rolled up, and as he flexed his fingers, the ripples in his muscles drew in her gaze. His lower half was getting stronger by the day, but his upper half was pushed to the limit each hour she wasn't working his legs. He was strong and fit, and she found herself wanting to run her hands across his tight skin.

"I'm going to head to my room," Chloe told him, hating that her breath was coming out too softly. She hoped he didn't hear the desire just beneath.

Nick winced, and she was immediately concerned. She stepped closer to him, her hand going out, but she pulled it back at the last moment. This was way past their therapy time, and she didn't need to be touching him.

"Can you rub out my shoulder first? I think I might have pulled something," he told her.

Chloe searched his eyes. She didn't see anything underhanded in his expression.

"That's because you push yourself far too hard. I've been telling you that for quite some time," she scolded him. She found herself moving behind him. He leaned forward so she could easily get to his shoulders.

Chloe's fingers were trembling as she rubbed them together to warm up. Though she'd touched Nick many times in therapy, this was different, more intimate. The lighting was low, it was late, and she was hot.

A jolt fluttered through her at the contact with his shirt. She could feel his body heat pouring through the thin material. She closed her eyes and inhaled his spicy scent, trying to get herself under control. She had to remind herself she was a professional, and she was simply helping a client.

When a shudder passed through Nick, she felt it reverberate through her entire body. She squeezed her hands over his tight muscles and tried to think of anything unsexy—doing dishes . . . taking out the garbage . . . clipping toenails. None of the thoughts helped her mind stray from her feelings of lust for too long.

Her thumbs moved to the bare skin of his neck, and she expertly ran them in circles as a low moan escaped Nick. It went straight to her core. Her legs were trembling as she continued with the massage, her mind alternating from wanting to flee the room and hide, or to lean down to taste his salty skin just below where his trim hair was cut.

"That's amazing, Chloe," Nick said, his voice a low growl. She was so out of focus, she had to concentrate to figure out what he'd said. Leaning forward turned out to be a big mistake. His scent grew stronger, and she found herself growing slightly faint.

"Um . . . what?" Chloe asked, her words barely a whisper.

"I love your massages," Nick told her. He reached up and clasped her hand, stopping her from rubbing his shoulder. She didn't know what to do.

"Let me finish," she told him, her voice a little stronger that time.

"Your turn," Nick said.

Chloe had no idea what he was planning, but suddenly his office chair spun around, making her take a quick step backward. Before she could retreat too far, he grabbed her waist and spun her, plopping her down in his lap. She landed with an oomph of air escaping.

"What are you doing?" she demanded, trying to get up.

"My shoulder is much better now. I thought I'd return the favor."

One hand was wrapped around her waist, locking her on his lap while the other slid up her back, and he began kneading her neck. Without her permission, a moan escaped. She *was* tense, probably more than he was, and the feel of his fingers massaging her was absolutely perfect.

She stopped trying to pull away from him without even thinking about it. It was so wrong for her to be sitting on him. It was far too intimate for a PT-client relationship, but when he moved the other hand that had been restraining her and began really kneading her muscles, her body turned into jelly.

Maybe minutes passed, maybe hours, but Chloe stiffened when she felt the warm air of Nick's breath brush across her neck before his lips followed in a soft kiss. His hands still rubbed her shoulders, but they were more gentle now—seductive.

She should rise from his lap. She knew she was playing with fire. She could feel the evidence of his arousal beneath her, and she knew he was more than capable of performing. This would be the time to thank him and then quickly run away.

But for some reason, she couldn't command her brain to tell her legs to move. She sat on him, limp and relaxed as his tongue swept across her neck and his fingers moved over her shoulders, dipping lower across the tops of her breasts.

Chloe's breathing turned shallow as she fought for control. It had been weeks of torture with this man flirting with her, showing her too much of his skin, pushing her to the limits of her sanity. She wasn't sure she could walk away—not tonight.

"I should go," Chloe said, but there was zero conviction in her voice.

"Don't fight me, Chloe. We both want this—need this, and I can't keep waiting for you to make that first move," Nick said as he trailed his lips along her neck before taking the lobe of her ear between his teeth and biting down.

One hand slid back around her as if he were afraid she was truly going to escape. She knew she could tell him to leave her be, knew she could stop this. She had several times in their short acquaintance. The difference was, she couldn't fight both him and herself any longer. She wanted him too desperately.

"You taste like sugar and smell even better," he whispered while his hand slid beneath her shirt and rubbed along the trembling muscles of her stomach. His thumb brushed the underside of one breast, and she felt heat surge through her core. Nick pushed against her butt, his arousal thick and hard. She knew what it felt like deep inside her, and she wanted to feel it again.

"Tell me to stop, Chloe, and I will," Nick said. The confidence in his tone told her he knew she wasn't going to do that. "It would be an excruciating night for both of us." He pressed into her again, just in case she hadn't managed to already notice his excitement.

A moan escaped her as his fingers climbed over the curve of her breast and he squeezed the sensitive flesh. She wiggled on his lap, trying to hold her thighs together to relieve even the slightest bit of the ache that was resting there.

"Damn, you are soft in all the right places," he said as his other hand came around and slipped beneath her shirt. He quickly grabbed her other neglected breast and squeezed before his fingers slipped inside the lacy bra and he pinched her nipples.

"Nick . . ." His name came out a low moan as her back softened into his chest, making her even more accessible to him.

"Tell me how much you want me to strip off these clothes," he demanded before expertly unsnapping her delicate bra. Without hesitation, he took the weight of her full breasts in his palms and rubbed and squeezed them until she was moaning his name over and over again.

"Tell me, Chloe, or I won't know," he warned.

"Please . . ." she said as she reached her arms up and clasped them behind his head, her back arching, her legs opening. She wanted his touch in so many other places on her body.

"Please what?" Nick said as he flicked his thumb across her nipple before his hand began moving lower on her body, stopping at the button on her pants.

"Please touch me, Nick," she whimpered.

He chuckled in her ear, and for the briefest second, she found herself mad at him, but then his fingers slipped between the waistband of her pants, and she sucked in her breath in anticipation.

The entire night she'd been restless, pacing the house, knowing this was what she wanted. She just hadn't been able to admit it—not even to herself. She didn't care if she regretted her actions in the morning. The pleasure he would bring her tonight made it all worthwhile.

"Your body is softer than satin. I can't get enough," Nick told her. His fingers were caressing her lower belly, not going deeper inside her pants.

"Nick . . . I want more," she told him on a sigh.

"You'll have plenty more," he assured her as he pulled his fingers away. She wanted to reach for him and lead him exactly where she wanted. But Chloe didn't have a lot of experience with men, didn't know how to show what it was she was craving. She truly wished she did.

Nick reached up and held her face, turning her so she was even more vulnerable. He leaned forward and pressed his mouth to hers, taking her lips in a gentle kiss that surprised her. She melted more fully against him as one of his hands cupped her naked breast and his tongue traced her lips.

She turned as far as she could, pressing her backside against his thickness while she connected with his lips in a hungry kiss. She pulled on the back of his neck, wanting him to devour her as she got lost in him.

Quickly, the gentleness stopped. Nick tugged on her hair while he took her lips more roughly and pushed his erection hard against her bottom. He was growing more excited, and she wanted him to lose control in her arms. She needed to turn around and press her breasts against him, open her thighs, and feel his hardness pushing against her. She wanted them to be locked together.

When he pulled back, she whimpered. "Nick, please."

He suddenly pushed her off his body, and for a moment she was confused and hurt, but then he did exactly as she was hoping and pulled her to him, quickly turning them both so she had her back to the desk as he scooted forward and pulled her into his arms and between his thighs.

She wanted her legs open, not his, but at least her tender breasts were now pressed against him, even if he was tugging on her to pull her down to his level. Thank goodness for tall chairs, was her only thought before he grabbed her head and ravished her mouth again.

Nick's hands gripped and squeezed her ass as his mouth traced hers, his tongue diving inside. He moved his fingers down and gripped her thighs before slipping between them and rubbing where she ached most.

She was so hot and wet, she was sure her pants were ruined, giving away how much she wanted him. She didn't care. She was almost delirious with lust. Her need was so strong, she doubted she'd ever be able to stop what was happening.

Nick's lips broke away from hers as he gasped, but his hands climbed back up her body. He found the *V* of her shirt and tugged, ripping the material, allowing him to view her swollen breasts and peaked nipples. He murmured his approval before leaning forward and taking one bud into his mouth.

His hot tongue danced around the puckered flesh, sucking hard, making her sway on unsteady legs. She was going to collapse, turn into a puddle, and melt at his feet.

Nick seemed to know exactly how she was feeling, because he released her nipple and grabbed her leg, pulling it up and making her straddle his lap. She moaned as her wet flesh rubbed against his arousal. She pushed against him, wanting their clothing gone.

Nick didn't give Chloe any more time to think, though. He grabbed her head and pulled her to him to meet his lips again while she pressed her aching breasts against his chest. She wanted them both nude, but she didn't want to part long enough to strip.

He took care of that for her. Reaching between their bodies, he ripped off his own shirt, then pulled her against him. The feel of her swollen breasts tightly pressed against his chest was delicious.

Chloe ran her hands across his strong shoulders, relishing the feel of his muscles. He continued tracing her lips with his tongue while his hands moved down and squeezed her butt. He pulled her next to his arousal and thrust his hips upward. They moaned together.

Chloe wrenched her lips from his and trailed them across his jaw, loving the feel of him clenching it as he tried to maintain some amount of control. It was a losing battle for both of them. She scooted back on his lap and bent down, circling her tongue around his hard nipple before she sucked on it.

His gasp of pleasure encouraged her to keep going. Sliding from his lap, she found herself kneeling in front of him, his covered thickness inches from her face. She needed to have a taste of him.

"Chloe," he warned. She wasn't sure what he was asking for—her to come back to him or to take his pants off. She chose to believe it was the latter.

She took her time sliding her hands across his thighs, edging closer and closer to where she most wanted to touch him. His fingers wound into her hair as he tugged her closer to him. She didn't resist.

Chloe leaned in and kissed his thickness, feeling him jump within his pants. She was floating in a happy delirium. Opening her mouth, she gently bit down on his covered erection and he groaned. Looking up she loved the sight of him with his head thrown back, a layer of sweat beading on his hard abs. He was magnificent.

Chloe quickly grew tired of teasing him and reached up to undo his pants. His breathing was labored as she pulled his zipper slowly down, finding his arousal straining against the black cotton of his underwear.

"Lift up," she told him. He didn't hesitate. With a quick tug, she pulled his pants and underwear away, his magnificent erection jumping out, inches from her watering mouth. Circling her fingers around his thick shaft, she pumped her fist a couple times before running her thumb over the bead of pleasure dripping from him.

A shudder passed through his entire body at her touch. He was so solid and hot. She used his excitement to lubricate him so she could move her hand more quickly up and down his thickness.

Chloe was wet as she continued playing with Nick. He was all man, his injury forgotten even as she felt the brace against her side while she drew closer to him. Nick wouldn't be kept down for long.

Unable to wait any longer, Chloe leaned forward and took his large head into her mouth, tasting his salty flavor as he pulsed against her tongue. She squeezed around the bottom of his shaft as she sucked him deep into her mouth, moving slowly up and down his velvety smoothness.

"Your mouth is so hot," he groaned.

With her lips fastened securely around him, she looked up again. This time his eyes met hers, fire burning from his dark green depths. The look made her stomach tremble as she watched him while sliding her mouth farther down his shaft, taking him into her throat and squeezing all that she couldn't fit with her hand.

His lips tightened at the pleasure she was giving him, and she couldn't tear her gaze away as she continued to suck on him. She slid her lips back to his head, swirling her tongue around his tip before taking him deep into her throat again—over and over she did this, growing even more excited as his eyes darkened to almost black.

"Stop!" Nick cried as she took him even deeper and flexed her throat. She felt a gush of warm fluid slide down the inside of her throat, and she would have smiled if her lips weren't tightly locked around him.

He pulled hard on her hair, forcing her to release him from the warmth of her mouth. She looked up and smiled while she licked her lips.

"You didn't like that?" she teased.

He growled at her as he gripped her beneath her arms and pulled her back up, turning her once again so she was against the desk. With a fast movement, he undid her pants and pulled them down her legs, leaving her bare to him. Easily lifting her up, he set her on the desk, then scooted between her thighs.

"Nick . . ." she groaned as he pushed her down on the desk, her body draped across the wood. He began kissing the insides of her thighs.

Chloe tried to lift up to watch him, but one of his hands pressed against her stomach, keeping her down. His hot breath washed across her opening before she felt the pressure of his tongue circling her sensitive heat.

She cried out as he sucked her into his mouth before laving his tongue across her folds. She was writhing on the desk as he brought her closer to the pleasure she so desperately wanted.

His fingers easily slipped inside her heat, and he pumped them in and out while his tongue tasted every delicate centimeter of her swollen flesh. His murmurs rumbled through her, and she was lost in the pleasure he was giving.

"Please, Nick, please," Chloe begged him.

With a hard thrust of his fingers, he sucked her swollen flesh into his mouth, and she screamed with the intensity of the release he gave her. She was shaking as her body clenched repeatedly.

Nick stood up and tugged on her legs, pulling her butt slightly off the desk. She barely acknowledged the movement. Then, he gripped her legs and thrust forward, sinking inside her as a spasm rocked through her, turning one orgasm into a second. It was almost more than she could take.

She whimpered as he began thrusting hard in and out of her body, her insides squeezing him tightly as he groaned and pushed faster and faster within her. He paused, buried deep inside her.

"You feel so amazing," he groaned as she clenched around him.

"So full, I'm so full . . ." she moaned, her breathing difficult as her body continued to fly higher and higher in her pleasure.

He began moving again, and their moans mingled in the air as he reached forward with one hand and squeezed her breast. The other gripped her leg as he thrust in and out of her.

Her body was so wet, he easily slid within her folds as he pushed her leg up, connecting them even deeper than before. She began to squeeze him again as another orgasm ripped through her. Never before had she felt such intense pleasure. She cried out, begging for mercy. But he wasn't willing to give her any.

The pleasure was excruciating as he continued filling her. Her arms were too weak to reach for him. She tried lifting them to no avail. He knew what she wanted, though, and he leaned down, stretching her leg even farther, giving her a whole new level of pleasure.

His lips clasped around her nipple, and he sucked while he pushed within her, grunting around her breast, his hot breath and warm tongue circling her.

With a cry, Nick pushed forward, the heat of his pleasure filling her. It sent her into another orgasm, and she squeezed him, taking every ounce of him deep inside her.

Nick fell forward, his body still connected with hers as he ran his fingers through her hair. They were both damp and spent. With a moan, he pulled from her, and she whimpered her disapproval. He sat back on the chair, tugging on her until she lifted up.

He pulled her into his arms and cradled her, his hands running softly up and down her back as he sucked on the tender skin of her shoulder.

"You are amazing," he said in awe.

She couldn't even form words to describe what had just happened. As the aftermath began to wash away, she tried to tug against his hold.

"No." His word was firm. She stilled in his arms. "You aren't running away this time."

She settled down in his arms and wondered what she was going to do. She wasn't quite sure. In the moment, it felt so right. But after she was satiated, she remembered who he was. No, he wasn't the monster she'd once thought he was, but his family was the enemy. Her father would never approve of her being in a relationship with him. Chloe didn't know what to do.

"We're going to go to bed together without any regrets," Nick told her.

Chloe wanted to do exactly that, but she couldn't voice her opinion aloud. He gently pushed her from his lap and then he stood. Taking her hand in his, he began walking slowly, leading her through the house to his bedroom.

She hesitated only a moment before entering his quarters. She stopped fighting as he pulled her into his bed. When she was tucked securely into his arms, her eyes drifted shut, and she fell into a deep sleep.

The next day Nick didn't allow her to pull away from him, and she appreciated it. That night, she again went to bed, falling asleep in his arms after they were both sated. It's how the next few days and nights went and those regrets Chloe felt she should be feeling never came.

CHAPTER TWENTY

Chloe was trembling as she hid beneath her bed. Terror filled her as she heard the footsteps coming closer. The only sound was that of deep breathing—controlled, almost excited.

She shook as she tried not to make a sound, but it was no use. The chattering of her teeth were like shotgun blasts, and her falling tears sounded like splashes in the lake, clearly giving up her hiding position.

Scooting back, her body scraped against the hardwood floor, and she had to put her hand over her mouth to keep from whimpering as the footsteps stopped at the edge of her bed. Maybe he wouldn't notice. The feet turned and she sighed in relief. Then he quickly dropped to the floor to check under the bed. She screamed when his face appeared, an evil smile overtaking his lips.

She struggled to get away from him as his hand reached for her. Pain was promised in his expression, and she kicked as she resisted. Normally she just accepted it, but this time, she wasn't going to cave so easily. She was stronger now, bigger. She didn't have to allow him to hurt her.

"Please, no!" she shouted. "I haven't done anything. Please." Her words turned into a sob as he pulled her from beneath the bed and pinned her to the ground, holding her arms in place. She kicked at him, bit down on his chest when he leaned into her.

"Dammit, stop!" The thundering voice shook Chloe as she snapped from sleep. Her eyelids lifted. Her body violently shook. Her vision was blurred by tears and she blinked several times, trying to focus. The man before her came in and out of her hazy focus.

"Please don't," she begged, half in and half out of sleep. She couldn't distinguish between her dream and reality.

"Chloe . . . Chloe . . . you need to wake up. It's me."

Tears streaking down her face, Chloe continued fighting, but her movements were growing weaker. She couldn't hold him off. "It's me. It's Nick," he said, his tone soft.

The voice finally registered as the last of her nightmare faded away. "Nick?" she said, the single word coming out as barely a whisper. "Nick." She said it again, trying to stabilize herself.

She felt immediately that it didn't matter how angry Nick was with her, he'd never hurt her—not physically at least. She was safe. She was safe. She was safe. She repeated that phrase over and over again in her head. She was safe.

Finally, the shaking in her body stopped, her tears dried, and she focused on the face hovering above her. He was looking down at her as if she were a rabid animal. Maybe she was. Years of abuse would do that to a person.

"What in the world happened in your dream?" he asked. He was still holding her. She wondered what she'd done to him that he was afraid to release her.

"It doesn't matter. It was just a nightmare. I'm okay now," she told him. "You can let me go."

He eyed her mistrustfully. "You hit me a few times. I'm not sure I should," he told her. His lips tilted up the slightest bit in a teasing grin. He was lucky he hadn't released her because she might have slugged him for that.

"I told you I'm fine. Let me go," she demanded, though her voice was still weak.

"What happened?" he repeated.

"It was nothing, just a nightmare," she said as she turned away. There was no way she was telling him she'd been reliving a real moment—the time she'd decided to defy her father.

"I don't think so," he said. "That appeared to be more than just a nightmare. I have the wounds to prove it." He pointedly looked down to his naked chest, and she saw the bite mark there. She was horrified she'd done that. Her cheeks flushed as she looked away.

"I'm sorry, Nick. I guess I didn't wake up quickly enough that time," she said.

"This has happened before?" he questioned. Her cheeks flushed even more.

"How would I know? I am asleep when it happens," she told him, tugging against his hold.

He finally released her arms, but he didn't move from where he sat on her thighs. The feeling of being trapped was beginning to make her panic again. She had to get away from him, and quickly. She didn't want to tell him anything.

"Quit struggling," he snapped and she stopped moving. "You are constantly trying to run as soon as there is light in the sky. This time you're going to talk to me."

His commanding voice made her automatically want to obey him, and that instinct infuriated her. She was no longer that helpless child, and she wouldn't ever be controlled like that again. Ironically, there was a part of her brain that mocked her because she was only with Nick because her father had placed her there.

She was still obeying, and she hated herself a bit for it. The difference between her father and Nick was that she trusted Nick. That was a humbling and terrifying thought. If she trusted him, then he had the power to hurt her. She couldn't afford to be injured any more than she already had been.

Their wrestling match had shifted the blankets, and now that Chloe was calming down she realized they were both naked. Her eyes drifted down his chest to his torso before she blushed and looked back up. She reached for the blankets in a tangle next to them and tried covering herself.

At this, Nick glared at her and yanked the blankets from her hands. Naked once more, he traced the curves of her body and then looked back up to hold her gaze in a defiant way.

"There's nothing showing I haven't already seen many times," he pointed out. She glared back at him.

They'd been on the couch earlier that night. She remembered falling asleep after another incredible sexual experience. He'd bent her over the couch and been so deep inside her she hadn't known where he ended and she began. Her cheeks flushed as she thought about it.

"How did we get up here?" she questioned. She tried to take her mind off the sex that she couldn't seem to stop having with him.

"We both passed out after our workout," he said with a smile. "When I woke up, you were shivering, so I carried you to my room."

"You could have injured your leg doing that," she chastised him. He raised his brow.

"You're the one who said I'm so much better that I really don't even need therapy anymore, so what are you worried about?"

"Just because you don't need me babysitting you daily doesn't mean you should act foolish and cause yourself to backtrack on your progress," she told him.

"Are you worried about me, Chloe?" he asked cockily.

"No!" she snapped. "Now let me up right now."

"Even if you say it in that forceful tone, it doesn't make me want to change my mind," he said with a chuckle. She wanted to smack him. He was making her far more violent than she ever had been in the past.

"Quit acting like an ass and let me go," she said, her tone calming.

"So you can run away?" he questioned.

He was right. She blushed again. They were getting nowhere with this conversation.

"Look, we've been sleeping together for the past few nights, but that doesn't change the fact that this is completely inappropriate," she told him.

"Maybe I want to be inappropriate," he told her.

"My feelings matter, Nick!" she snapped.

"Of course they do, but I don't think you have any idea what you want. You keep going hot and cold, dammit. Now tell me about your dream."

"We're back to that again?" she huffed.

"We never were off it. You just thought you could distract me, and I'd forget about it. I have the war wounds to prove it happened," he said.

"You're sitting on my bladder and I have to use the bathroom," she told him, embarrassed. She was horrified saying it. He chuckled, but finally released her as he turned over. She threw the blanket across him as she jumped from the bed, fleeing the room, but not before turning back to glare at him. The look of satisfaction in his eyes as they traced her naked body was unmistakable.

"I'll be waiting when you're done," he called out after her.

Chloe shut the bathroom door with satisfying force before she sagged against it and took in several deep breaths, trying to get her bearings. She was entirely unnerved. The nightmare had wrecked her. The conversation after had made it even worse.

The shaking in her body returned as her mind flashed through the images of only one scene of her father's abuse. Living with the man had been a nightmare, and it seemed she couldn't even get away from it in her dreams. Maybe it had been the stress she was under that had brought it all up again. She didn't know. All she knew for sure was that she wanted to get away, go somewhere, and curl up into a ball for a while.

Whenever she'd been young and frightened, she'd rolled her blankets tightly around her and rocked back and forth. She'd had her brother, but he'd been on the receiving end of their father's fists more often than she had been. She often wondered if Patrick blamed her for that. She'd always been too afraid to ask him, and now she'd never be able to.

Taking her time in the bathroom, she climbed into the shower and let the hot water relax her tense muscles. She didn't want to leave the safety of the closed room. She had no doubt Nick would be right outside waiting with more questions. What was she going to say to him?

She tried to formulate a story that would satisfy him. If she could just get through the morning, then maybe all this would end. Maybe she'd be able to walk away from this thing she had with Nick without getting scathed any more than she already was.

When she finally came out, Nick was sitting on the bed in a pair of low-riding sweats, his beautiful chest still bare, his eyes wary. Two cups of coffee sat on the nightstand, and Nick patted the spot next to him on the bed.

"Come have a drink with me, and we'll talk," he told her.

"We can talk in the kitchen," she said, a towel wrapped around her. She clutched its loose ends tightly to her chest with her hand. "I need to get dressed."

She scooted toward the door. Surely he couldn't be offended by that.

"No. I'm not going to let you run away and try to create a story. I think you owe me an explanation of what is going on in that head of yours." He looked relaxed, but she knew he would be ready to spring in an instant.

"I already told you I don't want to share with you. Why don't you quit being so pushy and accept that?"

His eyes narrowed as she took another step. "Don't make me get up and carry you over to the bed," he threatened.

She stopped walking, having no doubt he'd do exactly that. She gripped her towel like a life raft as she shifted on her feet, her eyes darting between him and the door. Nick sighed.

"Should I count?"

His words made her heart thunder with rage. "I'm not a damn child, Nick," she yelled.

"You could have fooled me. Stop behaving like a brat."

Chloe took a furious step toward him, and he smiled, mocking her, egging her on. She was barely holding on to her control as she shivered where she stopped herself.

"Do you enjoy intimidating people? Is that how you get what you want?" she asked.

"Sometimes," he told her. "But usually I don't have to resort to such methods. Most adults actually behave normally," he told her.

"You're an ass."

"Is that your go-to method, name calling?"

"I don't *ever* call names. You just bring out the worst in me," she admitted.

"Maybe we do it to each other because I don't normally have to work so hard to get someone to speak to me."

They glared at each other, at a complete impasse. Chloe sighed. Finally, she moved over to the bed and sat as far from him as she possibly could. She reached for her coffee cup and took a sip. He'd made it the way she liked.

"Thanks for the coffee," she told him, making her voice extra polite. He laughed, and she had to fight not to scowl.

"I want to know what you were dreaming about," he pushed.

"You aren't going to drop it, are you?" she asked.

"Do I seem like the type of man to let something go once I start?" he questioned.

"No. *That's* for sure." She didn't mean the words to be a compliment.

They were silent for several moments, neither of them speaking. Chloe wondered if she could just wait him out. Even as she had the thought, she knew that would never happen.

"I can barely even remember what it was about. I was just hiding from something in the dark, and then it felt like someone was grabbing me. When I woke up, I was having a hard time differentiating the nightmare from reality," she told him. That was an easy enough explanation.

"That makes sense," he told her, and relief washed over her. "But the panic and fear I saw in your eyes went beyond a normal nightmare. I think it was something more." Her hopes were shattered.

Nick grabbed her chin and forced her to look at him. She tried to hide what she was feeling, but his knowing eyes captured everything. Chloe didn't like how well he saw her.

"I don't want to talk about it," she told him as her eyes filled. She saw what appeared to be sympathy in his expression, and that look almost undid her all over again. Damn the man.

"I'm patient," he told her. "But I think you need to tell your story, you're just so used to pushing it back, you don't know how to begin." Chloe shook as he continued looking at her.

"Sometimes it's best to leave things behind in the dreamworld," she said, forcing her lips to turn up as if it were nothing more than a joke.

"What are you keeping from me?" he asked. The question was more for himself than for her, as if he was running the morning's events through his brain, analyzing her actions. She didn't like that either.

"Haven't you ever had a dream you couldn't explain?"

"Many times. Sometimes they are silly, sometimes terrifying, and usually there's meaning behind them. You've been hiding things from the moment we met, so you're either the coldhearted bitch you want me to believe you are, or there's something else going on."

He said the words so calmly, but they affected her more than if he'd stabbed her.

"Maybe that's exactly what I am," she told him with a hitch to her voice.

"I don't believe that," he reassured. "I think something else is going on in your life. I don't know exactly what it is, but I do know that I don't like to leave questions unanswered. I'm trying to find out if my effort to get to know you is worth it."

That hurt her more than anything else he'd said. Chloe had always been told she wasn't good enough, wasn't worth the trouble of raising, that she'd been a disappointment. For Nick to confirm that absolutely broke her heart. But did she truly want to try and change his opinion of her? In order to do that she would have to bare her soul.

She decided she could accept him believing the worst about her. "It's not even worth talking about," she whispered after several moments.

He waited, giving her a look that told her she was being a fool, and he wasn't going to even respond. She finished her coffee and sat there. Neither of them moved. Minutes passed.

"Fine. What do you want me to tell you?" she said with a huff.

"I want to know everything in that pretty little head of yours."

"That's not asking a lot or anything," she said with a false laugh.

"Chloe," he said with a sigh. "You're putting off the inevitable. You want me to trust you, but you're unwilling to."

"What makes you think that I can trust you?" she asked.

"I'm not the one of us who's hiding things. Whatever happened to you in the past, can't you see that you're safe with me? I don't think you ever feel protected," he pointed out, making her flinch.

"I don't even know why you're pushing this so hard. I don't know where to begin," she snapped.

"You can start by telling me what had you frightened. That's a beginning."

He wasn't asking for much, but the one thing he did want to know was the thing she absolutely didn't want to share.

"My father wasn't the nicest man," she began. She was grateful he wasn't touching her. "Growing up, he had high expectations of my brother and me, and we rarely met those standards."

She felt Nick tense beside her, but she didn't look at him. If she did, she would lose her courage, and then they'd be right back to arguing.

"My dad believed in using an iron fist. He'd punish us often. I'm sure it was no worse than many kids had it, but I was afraid of him, afraid of disappointing him."

"Where was your mother?" he asked. There was a simmering rage in his voice, though she could hear that he was trying to keep it from boiling over.

"She was the obedient little wife, always in the background. She would mend us when he'd go too far, but she'd always tell us we shouldn't disobey, that it was so much worse when we did."

"Was that what your dream was about?" he asked.

"One time, my brother and I got into some candy that was in the pantry. That was a definite no-no. I heard my dad screaming downstairs, and I hid from him under my bed. That only made it worse. When he found me, he dragged me out. I ended up with a broken arm that time. It was the worst punishment I can ever remember getting," she admitted.

"For getting into some candy?" he asked incredulously.

"I knew I shouldn't have," she said with a shrug.

"So you think it was your fault?" The words came out with acidity.

"I didn't say it was my fault. I'm just saying that I did something I knew would have consequences."

"How old were you?" Chloe still couldn't look at him. There was too much anger in Nick's voice, and that reminded her too much of her father. She was having a difficult time not flinching from him.

"I was eight, my brother was fifteen."

"So at eight years old, you were expected to fall into line at all times?" he snapped.

"At two I was expected to fall into line. By the time I was eight, I was expected to act like an adult. I knew right from wrong. There was no gray line with my father," she said with a sigh.

"How do you still have a relationship with the man?" His voice was incredulous. Of course he couldn't understand. He had a loving family who would do anything for him. No one with the upbringing she'd gone through could comprehend what that was like.

"He's my father," she said simply.

Nick took the empty cup from her shaking fingers. She hadn't even realized they were trembling. It didn't really matter, though. She'd given him information he could turn around and use against her. Maybe she deserved that. She wasn't sure anymore.

"I think I get it, Chloe," he told her.

"Get what?" she asked.

He lifted her and set her on his lap as he rubbed her back and pulled her head against the warmth of his chest.

"I think I understand why you're so afraid of opening up to someone."

There was so much sincerity in his tone, she didn't know what to do. She curled against him and accepted his comforting, for now, at least.

When Nick pulled the towel away and tucked her in beside him on the bed, she didn't try to fight him. The weeks before this moment had drained her, and the nightmare had taken the rest of her energy away. Talking to Nick had been more difficult than she ever could have imagined.

When his fingers traced her flesh, she let her mind empty and focused on nothing but what he was doing to her. She needed that. She needed him.

CHAPTER
TWENTY-ONE

Nick and Chloe sat at a café overlooking the beautiful Puget Sound. The wind gently blew as she brushed some wandering strands of hair from her eyes. It had been a peaceful day—almost too peaceful. It made her wonder when the other shoe would drop. At the same time, she tried to tell herself that was a programmed way of thinking and she didn't want to have these doubts.

Her job was going well, and she was enjoying her time with Nick. Did she think it would last forever? No. But it felt good for now, and that was important. Each new day began with how she wanted it to. She had to remember that, had to remember she didn't have to be controlled—not if she didn't allow it.

"Is it hard for you to look out at the water and not be on it?" Chloe asked.

Nick smiled. "Yes and no. It was really difficult when this all began. But having you around for company is making me much more of a land lover," he said.

Nick was a smooth talker, but his words were genuine. The way he looked at her sent her heart to fluttering. Maybe she was as foolish as she feared.

"You don't speak a lot about your Coast Guard work," she pointed out.

"I'm an open book. What do you want to know?" he asked. His eyes showed her he had nothing to hide. *She* did, though, and that was standing between them. She wished she was brave enough to tell him the whole truth. She was too happy to risk that.

"Tell me about some of your adventures," she said.

Their food had come and gone, but neither of them were in a hurry as they sat back and sipped on coffee, picking at their decadent desserts of powdered donuts with dipping sauces.

"I served up in Sitka for a year. It was always pretty exciting there," he said.

"Yes, you mentioned that it's extreme in Alaska," she said.

"The Coast Guard established an air station in Sitka in 1977. Since then they have saved over two thousand lives in the area. It's pretty awesome."

"I'd say so," she said. "Tell me about a typical day there."

"I wouldn't exactly say there were typical days, but I remember one night pretty clearly," he told her. "I was just getting to work for a twenty-four-hour shift. It was about three in the afternoon. First thing we always do is get into our flight suits and check out the weather. Most pilots for the Coast Guard really want to fly in Sitka or Kodiak, but we have to gain experience first. I had a lot of flight time, but I was still a copilot for my flights there."

"I can't imagine you taking commands from anyone," she said with a laugh.

"We're a team and we work together. It's not about who's giving the orders," he told her.

"Team player. I like it," she said.

"The team and I got suited up, then went to the Operations Center for our upcoming duty brief. Everyone was in good humor."

"I bet you all had tight bonds since you were in danger together so often," she said.

"Yeah, you have to rely on each other for survival. It makes you form a tight-knit group," he told her.

Chloe didn't have that same loyalty in her job. She worked more on her own. She did get along with a lot of the medical staff, but there were some who didn't think she was a real medical member as well. She'd bet there was some of that in the Coast Guard between the different ranks. She didn't point that out. It was a pleasant day, and she wanted to keep the conversation upbeat.

"Go on," she told Nick.

"Our OWS briefed us on airfield weather, the status of our choppers, and location of our command cadre."

"OWS?"

"Sorry. Operations Watch Stander," he said with a grin.

"I'll try to keep up," she told him.

"Weather wasn't the worst I'd ever seen that night, but on the east side it was pretty volatile. We had to really keep an eye on the cloud ceiling to know if it was safe to fly."

"Were there a lot of times you couldn't go out?"

"Unfortunately yes, but if there was a chance of us performing a rescue, we did it without hesitation. It was tough on us when we couldn't get out there."

"Did you have to wear a ton of gear the entire time on duty?" She'd seen it when going to the station with him, and it didn't look like it would be comfortable to wear all the time.

"No. We just have it at the ready. Our vests—the vest that saved my life—is equipped with a harness, so we can be pulled from the water if need be. We also have survival gear such as emergency flares and a mini scuba setup with about five minutes of air, depending on how quickly you're breathing, in our survival gear, too. These things can make the difference between life and death if you are stuck in the water."

"If you forget even one step, it could be death," she said in awe.

"That's true for any job, really. If you think about it, you could miss a step at the mall and go tumbling down and break your neck. There's always danger around us, we just have to be aware and prepared," he pointed out.

"True," she said, though that hadn't ever been anything she'd thought about before.

"After more briefings and getting our equipment ready to go, we waited around to see if we got a call."

"That sounds boring," she said.

"Nah. My philosophy is that only boring people get bored," he told her with a wink. She scowled at him. "I'm just saying that we have to make the best of any situation we're in."

"I guess I can agree with that," she said.

"About six that night we got a call from Juneau. There was a medevac launch requesting our services."

"Medevac?" she questioned.

"Yeah, we did a lot of transports like that in Alaska. We didn't always work out on the sea. Our choppers can fly in weather the hospitals can't," he told her.

"I guess it's safer than flying over rolling waves," she said.

"Not necessarily. This time it was an elderly woman who had appendicitis, and she needed to get to surgery. We agreed to pick her up."

"We got off the ground, and the weather worsened, but we were able to push through. We picked her up and got her to the destination. We refueled and grabbed a quick bite. Before we were halfway through the meal, we got another call, this time an older gentleman with a heart condition. It wasn't a particularly exciting night, but it was almost endless, and we were the only ones flying."

"I was hoping you were gonna tell me of an epic water rescue," she admitted.

Nick laughed. "The reason this night is so memorable for me was that our crew saved six lives that night. Our chopper was the only one willing to make the pickups and do the drop-offs. The weather worsened all night, and because my crew was skilled, no one died. It was a good night," he told her.

"I'm sorry, I didn't mean to put you down," she told him as she reached out to him.

"I didn't take it that way. I'm just saying that the most exciting moments in life can be those quiet in-betweens."

"What does that mean?"

"We have to appreciate the calm before the storm to make it through the turbulence about to come," he said.

Chloe realized she was falling more and more for this man who didn't belong to her. She wanted to categorize him into one box, but the more she learned about him, the more she realized she would never be able to do that. She just didn't understand what that meant. Maybe it was that she didn't want to know what it meant. Then she would have to face too many questions she didn't want the answers to.

CHAPTER
TWENTY-TWO

Chloe didn't know what to think about how her day was going. After a leisurely morning of making love and talking about nothing of importance, she and Nick had been in sort of a truce it seemed. They'd made a very late breakfast together and relaxed while watching a show.

It had taken her a while to calm the beating of her heart while waiting for the other shoe to drop, but they'd even done some physical therapy. This time while he'd been flirting, she'd allowed herself to enjoy it instead of fighting what she was feeling. The problem with that was the realization that she truly enjoyed being with him, but she wasn't sure how much longer their "relationship" was going to last.

One night, at about six in the evening, he walked in wearing a fitted suit that showed off his muscles to perfection.

Chloe's mouth watered as he stepped closer to her. The man was beautiful in a rugged way. He was wearing black with a splash of green in his tie that showed off the sparkles in his eyes. She wondered what was happening.

"You should probably go put on the dress I bought you," he said with a smile.

She looked at him with suspicion. "Why?"

"Because there's a party tonight. I had forgotten all about it until my captain called," he told her.

"I still don't know why *I* would be putting on a dress," she said with a raised brow.

"Because *you're* going as my date," he told her.

"I don't think that's the best idea," she said.

"Why not?" He seemed genuinely perplexed.

She couldn't tell him. She knew someone might put the pieces together, figure out who she was, and then everything would be ruined. So she offered a different excuse.

"We aren't dating," she told him.

He smiled. "If this isn't dating, I don't know what is," he said as his eyes traveled down her body.

She couldn't help but blush as his gaze fastened on her cleavage before moving down the rest of her frame. She felt as if she were wearing nothing at all. When his heated gaze met back up with hers, desire rushed through her.

This stunning man, who seemed to really have nothing at all wrong with him, wanted her—desired *her*. She couldn't seem to wrap her mind around it. But she also was a little euphoric from the feeling.

She was unable to take her eyes away from him as he moved closer to her. His strong hands wrapped around her back in a hug. She sighed with pleasure before his lips drank up the sound. By the time he released her, she was almost dizzy.

"What's the event?" she asked, already forgetting what he'd said.

"Just a get-together," he told her.

"Why are you so formally dressed then?" she asked with suspicion. He laughed.

"You don't like me in a suit?" he questioned.

"It's not that, it's just you don't really seem the suit-and-tie sort of guy," she admitted.

"Hey, I can clean up," he told her, taking her bottom lip in his mouth and tugging on it before kissing her again.

"You aren't playing fair," she told him as she ran her hands up and down his arms, loving the flex of his muscles.

"I play to win. I never said I followed the rules," he assured her.

"Fine, I'll come with you." Her words earned her a brilliant smile. She turned to walk into her room, and he swatted her behind, telling her to hurry.

Chloe was enthralled with the dress the moment she saw it. She had no idea when he'd managed to get it, but it must have been a while ago, because the two of them hadn't left the house all day.

She ran her fingers across the green material that matched his tie and sighed at how soft it was. Hurrying through a shower, she was anxious to put it on and see how it fit. When she looked in the mirror, she was delighted. It had been made just for her, hugging her curves in all the right places, having a slit up the side that showed off her thigh and ending just below her knees. It flowed against her legs, making her want to twirl in circles to see how high the material would ride.

She took her time with her hair and makeup, wanting to see satisfaction in Nick's eyes when she came into the room. Lastly, she slipped on the silver heels she'd found with the dress. After a last glance in the mirror, she returned to Nick.

She wasn't disappointed in his reaction. A low growl escaped his throat before he pulled her to him and devoured her mouth, his hands sliding down her back as he tugged her close, showing her the evidence of his excitement.

When he pulled back, she was breathless, and thinking twice about going anywhere.

"Maybe we should just stay in," she suggested.

His eyes narrowed. "Don't tempt me, woman. You look good enough to eat, and I'm already having a tough time figuring out how to show you off. I don't want anyone other than me looking at you."

His words made her feel warm all over. She leaned in and kissed him softly, thanking him. Then she willingly followed him to his old truck and took a seat.

They were late to arrive at the party, and immediately several men came up and grabbed his attention. While he was laughing at something one of the men said to him, Chloe smiled. Her heart was thundering. She was almost in shock as she gazed at Nick, the man who had changed her thinking, changed many views she'd had her entire life. She felt the color drain from her cheeks as she realized she was hopelessly in love with him.

She'd often wondered if she would ever know what it felt like to truly love another. She hadn't been taught the meaning of the word love, so how could she feel that emotion toward another person? But as she gazed at Nick, she knew beyond a doubt that she did indeed love him.

It was odd. In the movies, love was portrayed as this epic adventure that was so obvious it smacked you in the face. In reality, it snuck up on you. One moment you were living your life as best as you could, the next you were gazing at a face you'd looked at many times, but the feeling was different. It was as if he was the reason you were standing there, he was the reason your heart even beat.

It hadn't happened in an instant, she realized. It had taken time. It was little things that had slowly begun to add up—the way he smiled, the way he kissed her, teased her, made love to her. The way he wouldn't let her retreat or walk away from him. He was strong and self-assured, but he was also kind and compassionate. And she'd fallen for him. The thought was as terrifying as it was joyful.

A part of her was scared, but another part was hopeful. He wanted her. She knew that for sure. But did he want her for now, or forever? That was the question she didn't know the answer to. That was what she was afraid to know.

They did work well together, and they certainly were compatible in the bedroom, but up until maybe two weeks before, she'd thought he was her enemy. Her father had told her Nick was evil. Would Nick be willing to forgive all of that? To not see it as a betrayal?

Chloe left Nick to chat with his friends while she made her way to the bar and ordered a glass of wine. She didn't know any of the people at the party, but she was okay with being alone. She didn't need to have constant attention to feel good. Sometimes she preferred to stand back and watch how people moved, how they interacted.

She looked over at Nick again, and he laughed before looking up. His gaze found hers and he smiled. She was filled with joy. He stared at her for several moments before his friend regained his attention, and he went back to chatting.

Chloe beamed, feeling warm and secure.

"That's not exactly the expression I expect you to be wearing while looking at *that* man."

The curt words sent a chill through Chloe's body, and definitely wiped the smile from her face. Her infatuation with Nick had caused her to relax, to not be on guard. She hadn't even realized it until this very moment, but she was always looking around her, always aware of who was nearby.

It had been a lesson taught to her at a young age. She never wanted to be surprised. Being unprepared usually brought terror and pain. There wasn't a shiny gift at the end of an adventure, there was disaster. With stiff muscles, Chloe turned to find her father looking down at her disapprovingly.

It took everything inside her not to tremble in fear, but she placed a polite mask on her face before speaking to him.

"I didn't know you would be here," she said, her voice tight no matter how she tried to change it.

"*You* are the one not supposed to be here. *I* was personally invited," he informed her. "I've also noticed you haven't been checking in with me. I would have thought by now you'd have found information to help your brother," he spat cruelly. "But it seems you'd much rather be flirting with the enemy than taking him down. I know I raised you better than that, but I should have learned by now to expect to be disappointed in you."

Chloe was trembling as he finished speaking. She was afraid of falling apart in a room filled with people. She didn't want that to happen, didn't want to be afraid of this man who had terrorized her all her life.

"I'm not doing this," she said as she turned and walked away. She was scared but also filled with a sense of relief at being able to defy the man and have him unable to do a single thing about it. He couldn't take a swing at her in a crowded room because then the world would truly know what a monster he was.

Chloe didn't get far before she felt biting fingers on her arm. She was dragged through a door before she knew what was happening—before she was able to cry out. Not that she would have done that, she realized as her father shut them in a small, dark room where no one would see what was happening.

"What are you doing?" she hissed as she backed away from him. Without the eyes of the crowd on them, his face contorted, his true personality showing through loud and clear.

"I can do whatever I want to you," he snapped, still not yelling at her. He wouldn't want anyone passing the door to hear a commotion and come busting in. That might ruin his prestigious reputation.

"No you can't," she said, trying to be brave. "I'm not here alone. Someone will notice." Chloe could see how her words infuriated the man. He stepped toward her and she shook, but she kept her shoulders back as she faced the giant who loved to torment her.

"Have you lost your damn mind?" he hissed as he cornered her, his hand shooting out and slapping her across the cheek. Her anger and fright didn't allow her to feel the sting of his mark.

"What are you going to do? Beat me so when I walk out of here, I'm black and blue? How would you explain that?" she snapped, hating the tears welling in her eyes.

"I can drag you out of this building and make sure you regret your insubordination," he threatened.

"You can't take me anywhere ever again. I'm not some helpless child you can continue to abuse. Your son risked his life just to get away from you. I've tried my entire life to gain your approval. I've been afraid and cowered because of you. I've been unwilling to take risks in my life. That will never *ever* happen again," she assured him.

"You little bitch," he thundered, apparently uncaring anymore if anyone heard them. "Do you really think I'll allow you to speak to me this way?"

Before she was able to respond, his fist connected with her cheek. Her vision blurred as spots danced before her eyes. She didn't fall like he'd assumed she would, though—like she had done so many times in the past. She stood there, waiting for her vision to clear. When it did, he was looking at her with satisfaction.

She spat at him, turning that satisfaction to shock and then fury.

"You can beat me all you want, you bastard. I still won't ever kneel at your feet again."

The rage in his eyes told her she'd made a mistake. She'd pushed him too far. Even though a room full of people was just on the other side of the door, it would be too late before any of them could get to her. The only satisfaction she had was in knowing he wouldn't get away with it. They would see him exit the room, and then they would find her and know he'd done it.

She smiled, pushing him over the edge.

He lunged at her, and she stared him down, wanting him to see her eyes as he tried to end her life. He was the one to help bring her into the world, and he was more than willing to be the one to take her out of it, too.

Just as his hands were coming up around her throat, the door was thrust open, light shining in on them. Chloe watched in amazement as her father went flying backward, through the open door, landing with a thump on the hard floor.

Then it was Nick standing in front of her, his eyes filled with rage at her father but deep concern for her. He slowly reached out to her, his finger gently running down her cheek, making her flinch at the pain she hadn't even known was there.

"I'm going to kill him," Nick told her as he turned.

Panicking, she grabbed his arm to stop him. Though he could easily have stopped her, he turned back around, his eyes wild as he looked down at her hand.

"Let me go, Chloe," he warned. "I'm furious right now."

Even though she should be terrified, Chloe wasn't afraid, not at all. Instead of letting him go, she pulled him to her and threw her arms around him, holding on tight as she shivered in his arms. She almost expected him to push her away, but he wrapped his arms around her and kissed her cheek.

"I'm sorry, Chloe. I'm so sorry," he told her as his hands gently rubbed her back. She was so close to losing it, but she refused to let herself fall apart.

"It's okay. I'm fine. Just another typical meeting with my father," she said. That was what she was supposed to say.

Nick pulled back and looked into her eyes, the fury in his fading away. He gently cupped her uninjured cheek and rubbed her chin with his thumb.

"No, you aren't fine. That man has hurt you for the last time," he assured her.

She wanted to fall apart, wanted to let it all go and rely fully on him, but she was so afraid if she did just that, she would never stop falling. She had to maintain control. There was a commotion behind them, and only then did Nick let her go, carefully placing her behind him as he took her hand and stepped out of the room.

Chloe's father was getting up off the floor, his eyes furious. The entire room of people circled around, trying to figure out what was going on. Her father shot them both lethal stares.

"Did you see what happened? Nick Armstrong assaulted me," her father thundered.

Nick smiled at him, a cruel smile that sent a shiver down Chloe's back. She clung to his hand as she faced the fury of her father.

"Everyone in this room knows that's not the case. You hit your daughter, left your damn mark on her cheek. This is one assault charge you won't get away with, you piece of shit. I know you did a lot worse to her growing up, but this time you screwed up and did it in a room full of honorable people."

As Nick spoke, two officers walked up. Her father lunged at her and Nick, but the officers stopped him. When he noticed them, he tried to get himself under control, but it was too late.

The party was over. Chloe had to explain what had happened. Nick stayed by her side, her father having been physically removed from the party. People stood back, giving them room, but Chloe was mortified.

When it was all over, she was told she'd have to make an official statement, that she could file charges of assault against the man. She wasn't sure she'd be able to take it that far. At least she didn't have to decide that night.

She and Nick left the party, and he didn't make her discuss it any further. She was grateful for that. She didn't think she had it within her.

That night, Nick took her to bed and pulled her into his arms. She waited for him to strip her bare and take her, but he didn't. He simply held her. It was only then that she finally let herself go and cried until she fell asleep, all while he rubbed her back and told her it would be okay. It would all be okay.

Chloe wasn't sure if it ever was going to be fine. But for this one moment, she really did believe him.

CHAPTER
TWENTY-THREE

Nick walked into his attorney's office with a broad smile on his face. The man looked up at him as if he might be slightly insane. How wrong Paul was. Nick was normally a happy man. His depressed behavior after the accident wasn't at all usual, but he'd suffered the loss of friends, and his career had been put on hold. He'd decided from the very beginning he wasn't going to give into the injuries, but at the same time, he had been downcast about how long the recovery was going to take.

Nick wasn't exactly a patient man. He didn't like limitations—and a shattered kneecap certainly had limited him. But after the past few days of incredible lovemaking with his impossibly beautiful physical therapist, Nick was back to feeling like his old self. Maybe his brothers had been right in saying he'd just needed to get laid.

The thought made Nick smile even brighter. He knew the sex was certainly helping his attitude, but at the same time it was more than the sex. He really liked Chloe. She was sexy as hell, but she was strong and capable and didn't take any crap from him. Nick realized he thought of her as an equal. That wasn't something he could say about too many people.

It wasn't that he thought he was above others—he just held himself to a high standard and didn't allow himself to fail. Not too many were willing to do the same. Nick had no doubt Chloe would go the distance with him. That thought made his smile even bigger.

"What in the hell do you have to be smiling about?" Paul asked when Nick sat down in the chair across from him.

"My leg is feeling great, my arm's almost fully back to top strength, and I have a beautiful woman at my place I plan on enjoying the rest of the day with. There's a lot to smile about," Nick told him.

Paul's lips pressed together as a concerned pucker appeared between his brows. Nick wasn't going to let the man's pessimism affect him. He was in too good a mood. Sure, someone was saying he'd been drinking before the flight. But he wasn't worried about that either. He had friends in the medical industry, and they assured him there would have been something in his system when he'd been rushed to the hospital after the rescue if he'd been drinking. Of course there'd been nothing there.

"Nick, this case is far from an easy victory," Paul told him.

"Haven't you spoken with the staff who treated me after the accident?" Nick asked. Nope. Still not worried, he thought.

"Yes, but it took six hours to find you, another hour before you were in the hospital. You lost a lot of blood, were dehydrated, and severely injured. The other attorney is saying alcohol could have easily been out of your system at that point."

"Paul, my friend, I'm innocent. I was hurt and upset when this all began, upset that someone would accuse me of ever putting my team at risk, but I think I will be cleared of all wrongdoing," Nick said.

Paul's frown deepened.

"Nick, you aren't a stupid man, so pull your head out of your ass," Paul snapped. His words took Nick slightly aback and his smile dimmed.

"It's not that I don't realize how serious this all is," Nick assured him. "It's just that I know when it comes down to it, my commanders, my peers, my friends, and my family will all testify to my ethics. There is one person saying they saw me drinking. I can bring in a thousand who will say that would never happen."

Paul sighed. "The judge has it out for you," he said.

That stopped what Nick had been about to say. He frowned at Paul as he searched his mind for a possible enemy working in the JAG system. He had no clue.

"What's his name?" Nick asked.

"Judge Robert Williams."

"I don't understand. I don't recognize the name," Nick said.

"From what I've found, he has a vendetta against your family. I have also been told—but can't prove this—that he does whatever he's told by Mitch Reynolds."

That stopped Nick in his tracks. The name was too much of a coincidence. "Reynolds?" Nick questioned.

"Yes, and from what I've heard, neither of them like you," Paul said.

"Why?" Nick asked. None of this made sense.

"I don't know what the vendetta is about. Maybe you can speak to your family about this and figure it out, but when we met last week, Judge Williams made it abundantly clear to me that this *would* go to trial, that your name wasn't going to get you out of this one," Paul said.

"My name?" Nick felt as if he were in an alternate universe. "What in the hell does my name have to do with anything?"

"You need to talk to your family. We might be able to get this thrown out if it's a witch hunt," Paul said.

Nick was silent for several minutes as he sat back and tried to fit the pieces of this puzzle together. He had no idea what was going on. He didn't like the feeling.

"Paul, does this Reynolds man have family?" Nick didn't want to ask the question. He was sure it was nothing more than a coincidence. It couldn't be anything else. Even he wasn't that unlucky.

Paul looked at his notes. He didn't show surprise by the question. Nick must be modulating his voice well enough. That was good.

"Yes, he's married, has one daughter, and looks like a son, but *his* name isn't listed," Paul said.

The back of Nick's neck was tingling, and he felt a cold sweat break out on his brow. He didn't like the feeling at all—not one little bit. He also didn't want to ask the next question. But he knew ignorance wasn't an escape. It might work for a short time, but it wouldn't last forever.

"What's the daughter's name?" Now Paul gave him a quizzical look. "Why?"

"Please just give me the name?" Nick said. He found his perfect little world beginning to unravel again. He didn't like it.

"Chloe Reynolds," Paul said.

Nick felt the color leaving his cheeks. The smile that had been on him almost permanently for the past few days might never come back again. Nick believed in things like fate. He even believed in accidents. This was just too much of a coincidence for him to ignore, though. This was bad.

There was a judge who hated him, and *he* had a friend pulling on his coat strings who wanted to see him go down—and that man's daughter had been in his house for nearly a month where she could snoop through his things, spy on him, report back to the enemy. But after what had happened at the party a few days ago he especially didn't want to believe the worst. That man had hit Chloe. But had that all been an act for him to witness? He was terrified to believe it was the case.

Nick ran through his life during the past month. There was nothing Chloe would have found that even remotely indicted him. But that wasn't the point. He'd trusted her—had been falling for her. He'd been thinking she might just be the one he couldn't let get away.

Was it all nothing but a lie? Nick felt worse than he had while waiting to be rescued from the tumultuous sea that had been trying so desperately to pull him under the night of the crash. He felt a pang in his chest he didn't at all understand. He'd trusted her.

"What is going on, Nick?" Paul asked. He'd given Nick several minutes to process whatever it was he was trying to process, but the attorney was now growing restless.

"She's my physical therapist," Nick said quietly.

Paul didn't often react to things, but at Nick's words, his friend and attorney leaned back, his face a mask of shock. It was taking the man a few moments to form words. Now the man knew minutely how Nick was feeling.

"You're sure it's the same person?" Paul questioned.

"Yeah, I have no doubt. I knew before you said the name, I just didn't want to admit it to myself," Nick said.

"How involved with her are you?" Paul asked him.

Nick sighed. "We're sleeping together—I'd say that's pretty involved."

Paul sighed, and then the confusion evaporated and a little gleam entered the attorney's eyes. Nick had no idea what the man was thinking, but Nick was sure he'd want nothing to do with it.

"No," Nick said as he sent a glare the man's way.

"You have no idea what I'm about to say," Paul complained.

"I don't like the expression on your face," Nick told him.

"Well, too damn bad. I've been fighting a losing battle from the moment your case came up. We finally just got the upper hand," Paul said.

"How in the hell do you figure that?" Nick snapped.

"Because she doesn't know that *you* know exactly who she is. You can get information from her. Don't lovers have pillow talk after doing the deed?" Paul crudely asked.

"You're disgusting," Nick snapped.

"I'm also costing you a lot of money, so you should heed my advice."

Nick glared at the man. "I'm not going to continue sleeping with her, so there won't be any damn pillow talk," Nick pointed out.

"Yeah, I have a feeling you will. Don't tell her you know anything. Let it ride, and let's see if the judge will incriminate himself. This could go so much farther than a charge. This might reveal corruption in the JAG offices," Paul said, his voice a bit too excited at the prospect.

"I'm not playing this game, Paul," Nick threatened.

"Don't you feel a bit used?" Paul pointed out, hitting Nick right where it hurt. He wanted to throttle the attorney. Paul smiled. "This can be your chance for revenge."

"I don't want revenge. I want answers," Nick thundered.

"You can get both," Paul told him.

As pissed as Nick was, the seed was planted. And now that Paul had put the idea there, he wasn't going to be able to push it away. His chair scraped back as he shoved away from Paul's desk and stood. He turned to walk away.

"Think about it, Nick. If you blow this, we lose the opportunity."

Nick wanted to tell the man to go to hell. Instead, he paused in the doorway. He couldn't speak, but he finally nodded his head before exiting the office. Nick wasn't sure where he was heading, but he knew he couldn't go back home—not yet. If he went anywhere near Chloe while he was so pissed off, he might do something he would surely regret. Nick felt gutted. There was no other word for it.

He also felt achingly alone. Yes, he could turn to his brothers—to anyone in his family, but the one person he really wanted to go to was the woman he couldn't. His heart ached.

Turning, he began walking to the beach. At least that was a constant in his life. The sea would never let him down. He understood the sea.

He knew better than most that she was unpredictable and moody. He knew she would be honest with him. She could lure him in with her beauty and lulling waves. And then at the first moment she could, and she would, pull him down.

Knowing that about his beloved sea made him realize that he understood something about Chloe as well. She had managed to get to him and then she'd sucked him under. He hadn't been expecting her to turn on him.

CHAPTER
TWENTY-FOUR

It was late in the evening when Nick felt calm enough to go back home. He'd been gone a lot longer than he'd told Chloe he was going to be, and he knew she would be wondering what was going on. He didn't care. Let her wonder. She'd lied to him and he'd been nothing but good to her.

One thing Nick knew for sure was that he wouldn't be able to pull off the act of pretending there was nothing wrong. He'd never been a man who could openly lie. If there was a problem, he'd much rather face it head on. That was just who he was. He didn't want to allow a woman to change that about himself. He wouldn't let that happen.

When he pulled up to his place, though, he found himself sitting in his old Ford pickup truck wondering what he was going to say to her. Was she going to have a smile on her face, her arms open wide to him? Could he resist her if she did?

Somehow he didn't think that would be a problem. Sure, she'd stopped fighting him—for the most part—about their . . . relationship. He couldn't even call it that. They hadn't agreed to anything formal.

Hell, she'd barely agreed to sleep with him without a fight. But they were involved. He wondered how much of it had been an act.

The thought made him want to put his fist through the worn dashboard of his truck. That almost brought a smile to his lips. His brothers made fun of him all the time, that he chose to drive the outdated truck when he had enough money to buy out a car dealership. He didn't care. There were some things a man just didn't mess with—his transportation being the top of that list.

Finally, he decided he needed to look at her face, needed to figure out what she was thinking—feeling. She'd known he was meeting with his attorney that day. Had she been afraid? Had she worried he'd figure out who was behind the accusations sooner, rather than later? Had she realized that he eventually would put the pieces together? Had she been hoping she'd be gone when that happened?

She really should have been out of his home already. He didn't really need her services anymore. He'd just been afraid that the moment he freed her, she would run away and what they had together would be forgotten, so he'd been the one to delay letting her go. Maybe he was just as big a liar as she was. That thought didn't sit too well in his already aching stomach. Walking into the house, he didn't find her. Moving through the large space, he found himself beginning to worry. Had she left? Was she going to be gone before he got a chance to get an explanation from her? He was owed something. But if she were proven a liar, what good would having her around really be?

She was nowhere in the house. He went to her room, and didn't take his first full breath until he saw her clothes hanging in the closet, her toiletries sitting neatly on the bathroom counter. She hadn't left. The only place she could be was the dock. She often went there.

Walking much more quickly than he had when he'd made the first trek down to the dock with her by his side, he glided along the trail. He stopped when he turned the corner, his chest pounding when he saw her there, sitting on the end of the dock, her feet dangling over the edge, drifting in the water.

He wished the sight of her didn't take his breath away—wished she didn't affect him as much as she did. The woman had proven she couldn't be trusted, and though his brain was quite aware of that fact, the rest of his body, though, wasn't quite catching on. He had better pull it together.

Moving again, he saw her shoulders tighten up as he drew near. She was very aware of his presence, just as he always knew when she was near him. It was a blessing and a curse—far more of a curse now that he knew she was connected to his accuser.

Nick sat down next to her. His shoes came off, he rolled his pants up, and he dipped his feet in the water. He didn't say a word. He wanted to know what she was thinking . . . what she knew of his meeting that day.

He might not be able to pull off a deception easily, but he certainly could keep quiet for extended periods of time. Long moments passed with both of them looking out at the sun setting on the smooth water. She didn't reach for him, and surprisingly he didn't reach for her.

What frustrated him more than ever was how much he wanted to touch her—how much he wanted to feel the silky smoothness of her skin. What did she know? That thought repeated through his brain, thundered with every beat of his heart. How much of this was all a joke to her? Had she cared about him at all?

"You were out a lot longer than you thought," she finally said.

He heard the distance in her tone, the voice she used when she wanted to keep a wall up between them. It was the voice she used during his physical therapy sessions, the voice she used when he was flirting and she was trying to keep it professional—it was the voice he wanted to remove from their "relationship."

"Yeah, the meeting didn't go as I expected," he told her. He kept his tone calm, but he felt her stiffen next to him. He wasn't normally guarded. He really had no idea what she might be hearing in his tone. At the moment he didn't care all that much either.

"I don't want to draw this out . . ." she began.

Fury so hot he could actually see a red haze flash before his eyes ran through Nick. He wasn't normally easy to rile up, but after what he'd learned today, this woman who had deceived him was going to try to give him another speech about why they shouldn't be together. Instead of unleashing on her, he held his tongue and waited. She was silent as if she'd expected him to interrupt. He wasn't going to give her the pleasure of doing that. He waited, not touching her.

Nick felt Chloe's eyes on him before she looked away, her gaze focused somewhere out at sea. The moment stretched uncomfortably long.

"I'm not going to lie to you and say I haven't wanted to sleep with you, Nick. What we've been doing together is unlike anything I've ever done before—unlike anything I even knew was possible." She again went silent.

Nick absolutely hated how her words quickened his heartbeat. Paul had suggested she was a liar . . . and who knew what else. He shouldn't be affected by anything she said or did. He shouldn't even allow this conversation to continue. For some reason he did. He was curious. He'd thought he was getting to know her, at least enough to know she was a good person.

"Spit it out, Chloe." Again his words were calm, maintained. She didn't turn to look at him this time. Maybe it was easier for her to face herself if she wasn't looking at him, maybe looking him in the eyes was too much like glancing in a mirror and not liking the reflection gazing back at her.

"We both know this can't go anywhere. Of course in the heat of the moment we both lose our heads, we both forget the roles we've been assigned in life. But the harsh reality of the morning light tells me this is a mistake. No matter how much I might be enjoying our time together, it has to stop. We're in opposite places in our lives and there isn't anything good that will come out of this."

She took a shuddering breath, and Nick wondered if she truly was that good of an actress or if she had broken the rules by engaging with the enemy. He probably wouldn't ever know because, even if he asked her, he wouldn't be sure she'd give him the correct answer—the truth.

"Do you think I'm a snob or that I'm not good enough for you? I'm really confused by your so-called explanation," he said, this time unable to control the frustration and anger from leaking through. She seemed to shrink the smallest bit as she pulled farther away from him.

Nick tried not to care.

"I don't think either of those things," she said with a resigned sigh. "It is what it is. Just because someone might wish for a different outcome, that doesn't mean it will happen. I wanted to ride unicorns over a rainbow when I was a toddler, but no matter how many nights I wished upon a star, that dream didn't come true." She went silent.

Nick waited for her to continue, confused by her cryptic words. When she didn't speak further, he felt confused and his anger grew. He turned to her, even more furious when she refused to look at him.

"Did you seriously just compare sleeping with me to riding a damn unicorn over a rainbow?" he finally gasped. "I don't understand what you're trying to tell me. Good-bye is easy. You simply say *good-bye*, but your words are tangled in knots I can't comprehend."

Nick wished the lighting was better—wished he could see the light in her eyes, try to figure out what she was thinking, what she was feeling. But even if he were gazing directly at her, he had a feeling he would never get the answers he wanted. He was afraid he just couldn't trust her.

What Nick didn't know was what he was going to do with the information he had. He should kick her out of his house right now, go to her father—and the damn judge—and demand retribution. Even knowing this was exactly what he should do, Nick couldn't find himself saying the words that needed to be said.

For some reason, her ridiculous explanation of why she didn't plan on sleeping with him again was like a slap to the face. And since he'd already been kicked in the gut earlier that day, he had little tolerance for it.

Though Nick didn't want to admit it, he'd fallen for this girl. He'd given her a piece of him he'd never before given to anyone. He'd actually started to . . . like her. He wouldn't say it was love. Nick had never been in love before. He didn't really understand what it would feel like. He knew his brothers were in love with the women they'd married, but he'd never asked them how they'd known. Now, none of that mattered anyway. How could he give his heart to Chloe?

"It's getting cold outside. We should get back to the house," he said.

Nick stood up and waited. He didn't hold out his hand to assist her, though he had to shove both hands in his pockets to keep from doing so. He'd been raised to help a lady. And no matter how much Paul had implied that Chloe had proven she wasn't worthy of that title, he still saw her as a woman in need.

Her shoulders were slumped as she continued gazing out at the water. He didn't tell her again it was time to go, he just hovered over her. The discussion wasn't over, but Nick wasn't exactly sure what he wanted to say or do next. But he would feel a hell of a lot better if he could at least see her face.

After several moments, Chloe finally rose. Without looking at him, she began walking up the dock. He followed her, staying about a foot back the entire trail to the house. It felt like the damn green mile.

When they came in the back door, Chloe turned as if she were going to flee to her room. Nick wasn't going to allow that. Without saying anything, he took her arm and steered her into his den. She didn't fight him, but he felt the stiffness of her muscles as she reluctantly followed.

Nick took her to the couch and waited until she sat, then he moved to his bar and grabbed the good Scotch. Without hesitation he poured a glass and swallowed the amber liquid. The soothing numbness made its way down his throat but barely even touched his emotions. He'd probably have to down the entire bottle for that to happen.

"What do you want to drink?" The words were harsh. He didn't care.

"I don't want anything. I would just like to go to bed," she said. He gazed at her as she shifted, her head down, her fingers twisting in her lap.

Nick placed some ice in a glass and poured her some Scotch, then he walked over and handed it to her. She took it with a confused expression. But after he stood over her for a few tense moments, she lifted the glass and took a sip. Her expression soured as the burning fluid made its way to her gut.

"If you're trying to intimidate me, then it's working, Nick," she said after several more moments of silence. "I'm sorry I feel the way I do." The last part came out with a bit of bite. She lifted the glass and forced herself to take another swallow, this time making herself cough. He stood there and waited.

"You're employed by me, aren't you?" he said, his voice deceptively calm again.

His words startled her enough to get her to look up at him this time. Her rounded eyes took in his appearance for the first time, and he saw a flicker of fear in her expression. Maybe his fury wasn't hidden as well as he'd thought it was.

"Well, sort of," she slowly said.

"There's no *sort of* about it. You either are or you aren't. Were you hired to do a job?" Nick hadn't even known he could speak to someone so coldly before this moment. He didn't necessarily like what she was making him become.

"I was hired to *help* you," she said. "But you are fine now. I was going to tell you tonight that there's no need for me to be here any longer." Her words came out in a rush as if she might be afraid she wouldn't say them if she didn't speak quickly.

"The contract isn't up," he told her.

"Nick, you know you don't need my help. You're far enough now to do this on your own," she said on a huff of impatience.

"I say when I think you're done." Damn, his voice was like ice.

"You are just wasting more money by trying to keep me here," she told him with a bit of a glare.

"That's not your call to make, Chloe."

He moved back to the bar and poured himself another drink. The liquor still wasn't calming him, but he feared how angry he'd be without the numbing fluid.

"I'm not your prisoner, Nick. I can leave anytime I want," she informed him.

"Then go. Say good-bye to the deal you have with my uncle."

He was satisfied when he saw her flinch. She needed the bonus she was promised. Probably to use the money to screw over some other man. Why in the hell wasn't he kicking her the hell out of his house and his life? He honestly didn't know.

"I don't think it's a good idea for me to stay," she said.

Nick smiled. It wasn't a smile of friendship and goodwill. It was that of a predator about to strike. He wasn't willing to play the games Paul had told him to play, but he was certainly willing to get something from her before he sent her on her way.

Chloe lifted her glass and downed the rest of the liquid. He could see her nervously swallow as she shifted in her seat. He towered over her before leaning down, boxing her in. She gripped the glass tightly in her hands as he forced her to look at him.

Nick was silent as he read emotions flicker through her eyes: fear but also pain. If only he could rely on what he was seeing, but that was a huge risk. She'd been deceiving him, at least in part, for a couple of weeks. Could she be faking the emotions crossing her features now?

"Nick . . ." His name came out on a sigh. He moved closer. "I don't want to play games with you. I have no doubt it's something I won't win," she admitted.

He grinned at her. Maybe she wasn't as foolish as he'd been thinking she was.

"There's no doubt I'll win," he assured her.

"If you're trying to scare me, congratulations, you've done it," she said.

His smile grew, but there was no happiness in his expression.

"You should be scared, Chloe, you should be very afraid. I'm not even close to being done with you—not by a long shot. I don't like being lied to and I don't lose when I enter into a game. You started something with me, and now you'll damn well finish it."

He licked his lips as she gulped. If only he felt better.

CHAPTER TWENTY-FIVE

From the moment Nick had stepped out of the house, Chloe felt things were going to change—she felt it deep in her gut. The longer he'd been away, the more that feeling had grown. The day had become even worse for her when her father had called. By the end of that telephone call, she'd been trembling so badly she'd had to sit down, fighting tears she wouldn't allow to slip.

But the day had continued to pass and still no sign of Nick. He'd met with his attorney. With him being gone so long, she knew it was a bad omen—knew that he was likely aware of *who* she was. The first thought had been to run. She'd wanted to pack her things and leave.

Something had made her stay, though. She'd been afraid her entire life—afraid of her father's fists, afraid of failing the people she loved, afraid of ending up with the life her father said she deserved. She'd tried to make things better for herself, had gotten an education, had struck out on her own. But no matter how far she tried to get away, she couldn't fight who she was or the family she'd been born into.

So this time she hadn't run. It didn't matter if Nick hated her—that was expected. What mattered was she'd been hired to do a job, and she was doing it successfully. He should have let her go already. He was fine on his own. But for some odd reason, he wanted her around. Maybe he hadn't yet tired of the sex.

If Nick thought he could break her, though, he was very wrong. She'd been broken long ago, and there wasn't anything he could do to her that would make it any worse. If only there wasn't that small sinking feeling in the pit of her stomach telling her how very wrong she was.

She'd grown attached to Nick in the short time she'd been with him. She knew he wasn't responsible for her brother's death. If he were, she would have seen some sort of sign by now. But there was still that voice in her head—her father's voice that told her he might be guilty.

And now she was trapped in front of him, his arms caging her in. She could have gotten away, but maybe she really didn't want to. Maybe she was so messed up from the years of her father running her life, that she truly felt she deserved Nick's wrath. Chloe honestly didn't know.

The thing that terrified Chloe more than anything else was the fear that Nick would take so much from her, there wouldn't be anything at all left. She didn't think there was anything for him to take, but she'd been wrong so many times before. If he truly knew what an empty shell she was, he wouldn't bother with the game he was playing.

She had no doubt he would eventually tire of whatever it was he was doing, though. She had nothing to give him but her body. But maybe that was enough to someone like Nick Armstrong, who already had the world at his fingertips. Chloe was a convenient distraction for him while he spent the required time mending his body. She was the one there helping to set him free. When he was where he needed to be, he would quickly discard her—and that was okay. It was what was expected.

What Chloe had never figured would happen would be the feelings she had developed for him. She had thought when it was all done, she'd walk away the victor, Nick placed behind bars, her heart beginning to heal from the loss of her brother.

She now knew she'd been naïve and foolish. Her father had been wrong and manipulative. She'd been shallow to follow his orders. And who had she thought she was that she could go head to head with Nick? Maybe it had been her last attempt to become the person she'd always dreamed of becoming. But she cared about this man, something she'd never expected, and perhaps she was in love with him, and to him she was nothing more than a convenient lay. She was unsure of so much.

One thing Chloe knew, though, was that even though she could see the fury in his eyes, could understand how angry he was with her, she didn't fear his fists. If Nick thought for even a moment she was afraid he'd hit her, she'd probably send him staggering back on his feet. Instead of that making her feel better, it only made her guilt of ever suspecting him that much worse—because in addition to all his qualities he did have honor.

"I would pay money to know what is going on in that head of yours," Nick growled.

Chloe trembled as his deep voice rumbled through her, his hot breath cascaded across her face, the heat of his body surrounding her in waves. He might pay money to know what she was thinking, but she'd give up everything she had to keep those thoughts from him. He already had too much power over her. There would be no way she'd give him more or hurt him with the truth. It took great strength on her part not to reach out to him. This might be the last time they were so close—it *should* be the last time. She wanted to memorize him, to have something to dream about. It was a foolish thought, but her thoughts were her own and she could have whatever ones she wanted.

And even though she would miss this man when she did leave, she knew she had to leave sooner rather than later. It had grown too complicated. She wanted to scurry away and try, once again, to rebuild her life.

"Maybe I was thinking about the moment I can escape you," she said with just the right amount of bite she knew would infuriate him.

Nick's eyes narrowed as he pulled back from her. His hands trembled as if he wanted to reach out and shake her. Chloe was impressed with his control. She'd be black and blue if she'd said such words to her father. Why had she ever believed her father when he'd said Nick was the reason her brother was dead?

If Chloe truly wanted to cast blame on anyone, it would be on her father. He'd pushed her hard, and he'd tormented her brother. Her dad was the reason Patrick had joined the Coast Guard, that's why he'd taken the dangerous position of being a rescue swimmer. He'd wanted to impress the old man. And in death, her brother had finally managed to do so. So much so that their father wanted someone to be punished.

Nick paced in front of her, tossing his jacket on the floor, his tight shirt hiding nothing as his muscles bunched beneath the thin material. He was furious and confused and she could see he was trying to find the right words to hurl at her. She sat where she was, waiting. She'd earned this tongue thrashing, and she would take it gracefully.

When minutes passed in silence, Chloe sighed. She rose from the couch. He spun around and seared her with a look. She held her head up and faced him. He seemed surprised. Of course he was—he didn't actually know anything about her.

"Just tell me what you need to say," she said. There was strength in her words, though she didn't know where she was pulling it from. Inside she was a trembling mess, but she was tired of showing the world how weak she was.

"How long did you and your father plan on taking me down?" Nick finally said, his voice controlled even if his eyes were wild. This time she wasn't able to hide the tremble that racked her frame.

Chloe opened her mouth to answer him. She was prepared to tell him she'd been a part of the takedown from the beginning, but the words wouldn't come out. She tried again, and her throat remained closed. She couldn't say what she needed to say.

"What are you talking about?" she finally asked.

His eyes narrowed as he glared at her. He leaned in closer and she was afraid, but more afraid of hurting him than of telling him the truth. She didn't want him to keep looking at her with such hatred. It was killing her.

He went still as he stared at her. Complete disbelief lit his features as he searched her face. She understood it. She never had been a good liar. But right now fear overrode everything else.

He moved closer to her as if he were trying to analyze her. She could see how very much he wanted to believe her, but there was mistrust in his expression, too. He knew too much to allow her to get away with the lie, but if he wanted it as badly as she did, then she could understand why there was a part of him willing to let it go. That gave her hope, but she didn't want that hope. It was a lie, and it would come in and get her in the end. How could she ever start over with Nick with a clean slate?

"Please stop, Nick." The tremble in her tone frustrated her. She wanted to be strong now, emotionless. If only she'd learned that lesson years ago, she wouldn't have been hurt so many times in her life.

"I can't seem to stop," he said. There was confusion in his tone.

"I don't even know what that means," she told him as he slowly moved closer to her.

Chloe left her hand out in front of her, as if that could stop him. But there was nothing else she could do. The closer he got, the more vulnerable she felt.

He was slow and steady, making her feel like the zebra being circled by the lion. She wasn't sure exactly when the attack would happen, but she had no doubt it would. She was certainly the prey. Nick would always be the predator.

"I can't explain it," he said with a sigh. "I just can't seem to keep away from you." He moved closer.

"Stop!" The word came out forcefully. He paused less than four feet away. He was so close she could smell his natural cologne, see the laugh lines next to his eyes, practically taste his breath. It was too close for her to think straight.

Chloe was stunned when Nick did as she asked, stopping where he was. When his lips turned up into a smile, she felt her mouth dropping open. She didn't know what to think of this new turn in their crazy night.

"Why are you smiling?" she asked.

If he were yelling and screaming, she would know how to deal with that. With him switching moods so quickly, she was at a loss. His smile grew and then he leapt forward, making her heart thunder.

His arms caged her against the wall, his face leaning down. The look in his eyes was almost wild. Chloe wondered if he'd snapped, if he was about to strangle her. The thought wasn't so much terrifying as depressing. If she were to die right then and there, would anyone even show up at her funeral? Would she be missed? The thought was too depressing to even think about.

"Because I'm a fool," he told her, his hot breath rushing across her lips. Her body began to tremble, and she hated them both for the desire that began to flood her, the desire that overrode every other emotion she was dealing with.

His eyes swept her face before narrowing. A chill ran through her. This wasn't the same man she'd known for the past three weeks—the man whose family adored him. The person boxing her in was a stranger. And damn her, but she still wanted him, still didn't want him to push her away.

"I don't like being lied to. I like being used even less," he said. His words grew more husky. Her heart thundered as she stood motionless against the wall. "I thought you were different, but now I don't know what to think."

"What are you doing, Nick?" she asked, hating the fear in her voice.

"I guess none of it matters. We can both be monsters, and we're still drawn together. I don't understand it," he told her, his lips twisted into a smile that didn't reach his eyes.

"So you think you'll feel better if you punish me?" she challenged.

That wiped his smile away. He seemed taken aback by her words. His body loosened, and his face relaxed slightly. His mouth opened as if he wanted to say something, and then he closed it again. After a long moment he seemed to regain his footing. He moved closer again.

"Do you want me to back away from you, Chloe? Do you want this to stop?" he challenged. One hand moved to her shoulder, and she was still as he ran his finger down her neck, over the top of her breast, and across her nipple, which instantly responded. There was triumph in his eyes as she gasped.

"You're a bastard, Nick," she told him.

"I might be, but that doesn't change the fact that you want me," he told her.

She desperately wanted to deny his words. But they would both know she was lying, would both know it was nothing more than air escaping in a last attempt to save her sanity. She knew if she told him to let her go, he would do just that. And he wouldn't be any worse for the wear if she walked away. Only *she* would be hurting.

So what did that mean? What was she to do?

"Believing in magic doesn't make it real. You either grow up, as you so emphatically told me, and face reality, or eventually you'll crash and burn," he told her.

Sucking in her breath she glared at him. "Are you talking about yourself or me?" she asked.

"I guess that's yet to be seen," he said as if he'd already won his little battle. The problem with a war was that there had to be a loser, and Chloe had no doubt she was the only one to be defeated in this battle Nick had waged.

"I honestly don't know what you're expecting me to do," Chloe told him.

"You took a job. Are you going to see it through?" he asked.

Yes. He'd gone mad for sure. "The job is finished, Nick, and we both know it," she told him.

"Then walk away."

He backed up, leaving her enough room to scoot around him, but not enough space to think properly. He wasn't telling her to leave, but he was giving her the opening she'd thought she wanted.

Chloe told her legs to move, but she stayed glued against the wall. This was her chance to run, to try to gain a bit of freedom. The problem was that she didn't have anywhere worth running to. She hated the man standing before her, and yet she was also drawn to him in a way that didn't allow her to walk away.

"I didn't *think* you were going anywhere," he said. Victory was radiating from him as he stepped forward again, this time his body brushing hers, his lips an inch from her own. This time it was with purpose and desire.

Chloe now knew it was possible to hate and care for a person at the same time. Nick had brought something to life inside her, and she feared she wasn't going to be the one to walk away from it, even if she'd had every intention of doing so. They both knew she wasn't going anywhere.

No matter how much she despised what he was doing to her—to the fragile relationship they'd started—she still desired him, still craved him. She wanted to pull away but she wouldn't.

When his finger softly rubbed her cheek, Chloe realized a tear had escaped. She hadn't even known it was falling. His thumb wiped away the evidence of her weakness before tracing her lip. Something softened in his eyes, but he quickly pushed it away, the hardness she'd been witnessing the past few hours back in place. That was the last tear she would shed in front of him, she vowed.

He left his thumb on her lip, and she opened her mouth. It slipped inside, and she bit down on it with enough pressure to make him feel it. Instead of the gesture angering him, she watched passion flare in his eyes.

Of course. There was no other way for their night to end. Without sex, they were nothing. And sadly enough, she cared about him enough to want him to touch her, to want to feel that closeness she'd never felt with another.

"You have proven repeatedly that I want you, that you can have my body whenever you command. But that's all you'll get of me," she told him, needing to at least make it appear she was using him as much as he was using her.

He smiled, not at all offended by her words. The look on his face called her a liar. She held her chin up in defiance.

"You foolish, foolish woman. You just can't stop lying, can you?" he said, sounding almost amused. "It's not just sex between us. We both know it. Something is burning inside me I've never felt before. And I see the same thing in your face. You can lie to yourself all you want, but don't think I will believe it," he told her.

Chloe was melting. She knew it was the closest she'd ever get to hearing him confess to having real feelings for her. It felt like it was enough. Soon, she vowed, she'd be strong enough to not accept anything less than *everything* from a man. But she wasn't there yet.

"We shouldn't do this right now. Too much has been said—been done." It was a weak attempt, but she had to say it.

He moved in even closer. "No, we shouldn't," he admitted. But then his lips brushed across hers, just a whispering of skin against skin. It was perfect, and yet it wasn't even remotely enough. Chloe shook as he pulled her into his arms, his strength and passion overwhelming her. He pressed his arousal against her, sending heat straight to her center.

She saw the moment he decided he was done talking. And she felt relief. He leaned in and took her mouth, this time without hesitation. Anger, passion, and emotions flowed through his lips, poured through her veins.

Chloe reached up and grabbed him. She was through fighting.

CHAPTER
TWENTY-SIX

Control had come and gone. Nick was lost the moment his lips connected with Chloe's. Though he was sure she had deceived him, was in fact still deceiving him, he couldn't stop himself from wanting the connection with her, wanting to accept the lie.

There was something so vulnerable in the way she looked at him, in the words she so carefully uttered—especially in the things she didn't say. He'd noticed how she'd flinched at the mention of her father, saw the pain in her eyes at remembered memories.

He tried to push past that, tried to tell himself it was an act, that she was still playing a game. But Nick wasn't normally a hard man, and he tended to trust people. This time that trust had the potential to royally screw him, but right now he wasn't so sure.

As Chloe responded to him, wrapped her arms around him and held on tight, he became lost in her embrace, in the smell of her, in the soft sighs escaping her throat. He should pull back, should be the stronger of them both and walk away. But just because he should didn't mean he was going to.

Nick had been reckless his entire life. It's why he didn't fear hovering over a turbulent sea while winds threatened to pull him down. It was why he was the first to rush in as everyone else was running away. And now, he chose to stay because at least for this night he was all in. He wasn't going anywhere, unless it was to a bedroom.

For a brief moment he'd had the misguided notion he could maintain control over himself, but as that tear had fallen down her cheek, as she'd shuddered with helplessness, he'd been lost. She didn't realize how strong a hold she had over him. He would rather keep it that way.

Nick had no doubt she wanted him as urgently as he desired her. It was that desperation that had sent him over the edge of any reasoning. But there was a freedom in the desire. As he allowed his body to take over, his anger faded, his sense of betrayal diminished. There was one sole focus, and that was her—pleasing her, making her cry out, loving her, finding pleasure within each other. He would get lost in her and the anxiety would fade away. And eventually he would be able to let her go.

As Nick delved within her mouth, capturing her—taming her—making her his, his wild thoughts ceased spinning. She whimpered as his hand moved down her back, clutched her butt, and pulled her into his thickness, making sure she was aware of where this was headed. His body was pulsing with an unquenchable desire.

Nick's desperation increased as his fingers wound into her hair. He tugged hard, making her head fall back as he tasted his way down the smoothness of her neck. He couldn't get enough of her smell, her heat, her flavor. He was holding on desperately, too afraid to even think about her pulling away.

She gripped the back of his neck as her body melted against his, fully entrusting herself to him. Euphoria filled him at the trust, the desire, the need she had for him. She opened herself up, inviting him to do with her as he pleased. He became almost frantic as his hands and mouth made a trail across her skin.

Never had Nick lost control like he was losing it at this moment. But he had to bury himself in her, had to complete the connection. His body pulsed with the need to take her, to make them one, to make them inseparable. She was going to destroy him. He had no doubt about it.

Nick's heart thundered as he began tearing at her clothes. Somewhere in the back of his mind, he knew he should slow this down, he knew he should think about what he was doing. But that was the whole point. He didn't want to think anymore. He wanted only to feel.

Even if Nick did attempt to regain control, her desperation matched his own as her fingernails dug into his neck, her teeth bit his jaw, and her cries grew louder. For this moment, at least, they weren't enemies. They were desperate to take their pain away in the only way they knew how.

Their voices echoed through the living room as he gripped her blouse, his lips resting at the luscious *V* between her breasts. His tongue laved her skin. He pulled at her blouse and the material shredded, revealing her black satin bra. Pushing her arms against the wall, he leaned forward and licked the material, her nipples hard pebbles through the thin material.

She tugged on her arms, but he held them tightly as his teeth scraped the satin. When he bit down, her moan vibrated through him, and he added pressure, making her writhe before him.

Nick wanted the material out of the way, but he loved holding her in place. With his teeth, he tugged on the satin, moving it only a tiny bit. That wouldn't do. With a growl, he gripped the small piece of satin connecting the bra's cups and ripped the strap, releasing her beautiful, lush breasts.

Her entire body pushed toward him as he pulled her naked nipple into his mouth and sucked it before swirling his tongue in circles around the orb of her breast. He kissed his way across the deep valley before finding her other tasty bud and sucking it deep within his mouth.

"Nick, please . . . please let me touch you," she cried out, her voice unrecognizable.

In response, he sucked harder, ran his teeth across the swollen flesh, and swept his tongue in circles. She whimpered as she pulled to release her hands. Finally, he kissed his way back up her neck, pressing himself fully against her. He sucked her neck for a moment before trying to calm himself with a deep breath.

The air was scented by her floral fragrance, and it made him light-headed instead of calm. If he didn't have her soon, he would be on his knees begging her for release.

"Do you want me to finish this—to bury myself inside you?" he asked. He hated himself a little for the question.

There was no hesitation on her part. "Now."

He wasn't going to ask twice. With the same urgency he'd been feeling since he saw her sitting down on his dock, her feet dangling in the water, he gripped her pants and tore the button. In seconds, she was leaning against the wall, her skin completely bare to him.

She was vulnerable, needy, her skin flushed and hot. He'd done this to her—only him. As much as she affected him, he affected her just as much. Together they made magic happen—the same magic he'd mocked her for when she'd talked about wanting to ride unicorns. Nick couldn't even begin to think about that. Her words remained a mystery.

Lifting her into his arms, he quickly moved across the room and set her gloriously naked body on the cool leather of his couch. She didn't even flinch as she lifted her arms out to him, her mouth open, her eyes bright, her hands pulling him against her.

In awe of the beautiful display she made, he ran his hand down her perfect body. She was so silky, so firm, yet soft and lush in the right places. He could be happy doing nothing more than trailing his fingers against her skin night and day. When he reached her spread thighs, his fingers trailed down her wet heat.

Her back arched off the couch as she moaned, reaching for his fingers as he pulled away to hover over her without touching. She whimpered her disapproval as she reached for him.

How had he thought he could walk away without touching her again? He really wanted to believe he was doing it because he'd been deceived and he was owed this—owed her devotion to him. But he was the one worshiping her and he couldn't even feel badly about it.

Dropping to the floor, he leaned his head against her stomach and kissed the quivering skin. Her fingers wound into his hair as she trembled at the heat of his tongue and lips. Blazing a path of soft kisses, he reached the tight skin at the top of her heat and licked her, making her cry out as she tugged on his hair.

He'd been molten for the past hour, but as he lazily trailed his tongue down her slick folds, his urgency dimmed. He pushed her thighs apart, gazing down at her perfection. She squirmed before him, and he gripped her hips to hold her still before leaning forward and planting kisses up her center. He sucked her swollen mass into his mouth and swept his tongue over it again and again.

She cried out as he intimately kissed her heat before letting his tongue play in circles. He couldn't get enough of her taste, her smell, her moans of pleasure. He felt her trembling growing, and he thrust his fingers inside her, relishing her quivering flesh as she squeezed him.

"Let go, Chloe," he demanded before sucking her into his mouth.

With a scream, her body tensed before it began shaking. He sucked her flesh all throughout her orgasm, drawing it out as he drank her in. When her tremors settled, he laid his head against her stomach and closed his eyes. He wanted to give her pleasure beyond anything she could feel with another. He wanted it to just be the two of them.

That terrified him because he knew it could never be.

Before Nick was able to think too much more, he rose and quickly discarded his clothing. Chloe's eyes were half lidded, and she wore a pleasured little smile on her lips. He should walk away right now.

She held up an arm, inviting him to her, and he knew leaving had been a foolish thought. There was no way he was walking away—not right then.

With a gentleness he hadn't known he was capable of feeling during sex, Nick climbed on top of her, settling himself between her thighs. He pressed himself against her, pushing his hips against hers.

As the tip of him pushed inside her, her eyes shot open, and he found himself getting lost in her gaze. Her expression was glazed and happy, and desire was still sparking there.

With a slow, burning thrust, he buried himself within her. She gasped as her back arched up, her arms coming around him to pull him closer. Their lips connected, and he felt complete.

Time stopped having any meaning as he pulled back and slipped inside her body. Their gazes remained locked together as he slowly built their passion, their skin flushed, their bodies tightening. He didn't want it to end, feared what would happen when it was over.

But as he moved within her, there was no stopping the climax. She squeezed him and her moan was lost on his tongue. He let it all go, filling her with his seed, collapsing against her as he gave her everything he had.

Nick was spent. The chaotic, emotional roller-coaster ride he'd been on the entire day had ended in a way he hadn't expected. Shifting to his side, he pulled her into his arms while grabbing the blanket off the back of the couch.

He closed his eyes with her head tucked beneath his chin. All of their problems would be there when they woke. For this moment, he wanted to think only of the pleasure they'd given one another. Tomorrow would come soon enough.

CHAPTER TWENTY-SEVEN

Nick and Chloe didn't say a single thing after they woke up. He was almost scared of what her opinion of the events would be, and he figured it might be the same for her. Normally Nick wasn't a man to fear anything. But when it came to Chloe, he had to admit he was afraid of losing what they'd created.

Sitting in the kitchen, he looked up when she came into the room, moving slowly to the coffeepot and pouring herself a cup. Her shoulders tensed before she turned to face him. They gazed at one another, questions silently blazing across the space between them with no words uttered.

Nick wasn't sure how to break the moment. Damn, he hated feeling this way. When the phone rang, Chloe jumped. Nick just barely managed to keep himself from doing the same.

"Nick," he said as he picked it up.

"It's Paul, we have a meeting with the judge in three hours," Paul said without bothering with hellos.

"About?" Nick asked. His eyes never strayed from Chloe's. He couldn't read whatever it was in her eyes.

"It seems your uncle Sherman has managed to schedule it."

"You aren't inspiring confidence, Paul. Do you have a little more information?" Nick snapped.

"Just be at the courthouse in two hours so we can meet beforehand," Paul told him.

"Got it." Nick hung up. Chloe hadn't moved.

"I should get going, Nick," she said, her tone void of emotion.

"Maybe," he said. The single word made her flinch, and he found himself feeling a bit guilty about it, though he didn't understand why. There was no reason for that. "I have an appointment at the courthouse. I'd like you to come with me."

Nick was almost as stunned as she obviously was when those words came out of his mouth. Why was he taking her down there? Especially with an almost certain knowledge she was working with her father. Maybe it was because a part of him wanted it to not be true.

"I don't think that's a good idea, Nick," she said softly.

"Is there a reason you shouldn't go with me?" he prodded.

She looked down, and he wanted to demand she look him in the eyes, but he forced himself to stay where he sat. She took in a few deep breaths before looking up again, but this time she didn't quite meet his gaze.

"No reason," she said, her cheeks turning a bit red as she chewed on her bottom lip.

"Good, then it's settled. I'm going to shower." He got up and walked away before he said something he might regret later.

Nick avoided Chloe until it was time to go. He was a little surprised when he found her at the front door, clutching her purse in front of her as she shifted from foot to foot. This time she didn't argue when he walked to his old reliable truck and held open the passenger door. Instead, she slipped inside, practically pressing her body to the door when he came around to the driver's side.

Though the ride there was uneventful, Nick's muscles were tense as they parked and made their way inside the marble building. Chloe walked beside him, silent and chewing on her lip. Maybe he'd insisted on her joining him because he feared she wouldn't be there when he got back. It was inevitable that was going to happen anyway, but for some reason he wasn't yet ready to let it happen.

"Nick." The familiar voice of his uncle calling out to him pulled him from his thoughts.

Sherman, Cooper, and Mav were walking toward him. He met them in the middle, and they exchanged hellos, the atmosphere full of tension.

"What's going on, Uncle Sherman?" Nick asked.

"Let's have a chat in private," Sherman said.

"I'll go and get coffee," Chloe told him.

Nick didn't try to stop her as he moved in the other direction with his uncle and brothers. They found a waiting room, and Mav shut the door once they were all inside.

"The suspense is killing me, so it would be great if someone would start talking," Nick said.

"You'd better sit down," Sherman advised.

"I don't want to sit down," Nick thundered. "Just spit it out."

"Okay," Sherman said. "I've been able to speak to your brothers already, but since you're the one being attacked I began doing some digging since you told us about the allegations against you. You already know your grandfather was a horrible man, but it seems he was even worse than I really knew."

"What does our grandfather have to do with any of this?" Nick asked. This hadn't been what Nick was expecting.

"Unfortunately, it has everything to do with what's happening to you," Sherman said. "Your grandfather was in the military for a short time in his younger days."

"So what? We all know that," Nick said.

"He was in a unit with Robert Williams and Mitch Reynolds." The bombshell dropped and Nick waited.

"And I'm guessing things didn't go well?" Nick said.

"Apparently, the three of them committed a crime together, which your grandfather and Robert Williams got off scot-free for, while Mitch Reynolds received a dishonorable discharge. Your grandfather got killed before Reynolds could seek revenge, but he's been blackmailing Judge Williams ever since, has the man in his pocket."

"Why come after me?" Nick asked.

"Because the man is filled with hate and vengeance. He tried to go after your father and was never successful, so he set his sights on you. We've found enough evidence to meet at Judge Hampton's chambers. Neither Mr. Reynolds nor Mr. Williams knows what's about to happen, but your case is getting dismissed. The witness came forward and said he was bribed by Mr. Reynolds to testify against you."

Nick sat silently for several moments as he processed what Sherman was saying. It was a hell of a lot to take in. He should be feeling joy and relief, but all he felt was an ache that Chloe might have been a part of this conspiracy.

"Nick, your attorney is waiting, but I wanted to be the one to tell you," Sherman said as he patted his shoulder.

"We better get this over with then, shouldn't we?" Nick said, his tone devoid of emotion.

"Brother, this is tragic that someone has held a vendetta against us so long, but you're about to be exonerated of all charges. I would think you'd be a little happier," Mav said.

No one was smiling. "I think Chloe was a part of all of it," he finally admitted.

"How?" Cooper asked.

"She's Reynolds's daughter." The words were almost as quiet as the room after they were spoken.

"Damn," Mav said.

"Yeah," Nick agreed.

"Have you asked her about it?" Sherman logically asked.

"Not really. I'm afraid of the answer," Nick admitted.

"Since when have you ever been afraid of anything?" Mav pointed out.

"Since I fell for the girl," Nick said.

"I think you need to get answers before you make any judgments," Sherman advised.

"Let's get this hearing over with, and then I'll go from there," Nick said.

"That's a good idea," Cooper agreed.

They left the room, sober and silent.

CHAPTER
TWENTY-EIGHT

Chloe was waiting in the chairs outside the judge's chambers when they all walked out. His brothers wore smiles of victory, and Sherman patted his shoulder. They all turned to spot Chloe there, and the smiles fell away. She looked to the ground.

Even though victory was at hand, Nick had a feeling of dread that wouldn't go away. His brothers, Paul, and Sherman walked away to give them privacy. They were barely around the corner when officers came out with both Judge Williams and Mitch Reynolds handcuffed.

"I bet you enjoy seeing this, don't you?" Reynolds snapped at Chloe. Her head shot up and she looked at her father with both fear and hope.

"You've been arrested?" she said.

"It won't last," he thundered as he tugged on the officer. "You'll all pay." The officers dragged the two men away. Finally, Nick and Chloe were alone.

"Why did you want me here, Nick?" she asked as she rose to her feet and moved over to him.

"Because I think it's time you tell me the truth," he said. One part of him insisted on having the answers he needed, the other part wanted to bury his head in the sand.

Chloe searched his face for several moments before tears filled her eyes. That was the moment he knew everything was about to fall apart.

"I did know what was happening, Nick," she whispered. He tensed. He was no longer going to be able to deny her involvement in this if she was finally willing to tell him. His heart was aching.

"Explain," he said, his voice so quiet she had to lean in to hear him.

"My brother, Pat Edmond, was your rescue swimmer."

"But . . ." He went silent. That hadn't been what he'd expected her to say at all. It made no sense. He thought he'd already learned everything he was going to learn.

"My brother hated our father. He left when he was eighteen, changed his name. He kept in contact with me, but he didn't want anything to do with the old man. Or he told me that, but I still think he wanted his approval. I think he even changed his name to our mother's maiden one to get a reaction. When our father wouldn't even react to that, Pat joined the Coast Guard and took the most dangerous job he could find. Because of that he lost his life." She ended on a sob, but Nick watched as she tried pulling herself together.

"I didn't know," he finally said.

He took a step closer to her, and she backed away. Anger filled him. He'd been the one lied to, so why was she the one backing up? Maybe it was shame. She *should* fear that.

"I didn't kill your brother, Chloe. I'm sorry you lost him," Nick said as he took another step toward her. This time she didn't move.

"It doesn't matter, Nick. I lied to you, and you have your own secrets. I never should have taken the job, never should have agreed with my father. If you think hurting me will help you get revenge on him, you'd be wrong. He hated my brother, and he hates me even more. Both of us have been a disappointment to him our entire lives. He expects perfection, and we never could live up to what that meant in his eyes."

She spoke in a monotone. He could see this wasn't a great revelation. It was just simple truth. It didn't really matter in the end because there would be no winners. Her father would go to jail, Pat still had lost his life, and Nick and Chloe would go on with their lives, likely separately.

Nick's emotions were flowing through him. He felt pain and betrayal. But he'd known it was coming so it wasn't a shock. He almost hated her for admitting the truth. That made no sense whatsoever.

Even with all he'd already known, Nick was still thunderstruck as he gazed at Chloe. After all they'd been through together, he couldn't believe she'd been working for the enemy—that she'd been trying to take him down the entire time he'd thought she cared about him.

To her credit, Chloe stood there, tears streaking down her cheeks as she faced him. Her shoulders were back and she refused to look away. She wasn't going to hide from him anymore. Still, nothing could make this right—not in his book.

"I didn't know you when this began. All I knew was who I'd been told you were. By the time I figured out you weren't that person, it was too late, I was in too deep," she said, her voice hitching.

Rage filtered through him.

"So honesty and ethics mean nothing to you?" he thundered as he got his bearings. She winced at the fury of his tone. He felt a bit of guilt when he saw the look of pain cross her face, but he reminded himself she'd been putting him through hell with no remorse.

"I was doing what I thought was right, Nick," she told him. Finally, she reached out for him, and this time he was the one who took a step away. If she touched him he might lose it.

"I want you gone from my house within the hour. By the time I get home, I don't want a single trace of you left behind."

Her tears fell even harder at his words. Her hand slid to her side, and her shoulders slumped. She was defeated and she knew it. Nick wasn't sure if he wanted her to fight for them or not. There was too much anger raging through him.

"Nick, please understand . . ." She trailed off. What could she say, he thought snidely.

"I should have your credentials revoked," he snapped.

Her eyes widened and a new fear entered her eyes. He knew what her career meant to her, knew how much time and effort she'd put into it. It was a low blow, but he was pissed.

"Please don't do that. I never once tried to impede your care," she told him.

"What about my mental health? Does that mean nothing to you?" he growled. He took a threatening step toward her. She stood her ground and took the lashing almost as if she felt she deserved it. Maybe she did—maybe she didn't. He couldn't think clearly enough to know the difference.

"Yes, of course. But I didn't know. I was hurting, too. It was my brother on that helicopter with you," she said with a hiccup.

"And don't you think I question myself every single day?" he yelled. "Don't you think I miss my crew? I would have gladly sacrificed my life if it would have meant bringing back my team."

"I know that now. But at the time I didn't," she sobbed.

"You could have asked me. You could have taken the time to talk to me, instead of making your damn assumptions. Now, we all lose and the memories of my crew were drug through the damn mud because of your family vendetta."

He took a step back, afraid he was going to reach out and shake her. He shouldn't even be thinking about this anymore. The past week had put him through the ringer, and he was done with it all.

"I'm sorry. I'm so sorry," she said, her voice barely above a whisper.

"Just go, Chloe. Get the hell out of my life."

He turned and walked away, her sobs almost in tune with his steps. When he made it around the corner, he punched the wall, blood instantly leaking out of his knuckles from the force of his hit.

"That's not going to help."

The quiet voice made him spin around. His thunderous expression did nothing to intimidate his uncle, who was looking at him with bemusement.

"This isn't the right time to talk to me, Sherman," he snapped.

"Don't you dare talk to me like that, boy," Sherman told him, steel running through his voice.

Nick instantly backed down. He loved his uncle, and no matter how angry he was, he wouldn't take it out on him. Not after everything Sherman had done for him and his brothers.

"I'm sorry," he said, some of his anger draining. He could feel blood dripping from his fingers. He didn't care. He'd rather feel physical pain than the suffocating pressure pinching his heart. "I just thought she was different. I actually thought she might be the one," he admitted.

"I think she is," Sherman told him.

Nick looked up in shock. "How can you say that after what her family did to me—after what *she* did to me?" he asked.

Sherman smiled at him, that secret smile that showed a wisdom that could only come to a person through time and patience. He stepped closer to Nick and patted his shoulder.

"Have you ever made a mistake, Nick?" he asked, raising his brows.

Nick wanted to say, hell no, but he nodded his head. "Of course I've made mistakes, but I haven't made ones so epic that I dragged a person's name through the mud, a person who I professed to care about," he said.

"Chloe didn't know you, didn't know our family. All she knew was that your grandfather was an evil man who put her family through hell. Then she lost her brother while you were flying the helicopter. She didn't know her father had talked that man into lying. She thought he was speaking the truth. What if it had been one of your brothers who had died, and to your knowledge a person's reckless actions were responsible?" Sherman pointed out. "Would you rest until the guilty paid?"

Nick hung his head as a whole new rage flew through him. "If someone were responsible for the death of one of my brothers, I would tear them apart with my own hands," he said through clenched teeth.

"So with the information Chloe had, don't you think she acted accordingly?" he asked.

The rage instantly died as Nick felt hopelessness filling him. He didn't know how to respond to that question.

"I don't think I can forgive her," Nick admitted.

"Do you love her?" Sherman asked him.

Nick looked into his uncle's eyes before he turned away. His memories flashed over the past six weeks, over the laughter and tears, over the moments of just the two of them, over his need to be with her, noticing her smile, her laugh, wanting to bring those two things out more in her.

"I really thought I was falling in love with her," he said.

Sherman was quiet for several moments. People passed them, but no one said a word, they just went on their way. Nick was grateful for that. He wasn't in the mood to make polite conversation or be congratulated on his hearing.

"There are people out there who think I was drunk, who think I killed my crew. Even if I was developing feelings for her, she tried to ruin me," he said.

"Oh, posh," Sherman said with the wave of his hand.

Nick looked at him with confusion. "It's not something to brush off," Nick insisted.

"No one believes you did anything wrong. They know what happened. They know a grieving family was trying to find a reason they would never see their boy again. Over time, this will all go away. As for the girl . . . she will go away, too. You have to figure out what you feel, because if you don't stop this, she will be gone forever, and the love of the right woman doesn't come around too often."

"I can't forgive her," Nick said again.

"Then maybe you don't deserve her," Sherman told him.

Nick's fury rose inside him again, but Sherman simply shook his head and walked away. Nick wanted to chase after his uncle, demand he take those words back. It was Chloe who had proven she didn't deserve him, not the other way around. Why would Sherman say such a thing?

Nick decided he couldn't be in the courthouse any longer. He had to get out of there, had to go somewhere, anywhere where he could think without interruptions. As he rounded a corner, he saw Mav and Cooper speaking by the front door. They were probably waiting for him.

He slipped out the side door. He'd had enough advice from family for the day. It was time for him to hide away and figure out what he was feeling. Sherman's words wouldn't quit spinning around inside his head.

Damn the old man.

CHAPTER
TWENTY-NINE

"What in the heck is wrong with people that they would choose to go through this multiple times? I mean really? How do they bear it?" Chloe asked. There were no more tears left for her to cry, nothing else she could say, but somehow she was still managing to speak. It had been a month since Nick had pushed her from his life, and that month had been the slowest she'd ever felt time move.

She'd decided to make a stand with him, had waited at the house overnight, but he hadn't shown. That's when it had truly sunk in that he was finished with her. He'd been there for her when her father had punched her, had held her while she'd fought those demons, but knowing she'd been partly responsible for charges being filed against him had been too much. She didn't blame him. She just hurt that she'd lost him.

Since her crying jags had stopped, numbness had settled over her. She didn't hurt quite as badly on a daily basis, but she also wasn't able to feel joy or much of anything really. She went about doing her job, and she existed from hour to hour. She couldn't figure out why anyone would choose to fall in love. There was too much risk that it would all fall apart, leaving a person feeling the way she did right then.

"I know you feel like crap now, but I swear to you that the pain will go away," Dakota said. "It's either going to all work out and he'll coming running back to you, begging for you to forgive him for being such a blind fool, or you will find someone much better than him. Because if he doesn't figure out his life is meaningless without you, he's a fool and doesn't deserve your love."

"Nope. I'm done with the whole love thing. I gave it a shot, and it didn't work out. I refuse to ever fall in love again," Chloe told her with conviction.

"Ah, sweetie, don't give up on love. That's what life is all about. It sucks when it ends, but I don't believe there's a greater goal in life than falling in love and feeling that emotion that only one other can make you feel. It's too incredible," Dakota told her.

"The pain is so much worse than the feeling of love," Chloe emphasized.

"It feels that way now because you're focused on the pain. But we're not meant to be alone. We are supposed to be with someone who cherishes us. Too many times, people settle because they don't want to be alone, but being with the wrong person is just as bad as having no one at all because you'll always ache for something more. Don't give up on love, but don't give up on Nick, either. We need a champion in our corner, and I think he is yours. He's already proven that. He was hurt, and justifiably so, but he will get his head together. However, if he takes too long, I can go kick his ass if you want," Dakota suggested.

"I love you so much, Dakota," Chloe told her. "And even though these are all things you must say to maintain the best-friend code of honor, it's still very nice to hear them anyway."

"Take your time to feel better about you. You can't be with him because you feel it's the only option. But know it's his honor to be with you, not the other way around. You are so special and amazing, and just because you went through hell, you feel that you need to hide yourself, but don't do it anymore. Realize your own strength and relish in it."

Chloe didn't know how she'd ever lucked out enough to have Dakota as her best friend, but if she had to give up everything else in life, she could, and survive through it. She wouldn't make it without Dakota, though. She climbed from her seat and walked to her, throwing her arms around her, and fought off tears.

"I can't believe I ever wondered what love was like," she told Dakota. "Because I freaking love you to death. *You're* my soul mate," she said with a chuckle.

"Damn straight I am," Dakota said, tears in her voice. "And your soul mate wants you to have everything you've ever dreamed of having." Dakota pulled back and smiled at her. "Now enough of this pain-filled month. We're going to laugh like there's no tomorrow and do that dance thing people speak of."

Her crooked smile and her mucking up of the most famous of motivational quotes made Chloe laugh out loud. It felt good to smile.

"I promise I'm done with my pity party. What was I thinking?" Chloe said, trying to appease her friend.

"We don't think when we're hurting, we react. But I promise you, if we fake it for long enough, we create a new reality. So every morning you get up, you tell yourself it's a beautiful day, that the world is full of fun and adventure, and that the man of your dreams is going to show up with roses in his hand and sweep you off your feet. Then one day, it becomes reality," Dakota said.

"So if I wish hard enough, Ian Somerhalder will be on my doorstep with roses?" Chloe said with a dramatic sigh.

"If you wish it, he will come," Dakota told her with a waggle of her brows.

"Oh, Dakota, my dreams are finally coming true," Chloe said, her laughter becoming more real by the minute.

"Thatta girl." Dakota did a little dance around her, and Chloe rolled her eyes.

"I just need to breathe in and breathe out, and it really is going to get better. I told myself I would never be kicked again, and this has felt like I was kicked in the gut. That's why it's been so hard. But I truly am feeling better just having you here with me," Chloe assured her.

"Maybe we should just talk about my lack of a love life, and then we can both feel sorry for *me*," Dakota suggested.

"It really is sad for the rest of us normal folk that you haven't managed to settle down," Chloe said with a frown. "If a goddess such as yourself can't manage to find a man, I'm a hopeless case."

That was something Chloe had never really thought about before. Dakota was beautiful inside and out with her stunning dark hair, bright green eyes, and pixie-like frame. She was a dancer for the Seahawks on top of everything else she did. How in the world was she single?

"I'm alone by choice," Dakota assured her. "Why would I settle down with a frog when the right toad is out there?"

Chloe laughed. "It's a prince, you dork. You kiss the frogs to make them a prince."

"Oh, whatever," Dakota said with a wave of her hand. "Same thing."

"I love the fact that you just don't care. I am vowing from here on out to be just like you," Chloe said with conviction ringing in her voice.

"Oh, honey, if you want to be like me, you're setting yourself up for failure. I'm a mess," Dakota assured her.

"Then you're the kind of mess I dream of being," Chloe insisted.

"I'm erratic, and it's rare when someone holds my attention. I'm in love with football enough to slide into a slinky little outfit and strut myself on television during freezing cold nights, and since I can lift more weights than the average guy, I sort of intimidate them," she said with a sigh.

"You can lift more than the football players?" Chloe said with a mocking glance.

"Well, those aren't the average guys," Dakota said with a laugh. "And according to the press, we cheerleaders warm their beds nightly, so *I* would know."

This made Chloe laugh again. She knew her best friend, and she was anything but the kind of woman she was describing herself to be.

"Need me to kick their asses?" Chloe said, repeating Dakota's earlier offer.

"Maybe. I'll let ya know."

"Take me shopping. I think it's time to get the heck out of this house," Chloe said, and Dakota's eyes lit up. Chloe had said the magic words, ensuring her best friend would stop all talk of love.

"You know the way to my heart, woman," Dakota told her as she rushed to grab her purse.

Chloe could put on a smile and pretend to be happy. She'd done it for years. In time she knew her best friend was right, knew that she would truly believe it. Until then she was going to fake it 'til she made it.

CHAPTER THIRTY

Nick sipped his brandy as he ran a hand through his hair. Sleep had been a thing he'd once actually enjoyed. Sure, being part of the Coast Guard meant he could wake at a moment's notice, but since he'd walked away from Chloe, he was lucky to get a couple hours at a time.

His dreams were filled with the woman, and each time he'd wake up reaching for her. He'd been hoping he'd forget her, hoping she would become nothing more than a distant memory. So far that wasn't happening.

His brothers had called him every kind of fool, but he was stubborn, hadn't budged, not even when his favorite uncle had looked at him with disgust. His hair was too long, and his temper too short. Life pretty much sucked.

His captain was being an utter ass, still not letting him come back to work. He said that Nick's physical injuries might be healed, but he certainly wasn't mentally ready to get back in the chopper. Nick didn't know what the hell he'd meant. He'd yelled at the captain, and that hadn't helped his case. He'd been asked to leave until he got it together. His life, in other words, was in shambles.

Taking another drink, he leaned back in his chair. Suddenly, his door was pushed open so hard it slammed against the wall. Jumping to his feet, he got ready to do battle when a wisp of a woman stormed into the room, not even remotely afraid of the hulking man in fight mode. When his vision cleared he saw it was Dakota.

"Dakota?" he questioned. Maybe he was seeing things.

"I have a message for you," she said, rage practically pouring from her veins.

He was so taken aback by her words, he relaxed his stance and simply gazed at her in shock.

"What in the hell are you doing here?" he asked, this time calmer.

The small woman glared at him before she pushed him. She actually used enough force to knock him back a step before he caught his balance. Nick was slightly impressed even in his irritation over Dakota trying to push him around.

"My best friend is in pain, and it's all because of you, you . . . you . . . miserable pig," she sputtered, so angry she was having a difficult time speaking.

"What?" He was even more confused. "Is she okay?" His chest tightened with fear. Nick's short nails dug into his palms as he clenched his fists.

"No! That's what I'm saying. She's not okay. I've been trying to convince her for a month that you're either really stupid, or you're not good enough for her. She can't seem to believe either. So she cries all the time, but then puts on a fake smile when she knows I'm watching. I'm her best friend, and I can't help her, but you had zero trouble ripping her heart from her chest."

This wasn't the first time Nick had heard insults about the way he'd treated Chloe, but it seemed to be the first time he was listening. Maybe because it was coming from such a tiny package or maybe because he missed the woman so damn much. Either way he was trying to make sense of what he was feeling. The tiny woman pushed him again, and Nick almost smiled.

"Would you quit doing that? For such a small thing, you have quite the oomph," he told her.

That made Dakota's eyes narrow as she took a threatening step closer to him. He held up his hands. He was really trapped here. It wasn't like he could defend himself against her. He'd break her in two.

"You have put my best friend through hell. I should tear you apart limb from limb," she said, moving forward again. All Nick could do was retreat. She kept speaking. "You've taken the zeal out of her life, made her a different person. You're a selfish pig."

"She lied to me," he said, the same words having been repeated so many times, he felt like a broken record.

"Get the hell over it," she yelled.

"Just like that?" he said with sarcasm.

"Yeah, you're a big boy, put on your . . . your big boy, um . . . shoes on," she finished.

Nick laughed. He couldn't help it. The sound shocked him so much he jumped. He hadn't heard his own laughter in so long he didn't recognize it.

"What are you laughing at?" she thundered.

"Sorry," he said, controlling himself. "Don't you mean put your big boy *pants* on?"

"You're *seriously* correcting me when I'm about to beat you down?" she gasped.

"I'm not too worried about you hurting me," he told her. She moved forward and he continued to retreat.

He held up his hands. "Look, this isn't a fair fight. I can't hit a woman," he said.

"Scared?" she challenged.

He realized she was serious. That made him have to fight not to laugh again. This was one hell of a tough woman. If he weren't already in love with Chloe, he might have asked her out on a date.

His face fell at the thought. His muscles felt like they'd gone to jelly, and he was grateful there was a wall behind him when he sagged against it. Dakota stopped her pursuit as she looked at him quizzically.

"Are you having a heart attack?" she asked, not seeming particularly sympathetic if he was.

"No," he said, the word barely above a whisper.

"Then what is wrong with you?" she asked.

"I . . . I love her," Nick gasped. He felt as if his heart was pounding out of his chest as he said the words. Dakota glared at him. He looked helplessly at her. She didn't seem at all understanding that he was having a serious issue. "My chest hurts. I might be having a heart attack after all," he said, actually frightened.

She rolled her eyes, and he realized he was going to die with Chloe's mean best friend standing there watching. His legs gave out, and he sank to the floor. That was dangerous in front of this woman. She was going to destroy him now that he was so weak.

"You aren't having a heart attack, you moron. You're actually allow-ing yourself to feel real emotions," she said with a huff, though all the bluster had rolled away from her as well.

"*This* is because I said I love her?" he gasped. "Why would anyone want to fall in love if it feels like this?"

"Because it doesn't hurt when you own up to your feelings and confess them," she said with another eye roll.

"Are you enjoying this?" he asked, irritated at anyone seeing him this way.

"A little bit," she admitted, and then she smiled. "You've put my best friend through hell, but seeing as you're going through a lot of hell yourself, that makes me feel better. Besides that, I can see that you're going to make it up to her."

The last words came out as more of a threat than anything else. Nick smiled as the tightness in his chest began to ease. Maybe he wasn't going to die. Maybe he'd get the chance to make things right with Chloe. That would be a miracle at this point.

"What do I do?" he asked.

She looked at him as if she wasn't quite sure if he was honestly asking. He gave her his best trust-me smile and inwardly crossed his fingers.

"You run to her and beg with everything you have for her to take you back. You get down on your hands and knees and tell her you've been a fool, apologize for everything, even the stuff that's not your fault, and you pray she will forgive you and let you back into her life," she said.

He stared at her in a moment of confusion.

"I have never in my life gotten down on my knees," he said before he smiled. "Unless it was for the right reasons."

Dakota slugged him in the arm and he glared at her. She gave him the look right back, not even a little intimidated.

"If you're unwilling to do all it takes, then you sure as hell don't deserve her and you should just stay away," she told him.

She wasn't kidding. He could see it in her eyes. Why was it that everyone kept telling him he didn't deserve her? Maybe there was some truth to it.

Nick leaned his head back against the wall and thought about it. Was he willing to give up his pride for Chloe? Without hesitation he realized he was. He would do anything for her. He didn't want to keep existing in a world where she wasn't a part of his life. She'd stormed in during the worst possible time and had made the sun come out again. How had he not realized that much sooner?

"Tell me where she is," he demanded as he leapt to his feet. Dakota scrambled to hers, not liking the serious height advantage, though it didn't help much when she was up, not even with her heels.

"Why should I tell you?" she asked. She was analyzing him, and he realized he had to be open with her.

"Because I love her enough to do whatever it takes," he assured her.

She looked at him so long and intensely he began to squirm in front of her. He didn't want to mess this up. He could find Chloe, but he didn't know how long it would take him. And given the way he felt at the moment, he didn't want even one more day to go by without her in his arms.

"Please," he said, the word never coming out more heartfelt.

She sighed. "If you mess this up, then you're going to have *me* to deal with," she threatened.

Nick didn't tell her he found that amusing. He also sympathized with whatever man was brave enough to have to deal with her. She'd be a handful. He cringed. She glared. If she even knew the thought he'd just had, he'd get his ass seriously kicked.

Dakota took a piece of paper from her purse and wrote down an address. "She'll be here tonight." She held on to the paper as he gripped it. Their eyes met, and understanding passed between them.

Finally, Dakota let go of the paper. Then without saying another word, she turned around and exited his house. She didn't bother shutting the door. Nick chuckled. Dang, she'd been a whirlwind. And since he planned on marrying Chloe, he guessed Dakota was going to be a part of his life. That was a terrifying thought.

Nick quickly went and made a cup of coffee. He slammed it down before making a second. Then he rushed to his room. He had to clean himself up before he could go find Chloe. If she saw him in the state he was in, she'd most likely run in the opposite direction.

Of course that didn't matter much. He wouldn't ever be such a fool as to let her go again. Nick smiled as he shaved. He was going where his heart was leading him—and he felt good about it.

CHAPTER THIRTY-ONE

Chloe sat in the background as people laughed and talked, drinking and having a great time. Dakota's family was a bit crazy, but they were loving and wonderful, so much nicer than her own. They'd embraced her from the very first moment Dakota had brought her home with her, and they'd been wonderful to her ever since.

Even though she normally loved Dakota's huge family get-togethers, she was trying desperately to keep her smile in place this time. She was doing better, much better, in fact, than the previous few weeks, but it still felt like a piece of her was missing. And because of that, she was faking a lot more enthusiasm than she normally would.

She felt alone and wanted to go home, but Dakota had made her promise she would come. Maybe in an hour or so she could escape without it looking like she was running away. She'd have to wait and see. For now, she was there, and she was nodding at all the right times and laughing when expected. She was getting very good at that. Maybe she should take up acting as a second career choice.

It was just so difficult when she was in love with a man who didn't want to be with her. The sooner the emotions dwindled and died, the sooner she would feel better. It would happen in time. Dakota had assured her of that. She almost wished she'd never met him. But to wish that would be to take away her memories, and there was nothing worth taking those away. She'd rather suffer.

When it was safe to get up and move away, she feigned thirst and went to the large bar to order a glass of wine. Then she snuck down the hallway and slipped into Dakota's bedroom. Her friend was playing a wild game of Twister and most likely wouldn't notice her absence. She hoped at least. She was wrong. It didn't take two minutes for Dakota to hunt her down.

"You aren't having fun, are you?" her friend said with understanding eyes.

"Of course I am," Chloe assured her. "I just have a bit of a headache and wanted to come lie down for a minute. I promise I'll be back out soon," Chloe finished with a bright smile as she lifted her hand to her head to make the lie more convincing.

Dakota gave her that look only a best friend could manage and then smiled at her. She came and sat down next to her and put her arm around her, squeezing.

"I love you to pieces, but you've always been a terrible liar," Dakota told her.

"I think I've been doing exceptionally well," Chloe countered.

"Ah, sweetie." Dakota sighed. "It will work out. I think he's hurting just as badly as you are."

The words made Chloe want to hope, and that was a dangerous emotion. She couldn't afford to feel that way. It had been a month and Nick was still gone. It was over, and she needed to move on.

"This is a nice day with your family. Please don't let me bring you down. I promise, after I have a few minutes to myself, I will come out smiling and laughing. I might even beat you at a game of Twister," she assured her.

"I love that you think you can," Dakota told her with a laugh. "And though it goes against everything within me, I will let you be alone for a few minutes. But if you don't come out soon, I'll be back with Jell-O shots," she warned.

"That's a deal," Chloe said.

When she was alone again, Chloe moved over to the window and looked down below, gazing out at the city landscape. Cars were moving in and out of traffic, horns honking, people yelling. *Seattle is at its finest*, she thought. No matter how much she wanted to feel a part of it all, she just couldn't yet.

The door opened again, and Chloe plastered on a smile, getting ready to turn. Dakota hadn't given her much time at all. But a few moments were what she'd have to accept. Her friend was just too worried. As she began to turn, though, the voice speaking stopped her cold.

"I can't believe you found a quiet spot in this place."

Tensing, Chloe wondered if she was imagining things. Was she thinking so hard about Nick that she could hear his voice? Finishing her turn, she was stunned when she found him standing in the room with her. How many times had she longed to see his dark hair, those beautiful green eyes, and his perfect lips smiling as he gazed at her? Too many times to count.

She wanted to rush into his arms, but she crossed hers instead as she gazed at him warily. She didn't know what this was about, but instead of healing as she was supposed to be doing, this was going to set her back too many steps to fathom.

"What are you doing here?" she asked him, her voice controlled.

"I had a chat with your best friend earlier. She really packs a punch," he said with a smile as he rubbed his arm. "Literally."

Chloe looked at him in shock. "Dakota punched you?" she gasped.

"Yep, she sure did." The way he said it was almost as if he were impressed by Dakota. That seemed odd.

"I'm sorry about that," she said. "I really don't want to talk to you right now, Nick," she finished. She had to be strong, and being with him like this wasn't going to make her that way.

"I need to talk to you," he said as he stepped toward her. She began to shake. If he touched her, she was going to fall apart. She couldn't let that happen.

"We said all we needed to say," she told him. This had to stop now.

"No. We said things when I was angry. I'm sorry, Chloe," he said. Then he swallowed up the distance between them and raised his hand, touching her arm.

The feel was so intense, it felt like she was being scorched. Her throat closed, and she desperately fought not to cry. She couldn't fall apart, not now.

Then Nick dropped down onto his knees in front of her, and she didn't know what to do or say. She was shaking so hard now he was bound to notice.

"Please Nick, please don't do this to me," she said, hating it when tears filled her eyes.

"I really screwed up, Chloe. I'm so sorry," he told her as he reached up and brushed a tear away. That only made more fall. "I've been thinking of what to say to make it all better and I honestly don't know," he admitted.

"You don't have to feel bad. I lied to you. I can't use my lack of knowledge as an excuse. When I began to develop feelings for you, and I knew what was happening to you was wrong, that's when I should have stepped up to the plate and told you what was happening. But I was trying to protect only myself. I was more worried about how *I* felt. It was all about me. It's pretty black and white," she said.

"Nothing is ever black and white," he told her. "I've never been in love before—not once in my life, so when it began happening with you, I didn't understand what was going on. It took your tiny friend to knock some sense into me," he said with a chuckle.

Chloe was trying to process his words, but they weren't getting through to her. She looked at him with confusion.

"What are you talking about?" she asked.

He gripped her trembling fingers and looked up into her eyes. She was close to falling down to her knees in front of him.

"I love you, Chloe. I think I have from the moment you fell into my lap. You are strong and beautiful, understanding and sympathetic. You make me want to be a stronger person, and you scare me at the same time. I'm scared because I've always been strong on my own, and now I don't do anything without thinking about you. I thought that if I pushed you away, put all the blame on you, then I would feel better about myself, but I was so wrong to do that. You knew nothing about me when this began, and when you did know, you stayed, not because you had to, but because you wanted to help me. I knew that even when I told myself I was furious with you. I'm sorry, darling. I'm so sorry."

His eyes were shining with love, and as Chloe listened to him speak, she realized he was telling her the truth. She realized he was admitting he loved her. The overflowing of her heart took her breath away. She hadn't known it was possible to feel so much joy until this very moment. She was so in love with the man kneeling before her.

"You can't take this all on you," she said.

"I'm not. We both made mistakes. I get that. But I also understand that I love you enough to forgive you. I'm hoping you feel the same way about me."

She was trembling as she gazed at this man who was showing so much courage.

"I'm scared," she admitted.

He looked at her with understanding.

"I am, too." For such a strong man to admit that sent her joy so high, she wasn't sure if she'd ever touch the ground again.

"I love you, too, you know," she said as her legs finally gave out and she sank down to the floor with him. He took her cheeks in his hands and gazed at her with so much love she was blown away.

"I've messed up so badly, I wouldn't blame you if you sent me away, but if you give us another chance, I promise you that I will love you more than anyone else ever could. I promise to take care of you and tell you how much you mean to me for the rest of our lives. I don't want another single day to go by without you in it. I'm imperfect in every single way, but with you by my side, I want to make myself a better man," he told her.

"Oh, Nick," she sobbed as she leaned forward and pressed her forehead to his. Her heart was overflowing. "No one is perfect, that's what makes us all so unique. But I love you so much. It's been hell without you. I've felt so much guilt about how hard I tried to pull away from you, and about not fighting more to keep us together. I thought it was hopeless, and I gave up because I told myself I wasn't good enough for you. It was just more of my father's words whispered into my ear. But I won't allow that man back in my head ever again," she promised.

He pulled her face back so he could look at her again, and he smiled before he reached down into his pocket and pulled out a small black box. She shook as she gazed down upon it.

"When I decide on a course of action, I never go back," he said as he ran his fingers over the velvet. "I know I've been an idiot, and I know I have no right to ask you this." He stopped as he opened the lid of the box. A beautiful, round diamond sparkled up at her. "But I love you, Chloe, and I want you forever. As much as I know I'm not good enough for you, I won't leave your side until you agree."

That spark of will that turned her on so much shone in his eyes. He was determined. He'd chased her relentlessly the entire time she'd been at his house, and now that single-mindedness made her smile.

"Then I'd better say yes," she told him.

Hope shone in his eyes.

"Yes?" he gasped.

"Yes," she told him.

With shaking fingers, he slipped the ring on her finger. It was a perfect fit. Then he pulled her onto his lap and kissed her so softly, she melted against him. She sighed into his mouth and felt truly at home for the first time ever. She was his, and he was hers, and it was exactly where they should both be.

When he finally pulled away, they were both smiling stupidly at each other. That's when Chloe heard the clearing of a throat.

"I didn't want to interrupt. That looked hot."

Chloe flushed as she looked up and found Dakota in the doorway grinning at her impishly. Nick jumped to his feet, ran to the door, and surprised the heck out of Chloe when he leaned down and kissed her best friend's cheek.

"Thank you for all you've done. Now go away," he told her. Then he pushed her out the door and shut it, locked it, and turned back toward Chloe.

"Now, back to where we were," he said. He rushed over and lifted her off the floor. Neither one of them made it back down to the family get-together. And no one missed them.

EPILOGUE

Ace Armstrong's adrenaline was pumping as he wandered through the large mansion where his case was finally going to come to an end. It was almost over. He was afraid to even believe it.

For the past eight years, he'd been away from his family, making them believe he was a monster so they wouldn't get hurt. He couldn't do it anymore. Of those eight years, four of them had been working on one case—the biggest undercover operation ever performed with the CIA.

He'd been flying for a drug cartel gang for years, getting information back to his team whenever it was safe for him to do so, and integrating himself within the organization's ranks until they trusted him as one of their own.

Now he was at the home they thought was his, and all of the leaders were going to be in one spot for an operational meeting. Ace was cool as ice as he looked over everything, making sure not a single detail was out of place. All of them had to arrive so this case could be closed with zero loose ends. It was the only way he'd get his freedom back.

Trucks pulled up, carrying crates of alcohol and party supplies. The scene was being staged, the prison bars closing in on the monsters who were responsible for the loss of too many lives to count, hooking kids on drugs, murder, extortion, and so much more. This case reached all the way up to the executive level of the government.

Ace had been disillusioned in his years as an undercover CIA agent. When he'd walked out on his family so many years before, he'd been angry at his father's will, angry at his brothers for giving in so easily—but he'd planned on coming back. Then his life had led him on a different path.

The CIA had saved him and destroyed a part of him at the same time. He no longer trusted anyone, and his heart was cold and barely beating. Now that returning home was within reach, he wasn't even sure he could. His brothers wouldn't recognize him—hell, he didn't recognize himself when he looked in a mirror.

Moving over to the entryway, he did just that, staring at the unsmiling reflection of himself. Who was he? The green eyes were void of emotion, the jaw was set tight, his dark hair closely cropped and uncared for. It was his lips that surprised him most of all. They hadn't smiled in so long, he wasn't sure he knew how to work those muscles anymore.

He'd pushed his family away, sued them for his inheritance just to tighten the bolts on the coffin of their relationship, had crashed his brother's wedding when he'd been feeling sentimental, then had punched Nick in the face to make it worse. But oh, how he'd panicked when Cooper's plane had gone down. Instead of showing his face to Coop, Ace had found his brother's woman and attempted to kiss her. Was it all a show? Or was there some part of him that was truly the monster he'd wanted his family to believe he was?

Last year, his closest brother, Nick, had gone down during a Coast Guard rescue. Ace had been there for that, too, though no one had seen him that time. He'd managed to sneak into his brother's room while he was out cold, recovering. It was the first time in years Ace had felt the urge to cry.

But even if he could explain it all to his family, did he want to? Did he know how to? He didn't know who he was anymore, let alone how to describe himself. That didn't really matter, though, because he'd soon find out. The case would be over, and he had nowhere else to go—no friends, no lover, nobody.

Pulling himself back into the present, Ace composed his features, easily slipping into the role of a dirtbag with coldhearted precision. Soon, very soon, it would begin . . . and end. And then he would be going home.

ACKNOWLEDGMENTS

This was my fortieth book written. Wow, it seems so strange. But what a joy it is for me to write. I am so happy to be a part of the Montlake family. Everyone there has been so good to me and such a great support system. Thank you so much to my editors, Maria and Lauren, who always blow my mind with the amazing story ideas. This book wouldn't have been nearly as great without you both. Thank you to Ahn, Jessica, Sean, Chris, and everyone else with Amazon for making me laugh, listening to my ideas, and taking me in as part of the team. I have been writing for six years now, and I have found a place that I love and am proud to be a part of.

Thank you to my friends and my family. I love when we have storyboard sessions and some of the crazy ideas that come out of your mouths. If I wrote all the stuff that we talk about, especially when drinking wine, I would be creating an entire new universe with bubbles and glitter and unicorns. I'm always excited to put my fingers on the keyboard after we visit. Much thanks goes to my extraordinary husband, who gives me amazing foot rubs and supports me 100 percent. I'm a very blessed woman.

Most of all thank you to my fans, who continually support me, come to visit me at conferences, chat with me online, and make me feel like I can fly. I wouldn't get to do what I love so much if I didn't have you in my corner. I hope to have many, many more years to come creating these fantasy worlds.

TEASER

TURBULENT INTENTIONS

Book 1 in the Billionaire Aviators series

Tires squealed as a sleek silver Jaguar shot out onto the highway. An unsuspecting car cruising along slammed on its brakes just in time to avoid a wreck with the Jag. The four brothers sitting in the Jaguar didn't give a damn about the commotion they were causing.

This wasn't unusual.

They continued speeding along, trying to outrun the demons chasing them as they flew down the highway, hitting over a hundred miles an hour and continuing on, faster and faster.

It wasn't quick enough. They kept on going until they hit the edge of town in Bay Harbor, Washington, where they found a dilapidated bar with a blinking neon sign that had some of the letters burned out.

Cooper, who was driving, jerked the steering wheel and came to an abrupt halt outside the run-down building. "Good enough," he said. His fists clenched with the urge to hit something, or better yet, someone.

"Yep," his brother replied from the backseat.

Getting out of the car, they made their way to the entrance, an undeniable swagger in their gaits—a swagger that made people turn and watch them wherever they went. Though young, the Armstrong brothers already had a reputation in their small community for stirring up trouble.

When they entered a room, patrons would turn away, glancing back at them with a wary eye. The brothers were the first in for a fight and the last ones standing.

They were wealthy, and not above flashing their fat wallets, Rolex watches, and extravagant cars. They were also arrogant and hot-tempered, a foursome to both be leery of and look at with awe. Cooper was the oldest at twenty-four, each of his brothers one year, almost to the date, behind him: Nick at twenty-three, Maverick at twenty-two, and Ace, the baby, at twenty-one.

On this night, though, they were looking for more than just the usual trouble. They were out for blood, but the demon chasing them was relentless, and no matter how fast they moved, this was something they couldn't outrun.

Their father was dying.

Maybe it was the feeling of helplessness, or maybe, for once, it was not being the strongest ones in a room. Whatever it was, Cooper, Nick, Maverick, and Ace were scared, and because they wouldn't admit that, they were trouble to anyone in their path.

This band of brothers had always been revered as much as they'd been feared. They were tall, lean, and had distinct green eyes that hid their innermost thoughts but shone with a sparkle that most couldn't resist.

Walking indoors, Cooper sighed in anticipation. Smoke filled the air as loud music echoed off the walls. A few heads turned in their direction, and Cooper scoped them out, looking for a potential boxing partner.

The nervous energy rising off him in waves needed an outlet, so the first person that gave him the slightest reason would feel the wrath of his heartbreak, denial, and feeling of helplessness.

As if the patrons knew this group was up to no good, they cast their eyes downward, particularly annoying Cooper in their weakness to accept the challenge radiating off his entire body.

The boys ordered beers, then leaned against the bar, facing out as they scanned the crowd. None of them spoke for several moments, each lost in thought.

Cooper was thinking they might just have to give up on this place and find a new location when his gaze captured the angry look of a man shooting pool. Cooper smirked at the guy and practically saw steam rise from the man's ears. The stranger began making his way toward them. Cooper's fists clenched with the need to punch.

"You're the Armstrong boys, right?"

The man was swaying as he stepped closer to them, his glazed-over eyes narrowed. Cooper stood at full attention. This just might be the huckleberry he'd been in search of.

"Yep," Coop said, not altering his stance at all.

"I hear your daddy's on his deathbed." The man said the cold words with glee.

Maybe the man was too drunk to know exactly what he was doing, but instantly the four brothers stepped a bit closer to one another, their knuckles cracking, their collective breath hissing out.

"Maybe you shouldn't listen to gossip," Maverick said in a low growl.

"Oh, I don't think it's gossip. You see, your daddy has run over many real workingmen to get to the top of that mountain he's built for himself. And now he's getting the early death he deserves."

Nick instantly stepped away from the bar, but Cooper shot his hand out and stopped him. "He was looking at me, Nick," he said, his tone deathly low.

His brothers shot him a look, but then they stepped back, letting Cooper deal with his demons, and the drunken bastard before them, at the same time.

"Dave, come on. You've had too much to drink," a woman said, placing her hand on his arm.

"Get the hell off of me. I know what I'm doing," Dave snarled at the woman, pushing her away.

Cooper's fingers twitched in anticipation. He wanted to deck this asshole even more now. It was okay to fight with a man, but to push a lady around was never acceptable.

"Maybe you should lay off the lady," Maverick said. He wanted to push forward and take Cooper's place. Cooper looked at him and Maverick stepped back, though it was costing him to do so.

"Maybe you should keep your damn mouth shut," Dave said to Mav.

"This is Cooper's fight," Nick reminded Maverick when he began to shake with the need to hit this piece of scum.

Dave turned away from Maverick, his beady eyes focused again on Cooper. "Are you just like your daddy, boy? Do you like living off the men busting their asses for your family in those crap factories?"

"At least our daddy provides trash like you a job," Cooper said.

"Not that you would know. You haven't worked a damn day in your life," Dave snapped.

"Nope. And I have a hell of a lot more than you, don't I?" Cooper taunted him, making sure the man could see the gold Rolex he was sporting.

The man spit as he tried to get words out. He was furious. When Cooper pulled out his wallet and slapped a hundred-dollar bill on the bar and told the waitress to take care of the man's tab since he probably couldn't, Dave's face turned beet red with fury and embarrassment.

"I don't need the likes of you taking care of anything for me," he finally managed to sputter.

Finishing his beer in a long swallow, Cooper took his time before putting the glass down on the counter. The bar was strangely quiet as the patrons watched this scene unfold before them.

"So you're one of those guys who blames his lot in life on the big man in the top office instead of doing a day's hard work, huh?" Cooper said, a taunting smile on his lips.

"I like my damn life. I don't need some rich kid who doesn't know what work is telling me he's better than me," the man blustered.

"I *am* better than you," Coop told him with a wink he was sure would enrage the man. Just to add fuel to the fire, he pulled out a wad of cash and threw it at the man's feet. "Here's some spending money for you. Obviously you need the cash more than I do since I have a mountain of it back home."

"I'm going to enjoy kicking your ass, boy," Dave said, tossing his beer bottle behind him in his rage. Though he did look down at the cash longingly. Cooper would have laughed, if he had been capable of it at that moment.

His brothers didn't even flinch at the hundreds lying on the filthy floor, money that would be swallowed up the second the boys stepped away.

"I'd like to see you try," Cooper said with just enough of a mocking glow to his eyes to really infuriate the man. "Follow me."

His muscles were coiled and he was more than ready. He headed toward the door. He could do it in the bar or flatten this guy outside. Either way was good with him.

"You gonna leave the convoy behind, or do you need your brothers to save your ass?" the man taunted.

The fact that this piece of garbage was questioning his honor infuriated Cooper even more. He took a second before answering, not even turning around to face the drunkard.

"You obviously don't know me at all if you think I need any help kicking your flabby ass," Cooper told him. "Chicken ass," he then mumbled, knowing it would push this piece of trash over the limit.

The air stirred against his ears, alerting Cooper of the attack coming toward him. They'd barely made it out the front doors before the man swung, thinking that because Cooper was ahead of him he would get a cheap shot from behind.

He wasn't counting on Cooper's rage, or his soberness.

Spinning around, Coop threw all his weight behind a punishing blow that made brutal contact with the drunk's face. The resounding crack of Coop's knuckles breaking the man's nose echoed across the parking lot.

The man spit blood as he tried to get up before falling back to the ground. Cooper didn't give him a chance. In half a heartbeat, he was on the ground, slugging the man again and again.

"Should we stop this?" Maverick asked, leaning against the outside wall of the bar as patrons poured out to watch the fistfight.

"Not a chance. Hell, I'm hoping someone else mouths off so I can get a punch or two thrown in," Nick mumbled, looking around.

"It's my turn next," Ace grumbled.

Maverick held his brother back. "You'll get your turn," Maverick promised him.

No one was paying the least attention to the other brothers as the fight in front of them continued on the ground and Dave got in a good punch to Cooper's face.

Within a couple minutes, though, the fight was over. Dave was knocked out on the ground, and with the show over, the patrons of the bar lost interest and went back inside to their cold beer and stale peanuts. The brothers watched as Cooper slowly stood while spitting out a stream of saliva and touching his swollen lip.

A couple of men picked up Dave and quietly hauled him away. The brothers didn't even bother watching them go.

"Should we go back in?" Maverick asked.

"Yeah. I'm done with this trash. Maybe there's another idiot inside looking for a reason to get a nose job," Cooper said.

Before Nick or Ace could respond, Nick's phone rang. He looked at the caller ID and sighed. It rang twice more before he answered.

He was silent for a moment as the caller spoke. Then he nodded, though the person couldn't see him. "Yes, Mom. We'll be there."

He hung up. "We have to go back home," Nick told them. Even without the call, Nick was always the voice of reason.

"I'm not ready to go back there," Ace said, his eyes downcast.

"I can't," Cooper admitted. He couldn't allow the adrenaline high to stop, because then . . . then, he might actually *feel* real pain instead of anger.

"It's time," Nick said again.

They didn't want to listen, but they knew their brother was right.

It was like a parade down the green mile as they moved back to the car and piled in. They drove much more slowly toward home than they'd driven away from it, taking their time, none of them speaking.

When they pulled up in front of the large mansion they'd grown up in, they remained in the Jag, none of them wanting to be the first to open his car door. Finally, though, Nick got out, and the others followed. Their passage into the mansion was quiet, their shoulders hunched.

"Where have you been?"

They stopped in the foyer as their uncle Sherman busted down the stairs glaring at them. The urgency in his voice had them terrified. They knew time was running out.

"We had to blow off some steam," Maverick said, his hands tucked into his pockets as he rocked back and forth on his heels.

"Your father's been asking for you," Sherman scolded. "And there isn't much time left. Your mother will need all of you."

"We're sorry," Cooper said. The others seemed incapable of speech and just nodded their apologies.

Sherman sighed, not one to stay angry for long.

They followed their uncle up the stairs. None of them wanted to walk through that bedroom door. But they did it. Their father, who had once been so strong, was frail and weak now, the cancer taking everything from him, leaving him a shadow of the man he'd always been.

"Come here," he said, his voice barely a whisper.

Slowly, the four boys surrounded the bed, facing the man they would soon lose.

"Time is running out so I can't mince words," their father started.

"Dad . . ." Cooper tried to interrupt, but his mother put her hand on his arm.

"Let him speak, son."

Her voice was so sad that the boys turned to look at her for a moment, their shoulders stiffening before they turned back to their father and waited.

"I've done wrong by all of you," he told them, disappointment on his face. He looked extra long at the blood on Cooper's eye and sadly shook his head. "All of you."

"No you haven't, Dad," Maverick insisted.

"Yes, I have. You're men now, but you have no plans for the future. I wanted to give you the world, but you've only learned how to take because you haven't learned how to earn anything. I know you'll grow into fine men. I have no doubt about it. But please don't hate me when I'm gone," he said before he began coughing.

"We would never hate you, Dad," Nick quickly said.

"You might for a while," their father told them. "But someday you will thank me. I'm doing what I've done because I love you."

"What are you saying?" Ace asked.

"You'll know soon, son," their father said.

"Dad . . ." Maverick began, but their father shut his eyes.

Cooper willed himself to say something, anything to break this awful silence. But he just stood there, anger, sadness, fear flowing through him.

And then it was too late.

Not a sound could be heard in the room when their father stopped breathing. For the last time in each of their lives, the boys shed a tear as they looked down at their deceased father.

Then Cooper turned and walked out. He didn't stop at the front door. He didn't stop at the end of the driveway. He kept moving, faster and faster until he was in a full-blown sprint with his gut and sides burning. He tried to outrun the fact that he was a disappointment, that he'd failed his father. What if the man was right? What if he never became half the man his father was? He ran faster.

Still, he wasn't able to outrun his father's last words of disappointment . . .

◆　◆　◆

". . . And for my boys, I leave each of you, Cooper, Nick, Maverick, and Ace, a quarter of my assets, but there is a stipulation . . ."

It had only been a day since the funeral, and none of the boys wanted to be sitting in this uptight lawyer's office while he read a stupid will. It wasn't as if they didn't know what it was going to say anyway.

Their father, of course, had left his fortune to them; that is, what he hadn't already given them in their enormous trust funds, and to their mother and his brother, Uncle Sherman. They were the only living relatives—well, the only ones they knew about, at least. So this was a waste of all their time.

"Can you get on with this? I have things to do," Cooper snapped.

"You will learn some respect by the end of this," Sherman warned Coop.

"Yeah, I get it," Coop said. "Can I go now? I don't want to hear the rest."

"I think you do," their mother said.

Her sweet voice instantly calmed the boys. They did love their mother, had a great deal of respect for her, and listened when she spoke.

But they had hardened through the years, taking for granted what had been given to them.

That was about to change.

"You won't receive a dime of your inheritance until you've proven that you will actually better not only your lives, but the lives of others."

Cooper spoke first. "What in the hell is that supposed to mean?" He was up on his feet, his chair flying backward with the momentum. His brothers were right behind him.

The world was suddenly spinning and none of them knew how to deal with this latest news.

"If you will shut up and listen, then you will hear the rest," Sherman told them.

The four young men were obviously upset, but slowly they resumed their seats, all of them except for Cooper, who stood there with his arms crossed, daggers coming from his eyes.

"You have ten years to turn your lives around. At the end of that ten years, if you haven't proven yourselves self-sufficient, by working hard, being respectful to your mother and your uncle, and bringing something to the society that you live in, then your inheritance will be donated to charity."

The attorney paused as if he were reluctant to read whatever else was coming next.

"Get on with it," Ace growled.

"Your mother and I shared a wonderful, beautiful, exciting life together. A man isn't meant to be alone. He's meant to love, to share, to grow with a woman who will help guide him through the hardest parts of his life," the attorney began.

"What in the world are you speaking about?" Maverick snapped.

"Son, this is in your father's own words, so I would pay attention," Uncle Sherman said, his tone sad.

Maverick leaned forward, but he didn't seem to be hearing anything that was being spoken at that moment.

"Shall I continue?" the attorney asked.

"Yeah, yeah," Cooper said with a wave of his hand.

"You will receive your full inheritance once you marry."

Dead silence greeted those words as the boys looked at one another, and then at their mother, who had a serene smile on her face.

Finally, Cooper was the one to speak again. "Mom? What in the hell is going on?"

She gave her son a sad smile. "Your father and I have watched the four of you lose your way these past several years. He knew he was dying and he'd run out of time to guide you, shape you. He didn't want to lose you forever, as I don't. So he changed the will."

The boys waited for her to go on, but she sat there silently.

"We're rich without his money," Nick pointed out.

She was quiet for several moments. "Yes, Nick, you are," she finally said.

"Are you going to take away what we already have?" Maverick asked.

"No, I'm not," Evelyn Armstrong told them all. "You don't have to get your inheritance, though it makes your trust funds look like pennies, as you know. But getting the money isn't the point," she said with a sigh.

"What is the point?" Cooper asked, trying desperately not to yell, but only because his mother was in the room.

"The point is to grow up. You need to grow up," Evelyn said as she looked each of the boys in the eyes before turning to Sherman.

"Your father wants you to be good men. He's asking you to show your mother that you are," Sherman added.

"So, even in death, Father wants us to jump through hoops?" Ace snapped.

"No, son, even in death your father wants you to grow into the men you are meant to be," Evelyn told them.

"I don't need his stupid money. I have plenty of it that he's already given me and besides that I have my own plans. If he thinks I'm such a screwup, then he can keep it all," Cooper thundered.

"Agreed," Nick snapped.

"I'm not doing anything because someone is trying to force it upon me," Maverick said, joining his brothers.

"If he thinks we're such screwups, he can go to hell," Ace said, pushing it a bit too far.

"Ace . . ." Coop whispered.

"Save it, Cooper. You're always trying to be the leader, but this is crap. Yeah, I'm the baby of the family, but that just means that I've had to try to make up for every mistake that you guys have already made. I'm done with it," Ace bellowed.

"Calm down, son," Sherman said, rising and resting a hand on Ace's shoulder.

"No!"

Ace yanked away from Sherman and then moved toward the door.

"I love you all no matter what you choose, but I hope you'll listen to your father's last words and know he does this because he loves you," Evelyn said quietly, stopping Ace for a moment. Then his eyes hardened.

"I'm out of here."

Ace was the first to leave. He rushed from the attorney's office, fury heating the very air around him.

Cooper stood there dumfounded. What was happening? They'd not only lost their father, but they'd all just found out that they had never been good enough in his eyes.

"To hell with Dad—and to hell with this place."

Cooper followed his brother, though Ace was already long gone. It didn't matter. Cooper would prove himself, but he'd do it because he wanted to. He would never be someone's puppet—not even his father's.

ABOUT THE AUTHOR

Melody Anne is the *New York Times* and *USA Today* bestselling author of the popular adult series Billionaire Bachelors, Surrender, and Baby for the Billionaire, as well as the young adult Midnight series. She is also the coauthor, along with J. S. Scott and Ruth Cardello, of the Taken by a Trillionaire anthology.

Having earned a bachelor's degree in business, Melody moved on to a writing career in 2011. When she isn't living her dream as an author, she loves spending time with her family, friends, and pets while giving back to her small town through community work.

Melody has earned a spot on multiple bestseller lists and is a three-time Amazon Top 100 bestselling author. Learn more about her at www.melodyanne.com and follow her blog at www.authormelodyanne.blogspot.com.